Rebecca L. Frencl

Ascent
of the
Fallen

Cover Art:
Select-O-Graphixs

Publisher's Note:

This is a work of fiction. All names, characters, places, and
events are the work of the author's imagination.

Any resemblance to real persons, places, or events is
coincidental.

Solstice Publishing - www.solsticepublishing.com

Ascent of the Fallen

By,

Rebecca L. Frencl

Dedicated to

The angels among us.
The first responders who leap into danger to pull us out.
Particularly, this is for my brother and my sister-in-law.
They are among the bravest and the finest.

CHAPTER ONE

The buzzing whir of the stylus filled Rue's ears. He felt the burning nip of the needles as they dug and dragged in his flesh, inch by inch creating and crafting the artwork he'd commissioned. That bite of pain still felt odd. He'd cut his hand the day before and had watched, fascinated, as the blood dropped and pooled like ruby tears that glittered in the sun. He'd remembered to staunch the blood only after a woman passerby by had shrieked at the wound.

He sighed carefully, more to keep the artist from making a mistake, than from any pain. "You ok?" Joss, the tattoo artist, asked, lifting the stylus from Rue's flesh.

"I'm good." His voice was low, quiet. The spoken word felt unnatural even now – weeks later. Words seem to sit on his tongue, heavy and clumsy. After a second, Joss bent his head and the buzzing whir began again sending sharp little twinges to dance up Rue's spine.

It didn't hurt. It reminded him. Reminded him he was alive. Reminded him why he was here. Pain and penance, grief and redemption all seemed to meet here in the parlor as a reminder of his lost world was slowly etched into skin.

Later, when he shrugged his cotton shirt over the raw skin he saw the humans, Joss included, wince. "Don't that hurt, man?" One of the Spider Den's regulars, Locust, his own arm bare to the artist's needle, shuddered.

Rue shook his head. "It's nothing," he murmured and left the shop. Cold winter wind slapped him in the face. They knew nothing of pain. He squinted against the icy sleet soaking through his thin shirt. No, they knew nothing of pain, but, as he smiled at the storm, he knew that he did.

* * * *

"Dude," Herm shook his head, "he's a piece of work."

Joss nodded from his station, head bowed as he sanitized his tools. "You don't know the half," he muttered, peeling off his gloves.

"Seriously," Herm bent his head over Locust's arm trailing another long lock of hair on the busty mermaid he concentrated on meticulously carving, "does he ever say anything?"

"Not much." Joss shrugged. "Hasn't said much beyond what he wanted the first day."

"Paid cash," Locust nodded. Joss remembered – he'd been there that first day too. "How's he have the scratch if he can't afford no coat?"

"Speaking of scratch," Herm grumbled.

Locust rolled his buggy brown eyes, but he bumped his hips up to snag his wallet from his back pocket. "Yeah, yeah, yeah." He peeled four twenties away from a wad of receipts and papers. The cash disappeared in Herm's large paw.

"Winter storm that day, too." Herm's tongue peeked out from between his teeth as he hunched over, piecing in the more minute details of the mermaid's winsome face. He paused from time to time to peer at the picture of Marita, Locust's fiancee.

Joss looked out at the slushy mess slapping against the shop's windows. "Didn't wear a coat then either."

"Seriously, what's his deal, Joss man?" Locust swung his head around to keep the artist in his sights.

Joss dropped to a chair leaned back, tossed his heavy dreads over the back of the seat. He rubbed without thought at the rosary tattoo scrolling down his left wrist and over the back of his hand. "Don't know," he said at last. He looked once more at the wind-lashed street. "The man doesn't say much."

Locust grunted and turned back to watch Herm work. Joss noticed Marita's face starting to take shape. He closed his eyes. Working on Rue's art always exhausted him. He'd started telling Herm that Rue had to be his last client of his day. His mind moved away from the Spider Den's tattooed regular, Locust—to wonder about Rue out on the streets. Who was the guy? Where did he go? Joss flexed his cramped hands, the biggest question of all circling his tired brain. Why did the guy want angel wings tattooed on his back?

* * * *

So, this was sleet? Rue tipped his head toward the grim gray skies. Nasty pellets of ice slapped his cheeks, chin and eyes. He'd heard of sleet, watched the humans scurry from building to car and back again to stay out of it. Yet, the sharp little nips of ice invigorated him.

He shrugged. The freezing wet cloth clung to the work Joss had just finished on his back. He'd seen, in the angled mirror held by the artist, the clear outline of his wings. They would begin working on the individual feathers the next time. He rolled his shoulder blades feeling phantom muscles ripple. *Soon.* He permitted himself a small smile. *Soon.*

He bent his head like the rest of the lunchtime commuters around him, hunching his shoulders against the gale force wind whipping off the lake. The sleet soothed the lingering sting on his back. Physical pain was still such a unique experience. He had dealt out hundreds of thousands of punishments over the centuries, yet he'd felt no pain. It added a new dimension, didn't it?

Part of the problem too, he rolled his eyes heavenward. A large cold drop splattered on his forehead to roll cold and wet down his nose. *Thanks, Gabe.* Gritting his teeth, he continued his walk.

Compassion.

He snorted, watching a pickpocket dip a hand in a woman's swinging purse. The woman's bright red wallet disappeared into the boy's shirt. The latte-sipping businesswoman didn't notice. She chattered away on her cellphone as she strode by without a glance at the bum huddled on the ground near her impressive three inch heels, his inked sign running in the weather. She'd notice her wallet missing the next time she reached in to pay for a pricey coffee.

Rue worked a hand into his wet denim pocket. Change rattled at the bum's feet. *Compassion.* He frowned. *For whom?*

* * * *

Serafina watched the man in short sleeves and soggy gym shoes drop change at Mackey's feet. No coat, no hat, sleet freezing onto the ends of his dark blonde curling hair, but he'd given Mackey money. He'd given Mackey money when the well-heeled businessmen and women strode by, not even seeing the old man.

Swinging on her coat, she grabbed the Styrofoam cup of coffee she'd poured and ducked out into the cold jogging across Michigan to Mackey's side. She handed the old man the steaming cup. His teeth chattered on the lip as he took his first sip. "Did you see that, Fina?" he gestured with the cup his wide eyes followed the man fading away in the gray sleety day.

"I did, Mackey." She slipped a hand under the old man's elbow. "Come on, come wash up and warm up in the shop. Dan will take you over to Saint Mary's."

He wheezed as he got to his feet, following her across Michigan Avenue to her little shop tucked in among the Spider's Den tattoo parlor, one of Columbia's bookstores and the Artist's Café. "It's Tuesday, ain't it?" Mackey's voice creaked and he took another sip of hot coffee. At her nod, he smacked his lips. "They got meatloaf on Tuesdays at St. Mary's." He rubbed a dirty hand over his belly. "I always like a good meatloaf."

Dan's music choice of Metallica sounded sharply at odds with the careful displays of vintage gowns, hand bags and jewelry at Serafina's Treasure Trove Boutique.

"Through there, Mackey." She directed the man toward the tidy staff washroom. Even though at this time "staff" meant just her and her cousin.

"More strays, Fina?" Dan asked from his perch on the ladder where he was stringing tiny drop lights over her jewelry cases. The pinpoint lighting would shimmer over the jewels—both glass and real—like starlight.

"Could you take Mackey over to St. Mary's?"

He grunted in assent and screwed in the last tiny bulb. "Good to go here, Fina." He gestured to the switch. "I'll go trip the breaker. You hit the lights."

He bounced down the ladder and bounded into the back room. Serafina shook her head. He never walked. He was like Tigger from the Disney channel—why walk when you could bound? "All right, hit it!" he called, and she swept her hand over the switches.

Lights danced and twinkled around the ceiling and the tiny pendant lights over her glass jewelry cases made the necklaces and earrings shimmer. "Perfect," she whispered. "Just perfect." It was all coming together. She'd taken a risk and had dragged Dan in with her, much to his parents' dismay. She was thankful her young cousin was willing to spend so much of his off time between and after classes helping her set up and run the shop.

Dan's arm banded around her shoulders, his pointy chin settling on her head. She could feel his grin. "Looks great, cuz."

She squeezed his wrist. "Nice work, Danny. Thanks again." She felt him shrug as he turned away.

"What're family for?" He pounded on the staff bathroom door. "Come on, Mackey! Let's get a move on. You don't want them runnin' out of meatloaf, do you?"

As if on cue, the door opened. Mackey's white hair was a messy halo around his head. He'd scrubbed until his cheeks glowed pink. "I love a good meatloaf," he assured Dan. "My Mary made the best meatloaf." He groaned and rolled his eyes. "Make you cock up your toes and die it was so good." He blinked and looked around the shop as if seeing it for the first time. When he smiled, Serafina saw a full set of beautiful teeth. "Why, Fina, it's so pretty in here." He looked into one of the jewelry cases. "Why, if my Mary was alive and I still had the money my no good nephew stole from me, I'd sure as certain buy her something pretty from you." He tapped over an antique pearl necklace and earrings that shimmered in the new lighting. "They look just like angel tears," he murmured.

Serafina smiled. They were her favorites right now. She'd snapped them up, last time she'd been in L. A. Jane Russell's estate had been selling off some items and she'd bid on a blind lot and gotten lucky.

Dan bundled Mackey into the back room and out toward his hand-me-down Nissan. "Come on, Mackey, let's go. I've got a date tonight."

The old man chuckled, his grating wheeze made Serafina smile. "Oh, Fina," he called as he left, "that man, the one who gave me the money, I just remembered I seen him before."

Dan rolled his eyes behind the old man, keys dancing in his fingers. "Really, where?" she asked, ignoring her cousin.

He gestured to the right. "From the Den. Seen him a few times." He rolled his eyes. "Must be getting some extra fancy work done."

"Mackey," irritation tinged Dan's tone. "Hot date. Remember?"

"Keep your pants on," Mackey cackled at his own joke, but followed him out the back door.

Serafina pressed fingers to her forehead and wandered over to snap off the radio Dan had left blaring. A nasty little headache had started up again behind her right eye. Dan and his music. She shook her head. She looked over her shoulder at the darkening window behind her. The sleet had turned to rain, a cold winter rain that slid like tears down the large plate glass window. She was sure the weather wasn't helping her head, either.

She flipped the closed sign and dropped the blinds. It was miserable enough and late enough. No one would wander in now. She'd go upstairs, kick off her shoes and have a cup of tea. After another moment of admiration, she flipped off her sparkling lights. And maybe an Advil. Her head gave one more sharp pound. Make that three Advil.

She wandered the perimeter one more time, checking all the doors and windows. Dan had a slight tendency to open windows and not tell her. She remembered with a shake of her aching head, the one time he'd left her office window open and she'd needed to replace her computer after a particularly nasty rain storm.

Her headache gave another throb, and for a second Fina thought her eyesight grayed out. Another head shake sent a spear of pain so severe she lowered herself to the bottom step and just sat there for a moment or two, motionless. How much of this was in her head?

A few deep breaths, in and out. Memories of her childhood bubbled to the surface. Her mother had always been "ill." She remembered her mother fluttering around the house, dressed in a fluffy blue robe for most of Fina's childhood, claiming some indisposition or another. Her father had only rolled his eyes at the shelf full of pills and vitamins over her mother's dresser. She outlived him. An untimely heart attack had carried him off when Fina had been fourteen.

She remembered being alone with her mother, then. The sole recipient of the deep sighs, the tantrums, tears, the guilt trips that she swore went from the moon and back. She'd fled to a college dorm in Beloit as soon as she'd been able, coming home only when she hadn't been able to find somewhere else to hide. She'd crashed at Dan's house for several Christmases until she'd had the money to move into her own apartment, reasoning with her mother that they all went to Aunt Sarah's for Christmas anyway....

The pain faded and with a shaky little laugh she pushed to her feet. "Who knew that hypochondria could be inherited?" A tiny thread of fear wiggled through her. It was just a headache. Right? A migraine. Those were pretty horrible, she'd heard, and she'd certainly been under enough stress with fixing up the shop to bring on migraines.

After unlocking her cozy apartment above the store, she flopped on the couch, one arm draped over her eyes, as if with sheer will she could make the migraine disappear. If it happened again, she resolved, she'd go see a doctor. Once was a fluke. Right?

CHAPTER TWO

"You've been here how long and you've yet to find shelter?"

Rue turned toward the tart inquiry. Michael stood, framed in the street light, rain sheeting off the long trench coat, his wraparound black sunglasses out of place just south of midnight. "I thought you were supposed to keep your distance?" Rue pressed his back in the corner between the building and the dumpster. An overhanging fire escape protected him from most of the elements. A long stream of cold water ran steadily from above. He shifted his foot away from it.

Michael shrugged and took a seat beside him. They sat in silence for a few moments, the street light shining wetly in the alley's shadows. Rue felt irritation build, a slow burn beginning in his stomach to rise like gorge at the back of his throat. He couldn't take Michael's inhuman patience any longer. "Say what you've come to say and have done." His voice sounded like a low growl to his own ears. He pressed against the wall the rough brick scraped through his thin shirt. Pain blossomed, reminding him.

"How does it feel?" Michael asked without turning.

No need for clarification. He had been one of them for long enough. Long enough to know how much that one question cost. He shook his head, water flying from the ends of his hair. "I don't know if it's something I can explain to you." He flexed his hands, the long scab on the left one pulling open. Blood, black in the shifting light, welled and dripped.

Michael reached out touching his fingers to the wound. A tiny light, bright white, traced the cut. Rue felt a sharp burning and the ragged hurt drew together, the skin knitting tightly and leaving no trace. "How did it feel?"

He straightened his fingers one by one, searching for the right words. Words Michael would understand. "It burned," he finally decided. Michael knew about burning even though he had never felt the touch of flame.

"And this?" Michael held a hand out. Freezing run-off poured over his fingers.

"Cold," Rue told him. "If you were human you'd get frostbite."

Michael turned toward him. He tipped down the sunglasses, his shimmering silver eyes glowing in the dark night. "Ruvan, you are human."

Rue huddled in on himself. As if Michael's words were a reminder, the wind seemed to tear through him with more of a vengeance. A bone chilling river of water snaked across the alley to soak into his jeans. "Don't call me that anymore." His voice sounded harsh to his own ears.

Michael, those unearthly eyes unmoved, turned his face to the sky. The vault of the heavens remained dark. Neither the stars nor the moon dared show their faces in this weather. "I wondered how you were faring down here." His voice throbbed, making Rue's bones vibrate. "Sim doesn't think you'll make it."

He shrugged. "It remains to be seen."

"Are you any closer?" The words thrummed in Rue's ribcage. Light shimmered behind the sunglasses.

He darted a look down the empty alleyway. "Feel compassion for these fools?" He shook his head. "Sometimes I wonder why I'm even here." He gestured toward the bridge where he'd given money to the homeless man. "They ignore one another. They hurt one another. They treat their old and infirm worse than the dirt beneath their shoes." He felt his face twist into a snarl. "I should have been thanked for my zeal, not punished." Bitterness swelled.

Michael, his perfect features composed, sighed and rose to his feet. "That zeal and that attitude is what got you here in the first place."

"I am—" he choked, correcting himself. "I *was* the one who accounted their evil deeds at the gates of Hell itself!" He flailed one hand out, the gesture encompassing the whole of humanity. "I saw the worst of them." He glared up at Michael. "And the numbers? By the seventh heaven –" his voice dropped to an anguished groan " –the sheer numbers. How could I believe anything other than wicked in this world?"

Michael stood, silent, the streetlight shining on his tarnished gold hair. "Ruvan, for that you were sent to find the good." He knelt at the fallen angel's side. "You need to find your compassion. Find the good in the world." He smiled. "It's there. God willing, you will see it again."

Rue said nothing. Michael rose. He stripped off the trench coat, dropping it in Rue's lap. A shuddering rush of wind and his wings flared, nearly twenty feet wide and the color of shimmering moonlight. Rue shivered, the muscles in his back tightening.

Michael nodded, pulled off his sunglasses. Eyes like liquid silver glowed. "I'll see you soon." His voice thrilled like electricity through Rue's body.

Hunched over, Rue didn't speak. When he looked up again, the Archangel was gone. Rain hammered; a metallic tattoo on the fire escape overhead. He shrugged into the coat, sliding the sunglasses into the pocket. The scent of myrrh rose from the leather, bringing a lump to his throat. It smelled like home. He wrapped the coat around himself, tucked his hands up the sleeves, and lulled by the spreading warmth and the scents of home, drifted off to sleep.

* * * *

"Are we certain this will work?" Simeon's voice dripped concern.

Michael turned from where he still watched Rue huddled in the coat now from the place between the worlds. He wondered if the fallen angel could feel his presence still? Or had humanity lost the ability to sense the divine? "Nothing is ever certain," he replied in response to his colleague's question. "That is the nature of free will." He gestured to their fallen comrade asleep now in the darkness, the lines of bitterness smoothed from his face. "Ruvan is human now. He has all the ability to choose."

Gabriel strode forward to peer at the sleeping man. "He is strong," he assured them, his eyes blazing like twin suns. "He has always been strong."

"And stubborn," Nathanial added. They turned to the lord of the judges at the Gates of Hell. He was an unremarkable figure compared to heaven's princes. He did not have the gleaming eyes, the throbbing voice that could strip the flesh from men, the divine glow that wreathed them in eye-watering glory. He'd stood at Hell's Gate for millennia, he and his judges, weighing the souls who passed by sentencing them to heaven or Hell. And it was on his judgment they now relied. "I trust that stubbornness will ultimately help our cause."

Sim snorted, crossing his arms. "I hope you are right." The weight of warning pressed down around them. Nathanial simply nodded. Sim turned and in a bright flash of light disappeared—flashing from the plane of mankind back to heaven.

Michael shook his head. "Nathanial…."

The judge held up one hand, a simple gold band gleaming in the streetlights. "I understand. He's worried. So much is being left up to the free will of one man." He looked back through the veil between the worlds at Rue. One side of his solemn mouth tipped up in a humorless smile. "Have faith, Michael. I do." He nodded to Gabriel, then stepped between the veil himself, returning to Hell's Gate and the interminable line of souls waiting for him.

Gabriel and Michael stood in silence for a few moments, their silver and gold eyes watching the man on whom all their hopes rested. "I wish we could tell him," Michael murmured.

Gabriel shook his head. "You know why we cannot."

He nodded. "Yes. It just doesn't seem fair to use a colleague as a pawn."

Gabriel clapped him on the shoulder. "The greater good, Michael. It's for the greater good. You know that, I know that and Rue will eventually come to know that." He looked up to the clouded skies. "It's all changing and we need to be ready for it." He gestured to the man before them. "He will understand and approve when this is all done."

"Provided he chooses rightly."

"Indeed."

"Have faith, my brother."

Gabriel smiled and gestured Michael before him. "It's all we have." A flash of light saw them from the world of men back to the halls of heaven. They had more to prepare.

* * * *

She thought she was losing all the circulation in her wrists. The plastic Jewel bags dug in a little deeper as she struggled to shift just one more into her left hand so she could reach her keys. Dan was supposed to be on the lookout. She'd told him she was going to the grocery store. She hissed out an annoyed sigh, blowing one strand of irritating hair out her face. If she could just shift the bag with the milk.… She felt the thin plastic slide, felt it cut into her flesh and begin to split. "No, oh no…." Serafina bobbled, trying to save the milk, knowing deep down the gallon of two percent was a goner.

A hand shot out to save the bag right before it gave way. She turned with a grin and froze, her fingers numb from the weight of the groceries, her mind numb from finally meeting him face to face. Mackey's guardian angel, his hair a tarnished gold, his eyes hidden behind black wraparound shades, stood there, probably wondering if the blood had gone from both her wrists and her brain.

"Ah, thanks," she managed, mentally kicking herself in the butt for staring at him like a high schooler. She jerked her head toward the shop's back door. "Dan is supposed to be looking out for me, but –" a fresh surge of irritation had her kicking the door " –he's obviously goofing off!"

"Allow me." The man's voice was low and deep. She thought he was going to try and open the door, which wouldn't work since it was locked, but her fingers tingled when he lifted the bags from her overloaded wrists. She saw him give a slight frown at the deep red furrows the bags had cut into her skin.

She gave her wrists a quick rub then tugged the keys and opened the door. "If I weren't so stubborn," she laughed, "I'd have taken two trips." She gestured down the alley. "It's always such a pain when the car's parked all the way down there, especially in the winter." She waved him into the small break room. "Just drop those on the counter. Some of them go here, some upstairs."

He nodded and deposited the bags.

"Thanks," she held out her hand. "I'm Serafina, by the way. Serafina Kinnock, but most people just call me Fina."

He shook her hand and she felt the hard ridge of callous. "I'm Rue."

She waited a beat, but no last name was forthcoming. She smiled again, jerking off her watch cap to toss it on the cluttered countertop. "Thanks for the help, Rue." She could hear Metallica screaming in the next room and rolled her eyes. "My cousin had better be hard at work finishing the rest of my lights." She could almost feel Rue backing up toward the door, ready to make a break for it. She didn't want him to run, didn't want him to disappear into the bright winter sunshine like he had into the sleet that misty day, a couple of weeks ago. She picked up the coffee pot, rattled it. "The least I can do is offer you a cup of coffee, and you have to come see my shop."

His lips curved up in a tiny smile. It was such a sad smile, churning her imagination into overdrive. Finally, he tugged off the sunglasses. His eyes surprised her. With all that blonde hair she expected lighter eyes—blue or green, not a brown so dark they appeared black.

"Take a seat." She gestured to the old ice cream parlor table she'd bought at a flea market and refinished. "I'll make us some coffee, then show you my shop." She filled the pot, measuring the grounds carefully. "I've seen you around a few times." She jerked her chin in the direction of the Spider's Den. "I know Joss and Herm." She smiled, "In fact, Joss just asked me a couple days ago if I had anything that would wow Aisha for their anniversary." She knew she was babbling, but she also knew instinctively that if she stopped talking, he'd bolt.

"Do you have something?" his quiet voice broke her train of thought.

Serafina nodded. "I'll show you." She grabbed the frozen items from the bags on the counter, shoving them into the little freezer in the staff fridge. Seriously, her cousin had to lay off the Ben and Jerry's, she decided, tossing two mostly empty cartons in the sink to make room. "Let's let the coffee brew and I'll give you a tour."

He followed her through the door into the shop proper. She could feel the reluctance coming off him in waves. She didn't know exactly why this man intrigued her. She'd seen him a handful of times over the last couple of weeks. The first time had been in the sleet when he'd first given Mackey change. Afterward, she'd almost missed him. He'd acquired the long leather trench coat and shades, but he still stopped to give Mackey money every time. Once, she remembered watching out the shop window as he'd paused, hand in his pocket, at the spot were Mackey usually sat. She wanted to tell him that Dan had taken the old man to the shelter early that day. It had been bitterly cold and they'd been worried he'd freeze to the bridge. Rue's momentary pause had stirred something in her. For a split second, she just knew she was looking at a kindred spirit. By the time she'd gotten out the door, he'd been gone. Up and over the bridge, and nowhere to be found.

She wasn't going to let him get away so easily this time. She felt a connection to him and she wanted to know if it were truly there or a product of her always-overactive imagination. He stood awkwardly in the doorway, hands fisted in his pockets. "What do you think?" She spun gesturing to the whole shop.

Dan, up on a ladder again, ear buds in *again*, despite the loud music, twisted. She saw his foot slip. Saw the ladder tilt. And there was nothing she could do about it.

Rue moved. No, moved wasn't the word. Rue seemed to *flow*. One moment he was at her side; in the next he grabbed Dan, bracing him so he wouldn't crack open his head. Both men went down in a graceless heap.

Serafina's pulse bounded in her throat, pounded in her head. No, not a migraine now, she begged. I really don't have time for one right now. She raced to her cousin's side. "Are you two all right?" Her hands flew over her cousin's face, his arms.

"Get off, Fina, I'm fine." Dan flushed, his cheeks red with embarrassment and humiliation.

"Rue, are you…?" Her hands brushed his face and the words dried up in her throat. She could feel the scratch of whiskers, though his hair was light enough she couldn't see them. Those intense dark eyes of his pinned her, freezing her hands and words. He looked so lost. For a crazy moment she wanted to lean in....

"Jesus Christ, Fina," Dan scrambled to his feet, "you nearly gave me a heart attack!"

"Don't," Rue's voice sliced through the raging.

Serafina's hands dropped away, a blush burning her face. She let him help her to her feet. "It's ok, Rue, really." She glared at her cousin. "If you'd had the music at a normal volume you would have heard us." She flung a hand out toward the fallen ladder. "What kind of idiot has the music cranked *and* earbuds in?"

Dan kicked the ladder. "God, Fina...."

There was a hint of steel in Rue's voice when he broke in. "I asked you once, now I say again I will not tolerate such blasphemy." He turned that dark gaze on Dan. "Do not take the Lord's name in vain again." The words rang a warning through the sudden silence.

The bell over the shop door jingled. Joss hesitated on the threshold. Serafina couldn't tell if it was surprise at seeing Rue or if he could sense the sudden tension that filled the room. She ignored both men, turning to her customer. "Joss," she smiled. She took his hand, pulling him toward the first case Dan had finished lighting. "I was just telling Rue that I had the perfect anniversary gift for Aisha right here." Rue took the hint she threw and wandered away from her cousin. Dan's face looked angry, but slightly puzzled as he bent to pick up the ladder and his scattered tools.

Light swam over the creamy pearls. Joss whistled. "Man, Fina, they're gorgeous, but," he shot a worried look at her, "they're real, right?"

"Of course, they're real." She opened the case and pulled out the necklace. Pearls, cold, heavier than they looked, poured into her palm. "They're freshwater pearls. That's why they're so irregularly shaped." She played the necklace back and forth in her hands.

Joss looked like he was going to reach for them, then stopped himself, shaking his head. Snow melted, dripped from the ends of his dreads to spatter on his shoulders. "Nah, Fina, they're gorgeous, but they're way outta my league." He looked up at her. She saw the regret in his eyes. "I can't pay what these are worth."

She shrugged and turned toward the antique desk she used to check out customers. "Then pay what you can."

He continued to shake his head. "I can't do that to you. You're too nice as it is." He glanced over at Rue who had stood silent as a statue the whole time. "Serafina's our own little angel, round here." He gestured back toward the window. "You know she mother hens old Mackey out on the bridge most every day. She knows all the kids who dance on the street corners in the summer by name and hires them to wash her windows while she lectures them about staying in school."

She stuck her tongue out at Joss as she finished wrapping the necklace in pale green paper. "I've seen you do your share too." She handed him the package. "Joss can never turn away a girl scout."

He laughed and handed over his credit card. "That's the cookies, woman, not charity."

"Uh huh," she snickered.

"I need to go," Rue murmured. He nodded to Joss and Serafina. Dan gave him a half-hearted wave.

"Thanks for the save, dude."

The door closed on Dan's words.

"What up, Fina?" Joss asked with a jerk of his head toward the door.

She shrugged. "Nothing. Braniac here," she gestured to Dan, "was supposed to help me with the groceries. He didn't hear me pounding on the door and Rue gave me a hand."

Joss nodded. "Fina, you gotta charge me more than that," he protested the number on the credit slip.

"Just sign the receipt, Joss. And tell Aisha I said happy anniversary."

He shook his head. "You're going to run yourself outta business you keep up like this."

Her mind was already off the sale. "Do you know anything about him?"

"Rue?"

She nodded.

He gnawed on his bottom lip. She wondered if he knew something, he just wasn't telling. Finally, the artist shook his head. "Nah, not much. Dude doesn't say much even when he's in the chair."

Dan sidled up to the conversation. "I didn't see anything obvious. What's he getting?"

Joss didn't answer; he looked lost in thought. Serafina wondered what had brought Rue to Joss—maybe it was the religious leanings. Fina knew that Joss's left forearm had a beautiful angel, wings outspread, sword in hand, a rosary wrapped around his wrist to drape over his hand. His right forearm had a devil, all sly grin and dancing flames. She'd asked him once about his art. He'd told her they represented the two halves of man—good and evil with the head and the heart in the middle always being fought over. She'd been charmed by the story. What could Joss' left arm have to do with Rue? Was he getting an angel tattooed on him?

Her imagination spun into overdrive.

Maybe a tribute to a tragically dead younger sister? Maybe a reminder to follow the path of good after years of giving into temptation? Maybe….

Joss' voice brought her back. "Sorry, man, if the art's not out in the open, I gotta assume a client don't want to advertise."

Dan looked a little disappointed.

Serafina knew just how to distract her cousin, "Dan, I forgot to tell you. I needed room in the freezer so two of your ice cream cartons are in the sink."

"Fina!" He squawked and ran back to the kitchen area tossing a "See ya, Joss," over his shoulder.

"Seriously, he should weigh five hundred pounds," she muttered.

Joss reached out to cover her hand with his. "Fina, I don't know the dude's story, but honest, there's something odd about him. I don't know exactly what, but there's something off. Don't do anything stupid, ok?"

She smiled. "I'm just nosy," she assured him. "Now, get home and make sure you tell me how Aisha likes the necklace, ok?"

He paused a moment longer before shooting her a grin and leaving.

No, she was just curious. She remembered Rue's sad smile, his surprisingly dark eyes, and his odd warning to Dan. She was just curious, wasn't she?

CHAPTER THREE

He had shelter now. A room in what was called an SRO, single room occupancy building. The tall red brick building a few blocks away from the college teemed with other men: men whose luck had turned to the worse, men who struggled against the darkness in their own souls for redemption. Rue filled out the paperwork, startling the older black woman behind the desk with his lovely handwriting, and answered all their questions.

Yes, he was homeless.

No, he had no family.

The physician in charge of the physical had given him a clean bill of health, shaking is shaggy white haired head, murmuring about how he was in such good physical condition for being on the streets.

He was now the owner of a small room complete with bed, dresser, large mirror and refrigerator. He supposed he should put something in the fridge. He ran a hand over his chin. The growth of new whiskers scratched his palm. He was partial to Pepsi. He liked the way the bubbles burned. Maybe he'd get some to put in the fridge? A glance at the clock on the wall told him dinner was being served in the communal dining room. He could wander down and help himself. He shook his head. He was uncomfortable yet with the other men.

Rue could no longer see the sins of the men around him. He'd lost that ability with his wings when the Seraph princes had sentenced him to his punishment. However, he'd been on the job for a terribly long time. He knew, deep in his bones, that many of the men who sprawled on the couches in the SRO's lounge idly flipping channels were fighting with and against themselves every day.

He turned his back to the mirror inspecting Joss' work. If he looked closely enough he could see the individual spines on each of the feathers. Joss did beautiful work. He could almost believe that if he flexed his shoulders the furled wings would spring from his back. Joss was a good man, Rue decided. He understood, truly understood that man was the battleground for the soul. He recalled the artist's tattoos—the angel and devil—and the explanation behind them. He shrugged into the t-shirt they'd given him downstairs. Maybe Michael had been right.

Twilight darkened the sky beyond his window. He felt restless. Couldn't settle. Couldn't decide what to do. He paced from door to window and back. He could read one of the books on the community shelves downstairs, or play cards with a couple of the other men in the lounge, or zone out and watch *Wheel of Fortune*. Though he was careful now to keep his mouth shut and let the other men have a few chances at guessing the puzzles every once in a while.

No. He wanted to walk.

He swung on his trench coat. The scents of home had faded, but he was thankful to Michael. He wanted to walk. He needed to be out in the air. He loved the sharp bite to it—a cold so deep it made him choke out that first breath. But, heavens above, it made him feel alive! The biting nip of sleet, the gentle kiss of snow. Rue idly wondered what the other seasons would bring. Would he still be here when the sailboats currently dry-docked in the marina nearby skimmed the waves of the lake? Would he see the leaves turn golden, feel the summer breezes? No use wondering now. He would see what he saw. And learn to appreciate each season as it came.

Martha, the dragon at the gate, raised one dark eyebrow as he swung through the entry vestibule. "Goin' out late tonight, Rue," she observed.

He nodded. "I need to walk."

She chuckled. "There are just some who need to go out every day to make sure the world's still there." She shook her head. "You can take the boy off the street, but sometimes can't take the street outta the boy." She waved him through the glass doors. "We lock down at ten, Rue, you know that. Not here by ten you're locked out until the morning."

"I know." He shot her a smile. "Mom." He'd never been mothered and her concern warmed him.

She laughed at the joke and waved him away.

He wouldn't be back by ten. He needed more freedom than that. What was that she'd said? He needed to see if the world was still out there? Maybe he did. What did it mean when his world consisted of fleeting glimpses of a red-headed angel trying to save the city one soul at a time?

He'd seen her sprint through the traffic on Michigan a steaming cup of coffee in her hand to rescue Mackey. He'd watched her hurry out of her shop to help a woman who'd dropped her overstuffed purse chase down the last fluttering receipt. He'd sampled one of the brownies she'd dropped off for Herm and Joss. Chocolate chunk. He pressed his lips together in remembered appreciation. Heaven itself couldn't boast such a delicacy. Not that he'd have been able to taste them if he'd still had his wings. He pushed his hands deep into his pockets, willing them to warm up.

Maybe there was something to be said for humanity. There was plenty of bitter, he noted, watching a homeless man struggle to get comfortable in a nearby doorway, but as he remembered the warm chocolate coating his tongue, there was also plenty of sweet.

* * * *

Maybe this hadn't been the brightest idea. Serafina tucked her mittened hands under her arms to warm them and marched down the alley. It had seemed like a nice little short cut. Her shop and the cozy little apartment above it was just at the other end of the alley. She was near Columbia University, the Auditorium Theater right in the Loop. It should be safe to duck down an alley—even at midnight.

She hadn't anticipated the long shadows unfurling themselves from the side of one of the buildings to dog her steps. She kept her head down, her hand already fisted around her keys. They were just taking a short cut too, she tried to tell herself. The shadows drew closer, words and laughter materializing out of the darkness.

They chattered in another language, something she didn't understand, though she suspected it was something rude. She picked up her pace. The steps behind her quickened. Breathless laughter, the pound of running feet and she felt a hand wrap a bruising grip around her arm. Her scream choked off into a sharp squeak when the hands slammed her roughly into a wall, the building at her back. "Here now," the man holding her laughed, "why you in such a hurry?"

Another man, shorter and broader than the first laughed from behind him, "Yeah, me and my amigos just want to have some fun."

Serafina's eyes rolled. She counted three of them: the one who held her, the one who'd just spoken and a silent shadow as look out who danced a switchblade from hand to hand. She felt her heart hammer in her chest, the breath back up in her throat. "M-my purse," she stammered. The second man jerked the purse from her shoulder, the first didn't move except to flex his hands on her shoulders. "No jewelry?" One hand unzipped her coat, then scrabbled under her sweater searching for a necklace. He didn't find a necklace, but grinned at finding her breasts. She squeezed her eyes shut, shuddering at the bruising grope. Her mind spun, head pounding, what to do, what to do, what to do? Her arms shook and the scream welled up in her throat. The man assaulting her shifted his grip, letting her right arm loose.

She screamed, whipping the hand with the keys up to slam into the side of her attacker's head. He howled, swearing in something that sounded a bit like Spanish and fell away, blood blossoming in the street lights. She bolted.

"Get her!" Her attacker shouted, and Serafina poured on the speed.

She slammed against her building's back door, hands shaking, trying to fit in the key. "You hurt my cousin!" A hand snagged her hair, spinning her around. Her hat dropped to the slushy ground. The keys jingled musically to the pavement.

Her scream cut off sharply when he banged her head against the brick. Eyes rolling, she searched the shadows. Someone heard her, right? Right? Someone had to have heard her.

The bulk of the second man filled her vision. The thug holding her grinned and slapped her hard across the face. She whimpered. Sharp needles of pain lanced through her head. For a split moment streetlight gleamed across his face. Cruelty etched deep lines under eyes that glittered unearthly green in the uncertain illumination. A large hand reached over, but instead of hurting her, it wrapped around her attacker's throat and ripped him away. She dropped, her knees weak, to the cold alley. She scrabbled for her keys, clutching them in numbed fingers. With her own breath harsh in her ears, she fought to force her shaking hands to work. She heard grunts of pain behind her and the solid thump of a fist on flesh.

"Serafina," the low voice in the sudden silence stopped her. She'd only heard those tones once before, but she recognized them.

"Rue!" She turned, her voice a breathless squeak. "Thank God you were there!" Her keys clinked to the ground again.

She'd only seen him once since he'd helped her into the shop with her grocery bags. It must have been as he left the Den from his appointment to drop money in Mackey's cup. He'd cast a look over his shoulder at the Trove before disappearing for another week into the city.

Rue retrieved her keys and had the door standing open. "Let's get you inside and call the police." He looked back over his shoulder. She followed the line of his gaze to see the three men littering the alley way like so much garbage.

"Before they crawl away." She smiled, though her hands still shook. She looked up at him, "I think I still owe you a cup of coffee? Tea?"

She saw him hesitate, but he eventually nodded, ushering her up the stairs after firmly locking the door behind them. Her hands still shook when Rue opened the door to the apartment. She fumbled the phone. Rue caught it before it hit the floor. She laughed. It sounded shaky. "Why don't you go make that tea," he suggested. "I'll call."

She nodded and left him. Tea sounded good right now. She pressed fingers to her throbbing head. Tea with a little Irish in it sounded better.

* * * *

Rue dialed 9-1-1. He explained to the tired-voiced woman on the other end of the line what had happened. He'd been walking through the alley, a short cut on the way home, when he found a friend of his, also taking a short cut, being assaulted. He'd fought the toughs and left them in the alley—unconscious, but mostly unharmed.

He placed the phone gently on the table and looked around. Officers were on the way. Don't leave, he'd been told, they would want to talk to him. Rue figured the men had already crawled away, slithered back into their holes, but he'd do what he should. They wouldn't be there, he knew. He rubbed a hand over his face. The numbness of adrenaline began to fade and his shoulder started to throb. He'd been injured; a knife that had shimmered just for an instant in his vision changed into a claw, and had gotten past his defenses. The glittery gleam in the acid green eyes of the attackers, the flash of fang, the dance of flame... he shook his head. What did it mean? He knew the creatures of the dark sometimes slithered out of their holes between the worlds to play with humans, but why here and why now?

He wanted to rush back to the alley, hunt the shadows and blast the demon spawn into oblivion. Impossible now in this form. He could only follow the rules of his new human world. He ran a hand over his face, tired down to his bones. This attack didn't seem to be following the rules of humanity, but when had evil ever done so?

Glass clinked and he looked up, then ducked across the room to take the tea cups from Serafina. "Thanks," she sighed, dropping to the overstuffed sofa. She tugged a cork out of a bottle of good whisky, tipping a generous dollop into her cup. She shook the bottle. "It's not polite to let me drink alone." She smiled even though he saw the shock still in her eyes.

The weariness decided it for him. He nodded, holding out his cup.

She tossed a couple of blue pills into her mouth, chasing them with the liquor-laced tea. At his raised eyebrow, she blushed. "Headache. I get migraines. It's just some Advil to take off the edge." She dropped her head back to rest on the couch. "I think I'm actually going to have to go to the doctor and get something stronger, though. I've been popping advil like Pez and they barely do a thing."

He cradled the cup in his hands, leaning forward to brace his elbows on his knees. His right shoulder started to throb. How hurt was he? He was still unused to this new form. How much could it take before it ceased to function? What would happen if it did stop?

A pounding on the downstairs door and the muffled call of "Police!" shot Serafina into action and halted his musing.

"One minute!" she called down the steps.

He reached out, touching one hand to her wrist. "I'll go," he offered. He gestured to the couch. "Sit down."

Rolling his wounded shoulder, he bounded down the stairs. It pulsed in time to his heartbeat, becoming something he could ignore for a little while longer at least. A memory stirred. Some of the demonic denizens of the world between worlds were venomous. The wound gave a nasty throb as if to underscore his worries. Something to think about later he decided as he opened the door for the police.

The two officers regarded him with heavy eyes. He could see the weight of their jobs on them in the flashing red, white and blue lights from the cruiser parked across the alley. Window curtains twitched in upper windows, but no one came out. A glance down the alleyway proved that he'd been right. The men, or creatures, he'd knocked unconscious had managed to creep away before the authorities arrived. A long buried urge to drag them back for justice fluttered like broken wings in his soul.

"Do you need me to show you...?" he began.

The taller cop shook his head. "No need." He gestured behind him, "Mugging was interrupted." He jerked his chin toward the stairs. "The lady okay?"

"Why don't you come up and ask for yourselves?" Rue could feel irritation beginning to burn in his chest. Admittedly, they didn't have a chance of tracking and arresting the villains, but they weren't even interested.

"Might as well." The younger cop nudged his older partner. "Might be the break we're looking for."

The older cop sighed but nodded, gesturing with his flashlight for Rue to lead them up the stairs.

Back in Serafina's tidy apartment, Rue leaned against the wall next to the door. The burn of his shoulder wound was fading into sharp little shocks whenever he moved. Leaning against the wall, not moving was working for him right now. Serafina sat where he'd left her, the tea cup warming her palms. Light from the fringed lamp on the side table picked out the gold highlights in her red hair. He fisted his hands in his jeans pockets. His fingers itched to brush through the tangled mass. He wondered if it was as soft as it looked.

Her low voice trembled as she related the story. Had they found them? No, they hadn't. Of course, the police assured her, they would be on the look -out. Had she gotten a clear enough view for a line-up if it came to that?

They younger cop kept casting nervous glances over his shoulder at Rue. "Anything you can add, sir?" he asked, swiveling on the couch.

He shrugged and immediately regretted the move. He could feel blood slip warm and wet down his arm. Claws weren't usually venomous, he finally recalled. Only the fangs. Relief made his knees weak. "Serafina's covered most of it," he said. "I was cutting through the alley and heard the scream. I came running." His eyes moved from the suspicious younger cop to the older one doodling now on his pad. "I did what any upstanding citizen would do."

The older cop flushed and snapped shut his book. "Thank you, Mr….." he paused significantly.

"Rue." His voice was sharp in his own ears. "Just Rue."

The silence stretched thin between the two men before the older officer snapped it. "If we find anything we'll be in contact." His partner nodded to them and led the way out the door.

"I suppose I'll get going now," Rue murmured, pushing away from his slouch against the wall. He wanted to check the shadows one more time. He wondered if he'd still be able to sniff out their presence or if he'd lost that gift with his wings as well. It was late enough that no one should be able to see him crawling around the shadows.

Serafina's eyes had widened; her hand flew to her mouth but didn't muffle the gasp. "Heavens, Rue, what happened?"

He turned. A smear of red painted the wall like a careless child's art. "Hmmm," he-moved the wounded shoulder, feeling nausea now roil in his stomach, "it's worse than I thought." He gave Serafina a thin smile. "I wonder if I could have a bandage or two?"

She rushed to him, her face paling. Cold little hands guided him to the floor, tugging on his long leather coat. He shrugged it off, the scrape of the leather sending a new surge of pain down his arm. He closed his eyes, pressing his forehead into the plush carpet next to her coffee table.

"Let me... " her voice quavered, "just let me.... " Footsteps pattered across the room to disappear. Rue closed his eyes wondering if he wanted to see the gash. Not really. She returned with a bowl, bandages and disinfectant. He let her tend him, her competent hands soothing more than the gash.

"One of them had a knife," he muttered, a small smile curving his lips when she sprayed the disinfectant and blew on it like a mother for a child's scraped knee. She could understand a knife. He could almost believe that he'd imagined the claw now, with her hands moving on his skin.

"You should probably go to the hospital." She dabbed and blew again.

He grunted a negative.

"You should have told the police." She pressed gauze to the wound, binding it with medical tape.

With a sigh she sat back on her heels. He turned his head to watch her. Lamplight glowed behind her red hair giving her a halo brighter and more beautiful than any he'd seen in heaven. "Thank you," he whispered, sitting up. He needed to touch her. He took her hand in his and brought her fingers to his lips, an old fashioned gesture that he suspected she'd enjoy. Her cheeks reddened. "You're a ministering angel."

She tugged her hand away scooping up her supplies. "Let me look through the pile of things Dan leaves here. I'm sure he has an extra t-shirt." She paused, her eyes running speculatively over his form. "It might be a little tight, but should keep from getting you arrested."

He rose to inspect the damage in his coat. The gash was a straight line about three inches long. The wound was a constant burn, more irritating than anything now. "I'll get out of your way, then."

She paused in the doorway, a t-shirt twisted in her hands. "It's after two a.m., Rue. Way too late to go wandering the streets." She rolled her eyes, gave a nervous laugh. "You can bunk on the couch."

CHAPTER FOUR

Serafina stared at her ceiling and wondered if she
should have bolted her bedroom door. Though, against
whom? The t-shirt she'd given Rue had been way too tight
and had done little to stem the desire to run her hands
through that tarnished bronze hair and down that chest. It
had been a test of will to not trace the delicate feathers
inked so meticulously across his shoulder blades. She could
almost imagine the brush of feather on skin.

She bit her bottom lip and rolled over, pummeling
her pillow. Five-thirty in the morning. She'd dropped off to
sleep like falling into a well for about two hours. Dreams
filled with haunted dark eyes and the shadow of wings had
driven up her blood pressure and pulled her out of slumber.
Part of her wanted to be embarrassed that she was having
such dreams. But seriously, wasn't Rue the perfect
candidate for dreams? Mysterious, kind, a touch of danger
and God, he was gorgeous. A knight in shining armor,
who'd taken a knife for her, rescued her from a fate worse
than death and kissed her fingers with courtly old-fashioned
genteelness. Or was it that he didn't find her nearly as
intriguing. *Intriguing, hell*, she ruefully admitted to herself.
He was sinfully gorgeous and she was more than willing to
indulge in a little fantasy about him.

With another groan she levered herself out of bed. It
was useless. She was never going to able to be able to go
back to sleep. She inched the door open. She'd left her tea
on the side table. Perhaps the brandy-laced tea would help
soothe her into sleep. Or, she almost snorted, she could just
snag the bottle of brandy.

She went to the living room, discovering she needed
to step carefully around Rue. He slept on the floor,
stretched out on his stomach, his hair just long enough to
cover his eyes. No pillow but his crossed arms, Dan's shirt
draped over a nearby chair, his jeans low on his hips where
inked feathers disappeared under denim. The bandage

marred the smooth expanse of his shoulder, clearly visible in the gray pre-dawn light. Tiptoeing like a thief through her own living room, she knelt beside him.

She was just going to check the bandage. She acknowledged that lie as soon as she spun it. His skin felt warm as she traced the feathers. Would he have them colored in? She could see them, like hawk's wings, a beautiful blend of brown, red and gold darker than his hair. Joss did wonderful work, she thought.

She felt when he woke. The muscles under her hand tensed, braced, then relaxed one by one.

"It's lovely," she whispered, fingers trailing down his spine. He shuddered under the touch.

His voice was thick when he responded and her lower body tightened wondering if it were sleep or desire that roughened his tones. "Joss is an artist."

She traced another feather enjoying the feel of him. "He truly is. I think if I were ever going to be crazy and get a tattoo, I'd definitely go to Joss."

He turned his head, one dark eye gleaming up at her. "What would you get?"

She drummed fingers on his good shoulder as she thought, noticing with a little thrill that his pulse jumped in his throat. "I'm not certain." She smiled, trailing her hand down one inked wing. "Though I might get an angel." She shook her head. "Not one of those goofy little baby angels, but one of the sword carrying kind."

"Seraphim," he murmured.

She nodded, "That's the one." She tapped the art on his back. "That's what these are, aren't they? Angel wings…" She paused. "I thought for a minute they were hawk wings, but…."

He sat up abruptly, much closer than she'd thought. His hand closed over hers, warm and strong. "They're a reminder and a penance," he murmured, and she heard sorrow in his voice.

She raised her free hand to his cheek, feeling the warm scrape of his whiskers. In the cool gray light before dawn she leaned in. Be brave, be foolish, she thought, pressing her mouth to his. He froze and for a second she thought she'd read him wrong, but the hand that still held hers tightened and pulled her closer. His mouth opened and he responded, taking the kiss out of her control. She tumbled into his lap, feeling the hard press of him through her sweats. Her hand fell from his cheek down his chest. His heart pounded against her fingers and he groaned into her mouth.

He stopped her hand in its descent, pressing it against his stomach when she would have gone further. Blood pounded in her head, but it wasn't a migraine. Her pulse thrummed thick and warm, and desire pooled in her belly. "Rue," she whispered against his lips.

He ripped his mouth away from hers, burying his face at the juncture of shoulder and throat, the scrape of his beard, the harshness of his breath making her shudder. She gasped and pressed against him. He held her steady, just away from him, her hand still trapped by his. "Serafina." His voice was muffled by her skin, the words whispering across flesh. "This isn't what you want."

She shifted her position, straddling his lap and wringing a strangled groan from him. She grinned, wrapping her arms around his neck, pressing close. "Rue, I think this is what we both want."

His hands gripped her hips hard, making her heart leap. She could feel him poised ready to take, ready to give. He closed his eyes leaning in, his forehead touching hers.

"Rue?" she whispered. Her shifting made his breath shudder.

"Serafina," he said, his voice strained with need, "we can't be foolish." His hands flexed in defiance of his words, "No matter how foolish I want to be." His eyes opened and she could see desire and sad humor in them. "I truly wish... but...."

She closed her eyes, just letting the feel of him hum through her. "I..." she trailed off.

He brushed one hand up through her hair. "I understand completely." One side of his mouth quirked up in a self-deprecating smile, making her head swim.

From the bedroom her alarm sounded, the harsh squawking making her jump, breaking the mood. "Oh!" She twisted to look at the clock. "I'm supposed to meet a friend of mine at the gym this morning."

His hand settled warm on the back of her neck, keeping her against him for a moment before he nodded and leaned back. "I'll get out of your way."

She knew she should get up, get dressed and let him walk away. Fear shuddered through her that if she let him go right now she'd never see him again. She held him for a moment. "Will I see you again?"

She felt the hesitation in him. "I should walk out of this room and out of your life right now," he whispered, confirming her suspicions. She leaned back. He looked so torn.

"Please." She pressed a chaste kiss on his lips. His arms tightened for a moment.

"God forgive me, I don't want to walk away."

She pressed a kiss to his cheek. "Then don't." She smiled, feeling her heart lighten. "Come by at closing time. We'll have dinner."

He lifted her to her feet. "I'll be here." He snagged Dan's shirt, pulling it on.

She twisted her hands. "You promise?"

He swung the leather coat around his shoulders, not even flinching as he flexed the injured one. He lifted one of her hands to his lips. "I swear."

After the door closed behind him, she indulged in a little happy dance, boogying across the living room to the bathroom. Now, all she had to do was decide what to make for dinner.

* * * *

Rue watched her leave. Slouched at a table next to the window of the Artist's Café, he watched her walk down the street, her pink gym bag swinging behind her, her red hair pulled back into a bouncy tail at the back of her head. Her fluffy orange earmuffs should have been ridiculous, but charmed him instead. He warmed his hands on the cup of coffee he didn't want to drink. The last thing his system needed was more stimulation.

He closed his eyes for a moment, bringing the early morning back into focus. His body sprang to attention. In all his centuries, he didn't know you could feel so *alive*. Temptation had never tasted so sweet.

"Contemplating sin?"

Rue opened his eyes at the gravelly voice. The tall man, skin the color of polished ebony, eyes of shimmering amber, dropped to the seat across from him. "Feel free to sit down," the fallen angel muttered.

Azrael snorted, taking Rue's untouched coffee for his own. "You're treading a thin line, Rue."

He shrugged, feeling his wounded shoulder pull in response. "I'm living, Az. Living for the first time in my existence."

The angel sipped silently. "There are advantages to the life, I've seen." His golden gaze met Rue's. "I've seen more than most of you how much love affects them, how they cry when I come for them."

Cold fear suddenly gripped his bowels. He stared at the serene dark face of the Angel of Death. "Who are you here for?"

Azrael waved one hand, his silver skull and cross ring flickering in the late winter sunshine. "I'm not here on business." He gestured to the west. "I'm heading off to Loretto Hospital later, but I thought I'd stop in and have coffee with a colleague before getting on with my day." He grinned, making two women on their way to coffee counter stop in appreciation. One cold look from Azrael had them moving on shivering in the sudden chill.

"We're not colleagues anymore." Rue took back his coffee. It had been warm when Azrael had swiped it. A rime of frost now ringed the cup.

"Sorry about that."

"You're lucky I like iced coffee."

He clapped a hand to Rue's shoulder making the man wince. "You've changed, Ruvan."

A pulse of pain thrummed down the arm. He sipped. "Is that good or bad?"

Azrael remained silent for a moment, his gaze going distant. "I think it's for the best." A flare of freezing cold, a sharp burn of pain and the ache in the shoulder disappeared.

"Thanks," Rue said, his breath puffing white with frost.

"Don't mention it. Demon injuries have a tendency to infect more than not."

"So, they were...."

The angel pinned the man with a look, freezing him as easily as he'd been a deer in headlights. "Don't be a fool, Ruvan. You may not have wings, but you're not an idiot. You didn't lose all your instincts when the princes sent you here. Use them."

"Have there been more of these attacks than we knew about?"

A helpless head shake. "I wish I knew. I know that there've been more and more who I've had to attend to personally, but what it means, your guess is as good as mine. Keep your eyes open." Azrael checked his watch. "I need to get going. I have an appointment. Coffee's on me." He stood looking like he was trying to choose his words carefully. He shook his head, then nodded to Rue. "I'll see you soon."

Leaving those words to hang ominously behind him, Azrael ducked out the door, allowing himself to be swallowed in the early morning crowds.

Rue went back to the alley behind Serafina's shop. A cloying stench hung in the air. One a human would most likely attribute to the bins of trash against the buildings, but he knew that smell – the sweet, rotting smell of demon. In the bright light of day most of the ominous shadows had disappeared. One dark blot of shadow still sat under the fire escape where he'd spent his first night in the mortal realm. No amount of sunshine seemed to penetrate the shadow, but even when he poked a foot into the shadow, he hit nothing but pavement and had a passerby looking at him like he was crazy. Hunching against the cold wind streaming through the narrow alleyway, he left. If the portal were still active, nothing would be able to come through in the light of day.

* * * *

Rue filled his day with words.

He found himself standing before the imposing edifice of the Harold Washington Library. The vaulted red brick building smelled of books and dust and held a reverent silence he hadn't seen even in Holy Name Cathedral when he'd stopped by for a visit. Banks of computers stood to one side, but it was the stacks of books, stretching higher than a man could reach, that drew him. Students and the elderly camped at tables or sprawled on the floor in the stacks, surrounding themselves with words. Wires hung out of many an ear and one young man danced to a tune only he could hear.

Rue ran his hands over the spines of books. He'd seen few books in his place as a judge. Souls couldn't carry anything but their deeds in life. He'd read *them* like books. Too often in the last centuries he'd read the same stories.

Vice, greed, gluttony, waste and violence. His fingers trailed over the book spines. All that was here too. All those vices of human kind were contained in these pages. All the vices and all the virtues. Here too were stories of kindness, love, gratitude and redemption. Redemption. He sighed.

There would be no words of wisdom on the demons he'd seen last night. He would see nothing but mortal speculation and fiction on the subject, and possibly frighten his fellow patrons. He'd noticed in his weeks walking as one of them, that humans worried about quite a bit. He knew he would find little of demonkind here in the building dedicated to knowledge, but he could find humankind. Keep his eyes open. Follow his instincts.

Dust motes danced in the sunlight from the windows and he pulled a volume by the Bard. Sitting on the floor, Shakespeare's words flowing like water around him, he settled in. Portia's words echoed most clearly in his mind:

PORTIA: The quality of mercy is not strain'd,

It droppeth as the gentle rain from heaven
Upon the place beneath: it is twice blest;
It blesseth him that gives and him that takes:
'Tis mightiest in the mightiest: it becomes
The throned monarch better than his crown;
His sceptre shows the force of temporal power,
The attribute to awe and majesty,
Wherein doth sit the dread and fear of kings;
But mercy is above this sceptred sway;
It is enthroned in the hearts of kings,
It is an attribute to God himself;
And earthly power doth then show likest God's
When mercy seasons justice.

Mercy, he thought, running his finger over the word. Mercy is an attribute of God himself. Rue felt hollow. His shoulders itched, though it had been a week since he'd had a session with Joss. He'd been sent to find his own mercy, his own compassion. One could not judge when one had none, he'd been told. The Seraph princes had been very adamant about that.

He closed the book, replacing *The Merchant of Venice* on the shelf. A few stacks away he found Harper Lee. The Bard's words, Portia's words, were here too. Atticus Finch told his young daughter to walk a mile in a man's moccasins before she judged him. Rue tucked a finger in the book to hold his place, turning his face up to the light streaming in through the windows above. Despite the bitter temperatures outside, fingers of sunlight slipped warm and soothing over his cheeks. Benediction and blessing. The itch between his shoulders eased.

Replacing Harper Lee's work, he tucked his hands into his pockets prepared to follow the noble Southern lawyer's advice. Michael had been right. He needed to live, he needed to learn the true heart of mankind and find his own mercy and compassion, in order to win back his wings and bask once more in the light from heaven's throne. Live and learn, but stay aware. As it was written, there were more things in heaven and earth and, he added, all the worlds between.

* * * *

Joss was waiting for him. Fisting his hands in his pockets, he pushed back out into the late winter winds that whipped around the bases of the buildings. Buildings so tall they blotted out the sun and made dark valleys of the city streets.

Ears stinging from the cold, Rue pushed into the warmth of the Den. He looked around. The shop was quiet, empty. "Where's...?"

"Place to ourselves today. Herm's on vacay." Joss laughed. "Went on a single's cruise in the Bahamas. Like any woman in her right mind's going to look at that inked, pot-bellied bastard. Ready for color, dude?"

He nodded, glancing over at the colored sketch pinned above Joss' workspace. He noted that the sketch only appeared when he was there. He tugged off his coat, jerked his chin to the paper. "Why don't you keep it up all the time?"

Joss followed his gaze. "I figured your art was covered for a reason, man. Didn't want to advertise."

He pulled off his shirt, nodded. "You're a good man."

Joss rubbed a hand over his left forearm. "All I can do is try."

The two men stared at each other for a moment before breaking out into grins.

Joss snapped on his gloves, readied his equipment. "So, what's the story?" He gestured with the stylus he was filling with color.

Rue shrugged and turned his back to the man. "It's a long one."

"A lot of them are." The artist's gloved hand brushed over the new shoulder wound. "What's here, man? Didn't have this last week, but it looks too old to have happened recently."

He remembered the searing cold of Azrael's touch. He should have thought about that. Humanity wasn't comfortable with casual miracles. "I'm just a fast healer." The lie felt heavy on his tongue.

He could feel Joss weigh his words, and wondered if their new accord had already been broken? The whir of the needle punched the silence. "Must be another chapter to that story, huh?"

Rue closed his eyes, feeling the stinging nip of the needles. "You have no idea." They sat in silence for a moment. "So," he smiled, "did your wife like the gift?"

He heard the grin in Joss's voice. "Did she ever! Man, Fina never misses the mark. She's gonna run herself out of business with that big heart of hers, but she's a jewel."

Rue felt his blood run thick in his veins at the memory of her hands and mouth on him in the pearly light of dawn. "She is special," he murmured.

The stylus paused, powered down for a moment. He looked up, caught the speculative gaze and felt his face heat in a blush. "Yeah." The man's voice was serious. "She is special." The needles seemed to bite a little deeper, the pain a little sharper when he fired it up again. "We're real protective of her."

Message received. Loud and clear. "I know why." He tried not to flinch.

"You know her well?" Joss' voice was forced casual.

"We've talked on a few occasions. I helped her out a couple of times." Rue supposed he'd rescued her twice— once from her groceries and her own impatience, and once from the toughs. Which reminded him....

"Joss, have you heard anything about some guys in the neighborhood making trouble?"

He snorted out a laugh. "There's always guys making trouble. You got no job, no education and no support, you start looking at the street for answers. Why?"

"Fina was almost mugged last night."

"Shit!" The artist jerked away for which Rue was thankful.

He sat up, turned. "I was out walking last night." He shrugged. "Couldn't sleep, just wanted to walk." He looked at Joss and saw someone to whom he didn't have to explain the restlessness in his soul. "It was a good thing I couldn't sleep."

The artist's chin jutted out, a pugnacious bulldog looking for an ass to chew. "You get the bastards?"

His mouth stretched into a smile and he flexed his hands. Azrael might have fixed the shoulder, but he hadn't touched his raw knuckles. "We had words."

Joss grunted, "Good." He gestured for him to turn around. "Fina all right?"

"She's ok. A little shook up." He jerked his head in the direction of the Trove.

"Maybe I'll swing by later, check on her. Maybe take her home with me. Aisha wants to cook her a thank-you dinner."

Rue felt his cheeks heat again. "She invited me to dinner tonight."

Another long pause. The drone of the stylus the only sound. "Well," he said finally, "I hope she makes you her lasagna. That's a gift from God, right there."

CHAPTER FIVE

"Fina, where's my Metallica shirt?" Dan's voice floated down the back stairs. "I thought I left it in your room?"

She glared at the spread sheet on the computer screen. The numbers weren't staying in their nice neat rows. They kept jigging around. She pressed her fingers to her right eye. Was it her eye or the monitor? A headache began to thrum.

"Fina! Didn't you hear me?" Dan yelled again. "I need my Metallica shirt. What did you do with it? Chloe's waiting for me to pick her up for the concert."

Metallica shirt? "It's probably right where you dropped it," she shouted back. She needed to finish the invoices and get upstairs to work on her sauce. She wanted to make lasagna for Rue. He looked like he didn't get too many home-cooked meals, but this was just taking forever. A sharp spike of pain lanced behind her eye. She lowered her head to the desk for a moment.

Dan pounded down the stairs. God, he sounded like an elephant. "It's not there." She looked up. He ran his hands through his tousled hair, annoyance in his eyes. "I left it here 'cause I knew I had the concert. *You* had to move it."

"I didn't—" She broke off the snarl when the door jingled. She twisted the snarl into a smile which froze on her face when Rue walked in. She swore her head went numb as the blood dropped to her cheeks to light them in a glorious blush.

He swung off his coat. Dan's beloved Metallica shirt stretched across his impressive shoulders. The sound Dan made next to her was a growl mixed with a scream. She twisted to look at her cousin and was gifted with the most knowing and disgusted look in his repertoire. He looked just like his father, she mused.

She opened her mouth to explain, then realized it would sound worse than the truth. Let her cousin think whatever he wanted.

"Don't you have a concert to get to?" Frost rimed her tone.

Dan's glare raked over Rue. "Yeah, have a nice evening, Fina."

She bit her tongue as he stormed out. The back door slammed.

She rolled her eyes. "Never mind him. He's just in a bad mood."

He strolled over, draping his coat over a low tapestry back chair. "He's just protective of you."

She smiled and ran a finger down the front of his shirt, feeling his stomach muscles tense along the path. "Of course it could also be that you're wearing his favorite shirt."

He cocked an eyebrow. "Maybe I should give it back?"

She laughed and he smiled in return. "I needed a laugh today." She locked the front door, pulled the shade. "Well, closed for the day." She shook her head as she turned out the window lights. "It was a slow day."

She felt him step behind her, his heat warming her when he reached out to run his hands from her shoulder to her wrists and back again. The headache that had begun to wind behind her eyes started to unravel. "Troubles?"

She took a deep breath. "Not really. Just slow." She gestured at the window. "It was so gloomy today." She smiled and turned into his arms. "I guess I have the winter blahs." She let herself lean against him. Let herself wrap her arms around his waist and settle her head on his chest. She could smell her own laundry detergent on his shirt and some indefinable scent that could only be Rue. For one moment, she let herself dream. What would it be like to come home to an embrace, a warm shoulder, a kind ear every night? She'd never felt lonely before, but after tonight she wondered if she'd be able to say that again. There was just something about him.

She pulled back, looked up at him. "What is it about you?" she whispered. He tensed and her hands moved over his back to soothe. "Oh!" She exclaimed. "That reminds me... " She grabbed his hand in hers, pulling him toward the stairs in the back room of the shop. "I wanted to change those bandages."

He dug in his heels, making her stop. "Serafina." He gave her hand a little tug. "Serafina, wait."

He looked so serious. Her heart began to hammer, a nervous patter. He looked like he had that morning when she'd been so certain he was about to walk out of her life forever. "What's wrong?"

His mouth curved, sadly, sweetly. "Nothing's amiss. I just wanted to take you out tonight."

"I thought I'd cook for you."

He tugged her closer, one hand reaching up to fist in the riot of red curls that tumbled down her back. "We both know we won't be able to step away next time." He leaned down, pressed his mouth to hers in a chaste kiss that promised so much more. "You're a temptation."

She twined her arms around his neck, pressing closer. "Don't you ever want to give in?"

His eyes, dark and intense, focused on her mouth. His breathing changed and she knew his control was hanging by a thread. "More than you can imagine." He closed the distance and she shut her eyes, letting him take her under. He devoured her, his mouth desperate, hungry. She clutched his shoulders. Her head felt light and desire pooled in her center, wringing a groan out of her. If she could just get her hands to let go of him for a moment, just for a moment, she'd be able to.... He dragged his mouth away from hers, his hungry lips roaming her face.

"Rue, let's...." He cut her off with another brain-draining kiss.

He stepped away so suddenly she'd have fallen if the wall hadn't been handy. "I'm sorry," he whispered, his voice a grating rasp. "Serafina, can you forgive me?"

She leaned against the cool wall, feeling her heart leap and her system jitter in frustration. She tried to inject humor into her voice, though part of her wanted to scream. "Forgive you for which part, Rue? Attacking me or letting me go?" She fanned herself with one hand. "I can forgive one, but not the other."

His smile was all male satisfaction and made her want to scream at him for his damnable restraint. That old fashioned chivalry she'd so admired the night before was becoming a major stumbling block. "Let me take you out to dinner in apology."

After a moment, she nodded. "All right, you get your way." She grabbed the stair rail. "What do you say to Petterino's? Their lasagna's not quite as good as mine, but they'll do." She could sense his hesitation. She reached out, grabbed his hand. "I promise I'll behave."

"Hmmm," he mused, following her up the steps. "I hope I can."

She left him in the living room, perusing her DVD collection while she went and changed. The bold teal sweater hugged her curves and dipped low enough to tease the eye with a creamy hint of cleavage. Perfect. He seemed to like to bury his hands in her hair, so she left it down and brushed just a tint of color on her lips and cheeks.

He was standing at the window looking down on the bridge, the traffic snaking like red-eyed ants through downtown. "What are you thinking about?" she asked, grabbing her winter coat from the stand by the door.

He glanced over his shoulder, and she thought briefly that he looked like an illustration off of a vampire romance novel. Though she didn't recall any teeth. She ran her tongue over her own teeth, remembering the taste of him.

"What are you thinking?" she repeated.

"I'm thinking of the seven deadly sins," he answered, then stepped over to help her shrug into her coat.

She wrinkled her nose. "That's an odd thought, isn't it?"

He trailed long fingers along the swell of her cleavage. "I've one particular sin in mind."

She shivered her breath a little burst. "Ah, yes." Her voice was shaky. "Lust is one of them."

He hummed low in his throat, then turned away to open the door.

"Rue?" He paused, the hall lights highlighting his hair. "Is is always a sin? What about when lust is tempered by love?" She swept past him, determined to enjoy a night out in the theater district. She was happy for the slap of cold March wind. Maybe it would cool her blood.

* * * *

Rue thanked Michael once more for not only the coat, but the money that had been tucked in a tight roll in one of the pockets. Most of the money he'd been given when he'd been sent down was already gone—given to Joss and Herm as pay for returning his wings. He'd never thought he'd need money for more than that and a bite or two to eat.

He never thought he'd want to take a red-haired siren out for a night on the town. The restaurant, its walls covered in 1940s illustrations and its dim lighting made him feel right at home. The menu looked like it came out of an Italian grandma's kitchen and he chose the linguine when she teased him about missing out on her famous lasagna.

The red wine, a chianti, the waiter said, sat dry and fruity on his tongue. He wondered how the wine would taste with the flavor of the woman. He'd found himself craving the taste of Serafina more than anything he'd hungered for since being sent to Earth. He shifted in his seat, willing his rebellious body to listen to him. He was beginning to understand just why lust was one of the seven deadlies and why it was one of the sins he'd found most frequently on the souls of those he judged. He twirled more linguine around his fork. He could see too why this would be one sin they wouldn't repent of.

"Are you thinking more on deadly sins?" she teased, dipping a bit of bread in red sauce.

"How could you tell?" He leaned forward, hands playing with his wine glass.

She reached out, smoothing the line between his brows. "You have this little worry line right here." She pushed away her plate. "A latte, please?" She smiled at the waiter who flashed a brilliant smile at her. Rue thought the man's eyes lingered too long.

"You must be cold in that sweater. You should put your coat on." His own gaze traced the creamy swell of her breasts where they pressed against the teal fabric.

"I'm fine, Rue, and you're avoiding the question." She reached across the table to take her hand in his. "Still thinking on your sins? You're very kind."

He tugged away to drain his glass. "You don't know much about me."

She shrugged, leaned back. "I know I've seen you stop every day and talk to Mackey, not just give him money, but actually talk to him."

The old homeless man had been full of stories of his Serafina, how she was an angel as pretty as his own lovely Mary had been. He hadn't seen the old man in while, come to think of it, and Azrael had been nearby. "Is he...?"

Her smiled bloomed. "See what I mean? Mackey's fine. Dan and I got him into a shelter for a couple of days. We're hoping they can get him somewhere more permanent. He's getting too old to be on the streets." She took her coffee with a nod of thanks. The waiter hovered until Rue shot him a glare. "You saved my idiot cousin from himself." She sipped the foamy coffee. "That was an impressive move." She swirled whipped cream up with a finger, licking it clean. "Finally, you saved me."

He felt all the blood drain into his lap with that last move and the look on her face had him convinced that she meant for that to happen. "You don't know...."

She squeezed his hand. "I don't need to. I know there's a story." She tipped her head to the side, studying him as he'd studied the wild red slashes of paint on canvas at the Art Institute several weeks before. "Everyone has a story. Some of the stories are little more exciting than others." She offered him a sip of the latte. "I have a feeling your story would be pretty exciting."

He drank, letting the warmth soothe the razors he felt lining his throat. "It's definitely stranger than fiction." He handed back the cup. "What's your story?"

"Very pedestrian," she snagged the bill before he could. "You could say it would be in the typical Midwestern section of the library."

"Lake Woebegone?"Rue waggled his fingers for the leather folder.

She shook her head, ignoring his bid for the check. "Not quite that quiet, but pretty close." He sensed that there was more there, but understood that she didn't want to get into it. He felt an odd desire to know what dimmed the light in her eyes, however briefly.

Glancing at her watch, she nodded toward the street. "Want to catch a movie?"

"Don't you need to open your shop tomorrow morning?"

She slipped into her coat, taking the arm he automatically offered her. "The good thing about being the boss is that if I want to open a little later, I can. It's Saturday tomorrow, not much action in the Loop in the morning. Besides –" she pressed closer, and it was the most natural thing in the world to slip an arm around her, " –if we go a movie we can sit in the back and neck."

The images playing in his head stopped him in his tracks.

She danced in front of him, ignoring the crowds pouring out of theaters into cabs. "Rue, you all right?" She smiled, wisps of red hair escaping from her hat to dance in the playful breeze. She looked full of mischief. "If you're worried about those sins again, I can probably behave myself."

She grabbed his hand, tugging him behind her. "God in heaven, I hope not," he prayed.

CHAPTER SIX

The movie had included quite a few explosions, a hero who lost his shirt pretty early on and a heroine whose own ensemble grew more and more tattered as they ran from the invading aliens, blasting as they went. Rue remembered very little of it. Serafina had kept her word. She behaved. He hadn't. He'd been much more interested in the feel of her mouth under his than in how a man improbably called The Rock drove off alien hordes.

Martha had looked at him quite knowingly when he'd strolled in that morning. It had been too late to return to his SRO, so he'd slept in the alley behind the store, under the fire escape where Michael first found him, his eyes trained on the stain of shadow. Nothing had attempted to creep through, though the fact that it was still there that morning when dawn painted the sky, worried him. Normally, the entryway closed behind them to fade with the sun. That it hadn't, told him the demonkin had unfinished business.

Water dripped from the ends of his hair. Showers were still a human marvel to him. He stared at his reflection, shaking hair out of his eyes. He'd had to do that much more often. Perhaps it was time to have it cut? He grunted, picking up his razor to shave, something else he'd never had to worry about when he'd had his wings.

Sunlight danced through the dust motes on the bed. With a frown, he glared at the glittering shimmer as it coalesced and solidified. He hitched the towel tighter at his waist as the figure cleared. Aniael lounged on his bed, making no pretense at humanity. Her robe shimmered unearthly white, her wings of dusky gold folded gracefully at her back and draped across his plain covers. She fluffed her white-blonde hair, the look in her unearthly blue eyes just a bit challenging.

"What, no halo?" he drawled, folding his arms at his chest, leaning against the dresser.

"I'm trying to be subtle." Her voice echoed chorally, making him wince. She smiled. "Sorry," she said in a much more human tone.

"To what do I owe the pleasure, Ani?"

"You'd think you'd be happy to see me, Rue." She stood, one wing clearing the small table at the bedside. A water glass tumbled to the ground soaking the hem of her robe. "Oops."

"Furl them, Ani." Was she trying to tease him with her wings? His shoulders ached, muscles protesting as though they wanted to flex their own feathers. Old regret stirred. "What do you need?" He turned his back to her, pulling a shirt out of the dresser.

"Ooh!" Ani breathed. Rue felt her cold little fingers trace the art on his back. "They're just like yours were, Rue."

He stepped away, pulled on the shirt. "That was the idea." He held up a pair of jeans. "Do you mind?"

Ani rolled her eyes, but turned her back. "You humans and your fig leaves."

Not trusting the mischievous angel, he yanked on the clothes. "All right, you can turn around and tell me what you want. Women aren't allowed up here, so hurry it up."

Keeping her wings tight to her back, she faced him. "You've changed, Ruvan. Azrael told me you had, but I didn't believe it until I felt your heart tug me here."

He pressed a hand to his chest as though he could stop the traitorous beat of his own heart. "I don't...."

Her eyes no longer dancing with trouble, she stepped forward to catch his hand in hers. "Don't lie, Ruvan, not even to yourself." She shook her head. "You know who I am and I'm here to warn you."

"No warning is needed. I understand." He kept his voice flat. Any human would have understood the tone –

case closed, don't go there. She wasn't mortal and had an inhuman tenacity.

"You're at a crossroads, Rue." She pressed, "Trust me. I'm love's herald and I can see it as clearly as though it were written in front of me. You have a choice to make. Soon. You can choose to love one woman. Choose to stay here with her and give up your wings, become as mortal as she, set to face the judges at the end of your time here—a number of years or days that only Azrael knows." She stopped as if to give him time to see it.

He closed his eyes. Imagining. To love Serafina. To have her for his own, make a life with her. To wake to sunlight, gray skies, softly falling snow – all with one woman in his arms. To experience all the seasons he'd dreamed about with her hand in his. He could see it. Smell the scent of her hair and feel the shape of her pressed against him. Love. One of humanity's own miracles.

Ani continued. "If you do, you will never again be one of heaven's princes. Never again – " she fluttered her wings, the scent of myrrh rising from the feathers, "will you sit at the Father's feet."

Now, too, he recalled the feel of wind in his wings, the eternal companionship and comfort of his fellow seraphs. The overwhelming joy that shot like a pain through his very human heart as he recalled the beauty of the heavens and the love of the Father. The love that was the light, the center of his whole world, was merely a faint warm echo now. He'd felt it dimly when he'd stood in the Cathedral, colored light from the stained glass windows fracturing around him. To feel that again... he felt his breath catch.

"Humanity is flawed. You can choose to revel in the flaws or you can resist the temptation to love one woman for the love of all humanity." She gave him a small smile. "You know as well as I do that there are some sins you will not repent of when the time comes." He remembered something Serafina had said to him. "Is it always sin, though, Ani? You're the Angel of Love. What purer expression of God's gift to mankind is there than love freely given and freely received?"

She shook her head. "I can't say. I'm not a judge, Rue. You would know that far better than I. All I know is that you will have to choose. Soon."

He said nothing.

She rose with a sigh. Standing on tiptoe she kissed his cheek. "Heaven's blessings be on you, Rue. No matter what you choose, remember I wish you love. The love of one woman or the love of heaven's light."

Anieal fluttered her wings, the light building around her. He squinted and turned away. When he looked back, she was gone. A single amber feather was left to mark her passage. He picked it up, turning it over in his hands.

She was wrong, he realized.

Anieal, the Angel of Love, was wrong. It wasn't so much a choice of the light of Heaven or the love of one woman, for what was love but a reflection of heaven's light?

God *was* love.

He'd stood at the foot of the Lord's throne and in the circle of Serafina's arms and found love in both places.

Perhaps those who were too close to the light of heaven were blinded by its brilliance? With a smile, he placed the feather reverently on the dresser. He had a choice to make and a life to live.

* * * *

Shadows.

Creeping shadows crawled across the surface of the X-ray. Serafina shivered in the doctor's cold office, hugging herself as though that would keep her from flying apart. The little blurs seemed so small, so harmless, but they were like the fingerprints of the Angel of Death.

"Ms. Kinnock, Serafina, there are quite a few things we can try." Doctor Castor, one of the neurology specialists from Northwestern, leaned forward, his dark eyes earnest and kind. He pointed to one of the shadows. "This tumor, right over your optic nerve, is the one I find most troubling. I would like to start you on a drug therapy we've found to be very beneficial, right away. It could go a long way to shrinking it enough for radiation and chemotherapy to do the rest." He made a sweeping circle over the trio of tiny spots at the back of the picture. "Chemo and radiation should take care of these glioblastomas, so we'll table the idea of surgery right now." He flicked through several screens on the tablet balanced on his knees. "I'd like to get you into the treatment center for your first treatment as soon as possible." He stopped and reached out, covering her cold hand with his. He let his hand rest there, warming her fingers for a moment until she lifted her gaze to his. "Serafina." His smile was reassuring. "Northwestern has one of the best cancer centers in the nation. You're young, strong and determined. That counts for a lot."

She nodded. "I know, and I keep hearing about how we're learning new things every day."

The young doctor nodded, though said nothing about that. "We're going to treat this aggressively." He tapped a few things on his tablet. "I've sent the prescriptions down to the hospital pharmacy. I've also contacted the home care liaison and the oncology specialist. I want you to talk to Susie Mosswell today. You need to know exactly what you're looking at, here. She's a patient care facilitator. You may need to arrange for someone to help you at home—anything from feed the cat to driving you to your appointments." He patted her hand again. "We'll take good care of you."

The little ball of ice that had formed in her stomach the moment she'd seen those little shadows began to melt. They were going to help. There was something she could do. There was hope. What was that old saying? Where there's hope there's life? She turned her hand up, taking the doctor's in hers. "Thank you," she whispered. Her lips tipped up tremulously. "I don't have a cat, but I do have a shop that needs tending."

Dr. Castor chuckled. "Well, Susie can probably help you with that too."

She grabbed her purse. She could feel her insides quake. She didn't really want to go downstairs and listen to another sad-eyed, well meaning person who wasn't looking at a life in the shadows of illness. She'd smile and listen. Fill out their paperwork and pray her insurance company didn't drop her. She rubbed her fingers between her eyes. Weariness more than pain right now. So much to do, so many decisions to make. A little part of her wanted to play the little kid and pull the covers over her head. If she didn't look, it didn't exist, right? No, not in the grown up world.

Two hours later, she walked into the back door of her shop with a folder full of papers and a purse rattling with pills. Enya's soft strains floated in from the shop. Dan's girlfriend Chloe must be over helping him out. It was the only time he stuck with Fina's musical choices for the shop.

She crept up the back stairs not wanting to see her cousin, not wanting to think about everything right now. She just wanted to shove all this stuff into her underwear drawer, the one drawer Dan would never think of pawing through, and forget about it for a while.

She closed the bedroom door behind her, settling on the bed. She'd washed the shirt Rue'd been wearing the night he'd stopped the mugging. There was still a gash in the shoulder, but she thought he might want it back so she'd put it at the foot of the bed hoping to see him soon. She picked it up, buried her face in the fabric and let herself go.

She wept loudly, long, and messily, muffling the sobs in Rue's shirt, wishing it still smelled like him. Head throbbing, eyes red raw, she lay on the bed watching the sunlight move across her floor, the shirt still clutched like a talisman to her breast. She reached for the phone on the bedside table. Dimly she heard the phone ring down in the shop.

"Serafina's Treasure Trove. Chloe speaking, how may I help you?" Dan's girlfriend had one of the bouncy chipper voices that worked so well for this. She really was a sweetheart, though Fina just couldn't bear to face such cheeriness right now.

"Hey, Chloe, it's me."

Concern tinged her voice, "Fina, is everything ok? Do you need Dan to come get you from the doctor's?"

"No, no." She forced her tones to be casual. "I'm already home. I went right upstairs. The doctor ran a lot of tests and gave me something for the pain." There was something for the pain in her bag, wasn't there? "I just want to lie down for a while."

"Sure. I get it." She heard an impatient little huff. "Dan, your cousin's tired. Don't you go up there. Fina, he has a question." She heard a mumbled exchange and the phone thumped as it changed hands.

"Fina," Worry tinged his tone. "You ok?"

She smiled in the fading light. "I'm better now." She was, wasn't she? Now that they knew, it would all be better. She'd tell him later, just not now. "I'm just really tired right now."

"All right. Chloe and I will finish up here." He paused. "Do you want us to stick around after? We can order Chinese and watch some screen. I'll even let you pick out a chick flick and I promise I won't gag."

She thought about it. She didn't really want to be alone with her thoughts, but she didn't want to have to keep up the façade either, and she was in no way ready to really tell her beloved younger cousin. If she told him, he'd tell the family and she'd have to deal with his hysterical mother and her self-absorbed one descending on her before the week was done. She could only imagine her mom— fluttering around having her own 'issues,' countermanding the doctor's orders and telling her what she should do. "No, don't worry about it, Dan. I'm all right. Besides, didn't you and Chloe want to catch 7th Heaven at the Snuggery tonight?"

Silence on the other end. She closed her eyes, imagining the tense conversation happening over the covered phone. He was back. "All right. You win. I'll leave you alone tonight, but I know something's up with you, Fina. I have my cell on if you need me. Just call and we'll come back."

Like he would hear his phone at the club, but it was a nice thought. "Thanks, Dan. I'll be fine."

"'Night. I'll come by early tomorrow, bring you those donuts you like."

"Sounds like a plan." She clicked off, letting the phone rest beside her. Toeing off her shoes, she curled up and fell asleep to the sound of the traffic on the street outside.

* * * *

The pounding on the back door of the shop woke her. Groggy, she sat up and fumbled for the light. Eight pm. She'd been asleep for about three hours. "All right, all right!" she yelled down the steps. Dan must have forgotten something, along with his key.

She brushed her hair away from her face as she wandered down to the break room. She checked the peephole out of habit and froze. Rue stood on the stoop, the streetlight bright on his dark blond hair. Tugging at her wrinkled shirt and hoping she didn't have pillow marks on her face, she fixed a cheerful look on her face and opened the door.

"Rue, I wasn't expecting you today."

"You look tired." He stepped in and reached out to brush a hand over her cheek, closing the door behind him.

She closed her eyes, leaning in to the touch. "I am. I had a doctor's appointment and it just wiped me out."

His hand froze. "Are you all right?"

"It's..." She shook her head and pulled back. "I don't want to talk about it. Let's go upstairs. Are you hungry? I can fix something."

She didn't let him respond, didn't really look closely at his face. She didn't want to see any pity or concern there. She'd put it away for tonight.

He caught her on the steps; a simple tug on her hand stopped her, had her turning to face him. "Serafina." He looked so serious, so intense. "Whatever secrets you have are safe with me." He pressed her hand to his chest. She felt the thick beat of his heart. "I will keep your secrets close. You've no idea of the secrets I have."

His eyes were filled with them. She could see their weight pressing down on him. She wanted to comfort and be comforted. She wanted the illusion of forever right now. "Rue," she said. She lifted her free hand to his face. "Rue, please stay with me tonight?"

He kissed the fingers she danced over his mouth. "I'll stay as long as you like."

He swept her up in his arms, making her smile. It was so dramatic, so old fashioned romance novel, so... Rue. She twined her arms around his neck, settling against his shoulder with the warm of glow of belonging, and yes, she admitted to herself, love settled around her. She didn't know really when it happened, but it had. Maybe it had been the first time she'd seen him slipping money into Mackey's cup before disappearing into the sleet?

"You sure you're not hungry? I still owe you dinner."

He kicked the door closed behind him. "I'm hungry all right," he murmured and let her slide down, keeping her as close to him as skin. She felt every nerve ending in her body sit up and take notice. Her heart thrummed in her chest and for once it didn't make her head ache. Her hands crept around his neck and that was all the urging he needed.

The hesitancy, the reluctance she'd felt in him before had disappeared. His hands molded her to him. His mouth was a fever on hers. She tried to concentrate, tried to draw out the experience, remember every moment, but his hunger pulled her under. All she could do was cling to him, swept up in the heat.

His coat hit the floor. She yanked up his t-shirt, running her hands over his stomach, smiling against his mouth when she felt him suck in air. His hands fisted on her shirt. With a yank, buttons flew and he dropped his head from her mouth to her throat, his hands at work behind to unhook her bra.

They made it to the bedroom, leaving a trail of clothes behind them. Her hands molded his muscles, the strength of him thrilling through her. His hands and mouth roved over her, lighting fires in her blood. She writhed against him, hands fisted in his hair as he licked over her hip teasingly. "Rue, for the love of God, please?" she begged, yanking him up.

His eyes, as heavy with desire as the rest of his body, met hers. "Truly?" His voice was a harsh rasp against her mouth.

She couldn't speak – the feel of him pressed against her was too much. All she could do was moan as she wiggled, trying to take him in. With a deep breath he filled her. Fina's nails bit into his shoulders as he froze, just over her, eyes closed, head thrown back as he seemed to absorb the feeling.

She gave an impatient wiggle and he groaned, buried his face against her shoulder, his stubble shooting shivers through her as he began to move.

CHAPTER SEVEN

Rue felt his heart hammer in his chest. His brain still wasn't functioning and his hands kept moving over Serafina's back. He'd rolled, bringing her with him. She lay sprawled across him, her head tucked under his chin, her hands tracing idle designs over his bicep, scattering his wits every time he tried to gather them.

Nothing in all of his centuries could have prepared him for the elation, the exhaustion, the sheer joy in the physical. Laying there with this woman in his arms was worth losing his wings. The judges didn't need him. He closed his eyes, pulling her closer. There were many judges, but only one Serafina.

"Tired?" Her words whispered across his flesh, stirring desires he'd thought fully sated.

"Happy," he replied.

She scooted around to rest her chin on her stacked hands. Her kiss-roughened lips curved into a smile, beautiful with a touch of wicked at the edges. "You look happy." She reached up to trace the lines of his face. "You look happy for the first time since I first saw you."

He ran his hands over her shoulders, enjoying the feel of her smooth warm skin. "Did I look so miserable then?"

She didn't speak at first. He could all but see the wheels turning in her head. "You looked lost," she finally decided.

His hands buried themselves in her tumbled red curls, tugged her forward. "I'm found now," he whispered against her mouth. He felt her shift, closed his eyes as her heat closed around him and she began to move.

Dark humor and desire threaded through her voice. "Look at what I've found."

Need was a storm shuddering through him. He'd ridden the lightning and flown with tornadoes. He'd stood for centuries at the threshold of Hell and sentenced the worst of mankind. And nothing, nothing in all these long centuries could have prepared him for the temptation of woman.

Hours later she slept curled up on her side, her bottom tucked against his groin. Rue couldn't sleep, fearing that if he closed his eyes it would be nothing more than a dream. He'd open his eyes and find himself at the iron gates of the underworld, a line of souls stretching as far as he could see into the distance.

"It hasn't changed much." The grating voice made him jump. Naya'il, Angel of Testing stood at the window. "Come talk with me, Ruvan." The eyes he raked over Serafina's recumbent form were more pitying than anything else. "The woman won't wake."

He hitched on his jeans following the tall, thin figure into the living room. He mused that when humans had come up with their view of the Angel of Death they must have seen Naya'il instead of Azrael. Naya'il seemed to match the Grim Reaper image much more closely. His skeletal build, deep set eyes of burning crimson and long white hair spoke more to human fears than did dark haired, golden eyed Azrael. Then again, he was the angel of tests, the angel who brought humanity trials and tribulations. He was the one who piled on the misfortunes to temper souls and strengthen spirits. Too often humans broke from the weight of the burdens and wound up in front of Rue and his brothers at the broken gates of Hell.

Fear, icy cold, gathered in his stomach. He and Naya'il had worked together closely in ages past, though having made the decision to stay human, stay with Serafina, the angel should have no further business with him. Unless... he was here with a test.

"How can I help you, Naya'il?" He struggled to keep his voice neutral, the tone of a colleague as opposed to supplicant.

The grim specter turned, red eyes boring into him. He could almost feel them measuring his soul. Felt them find him wanting. "You're making a mistake here."

Shame flushed his cheeks red. He raised his chin, defiance making anger fire in his blood. "It was my decision to make."

Naya'il snorted, snapping his fingers to will a long silver cigarette into existence. The scent of frankincense filled the room. "I don't mean you giving into lust." He rolled his burning eyes, amusement lighting sparks of gold deep in their depths. "Honestly, I don't even know why lust became one of the seven deadly sins. It's quite vital to the continuance of the species." He gestured with the cigarette, trails of smoke hanging in the air. "I think that has more to do with early man's fear of his own urges than anything else." One side of his mouth lifted in a sinister smile. "Or the fear of woman, more like. You know as well as I do, Ruvan, how often those urges lead to more destructive and violent ends."

Had he ever understood? Ruvan thought he now knew how man could be driven. A man not nearly as controlled, not nearly as aware could easily be led about by those urges. And the desire to defend? He shook his head. Well, he could now understand how a man might commit murder to defend those he loved. Regret burned through him, sour as bile. To think he'd sentenced those men as murderers; sent them to rot in a darkness of their own making, cut off from the very things they'd killed to save.

"Now do you understand why I said you made a mistake?" Naya'il waved a hand, vanishing the cigarette and the smoke, leaving nothing but the lingering scent of incense on the air.

"I think it's for the best that I give up judging, Naya'il." Rue finally admitted sinking down to the couch. "I just realized how harsh I've been for the past century or so." He shook his head, fisting his hands in his own hair.

"Nathanial shouldn't want me back." He paused, thinking for a moment on Nathanial, the Angel of vengeance and fire, the Archangel who oversaw the judges at Hell's Gate. He'd been the one to suggest Rue's punishment for zeal to Gabriel and Michael. He'd urged them to this course of action. "He was trying to get rid of me all along, wasn't he?" Despite his decisions, despite his resolve, he felt his heart flutter as regret and betrayal surged through him.

Naya'il gave a disgusted snort. "By the light, Ruvan, you've always been stubborn. It's one of the traits I've always admired about you. But –" Naya'il reached out grabbing his shoulder forcing him to look up " –don't be a fool. Nathanial sent you down here so you could find your compassion. So you could see, really see, what it was like to be human. So you wouldn't judge those who had loved – " he gestured to the room behind them, the room that still smelled of sex and woman " –to the pits with those who had abused and twisted love." He smacked Rue in the chest, knocking the man back. "It's not the same. Something *you* now know, but –" those burning eyes flared " –the other judges *don't.*"

"Nathanial wants me back?" Something stirred deep inside him. His shoulders itched, muscles twisting. Indecision as sharp as a blade sliced into him.

Naya'il knelt before him. "Nathanial understands what it is like to despair, to think nothing but evil of mankind." The angel took a deep breath. "He also understands what it is like to walk among the humans, to live, to love and to bring that compassion back to the judges."

Rue's breath stopped up in his lungs. Seconds ticked by until spots danced in front of his eyes and he realized he'd forgotten to breathe. Several things clicked into place, pieces to a puzzle he didn't even know he had been looking at. "Nathanial?" His voice squeezed past the shock.

Naya'il nodded. "It was more years ago than even you can count, my little judge."

He shook his head. Confusion, desire, regret, and shattered contentment swirled inside him, a messy stew that he admitted could only prove his humanity now. "I don't...." he trailed off, his eyes going to Serafina's door. His heart ached, actually ached, to think about leaving her behind, yet there was a different kind of ache, perhaps deep in his soul, at Naya'il's words.

"It's a test, Rue." Cold hands rested on his. "You knew it when you saw me." He patted the man's hands, leaning back. "You have a choice to make. You thought you'd already made it after Anieal came to you. You didn't have all the pieces yet. I've given you more."

Naya'il rose, gathering his long cloak around him. Light from the streetlights outside shadowed the hollows of his cheeks. "I'm still missing a piece or two, aren't I?" Accusation shaded Rue's tone.

"You always were quick." Naya'il gestured to the front window. "Keep your eyes open. You never know when another piece of the puzzle will fall into place."

Rue went to the window, pressing his hands to the cold plate glass, eyes trained on the street below. He saw nothing but the street, the bridge, and the huge bronze statue of a woman, her outflung arms turning to wings against the dark heavens. He turned back to ask, but Naya'il had vanished. With a frown, he decided to tuck it all away for a while. He had a warm woman waiting in bed.

Cold prickled over the nape of his neck making his hair rise. He glanced back over his shoulder at the street. A shadow unfurled from the base of the statue and coalesced into a form with amber eyes and wings of purest night. He and Azrael stared at each other for a breathless moment before the Angel of Death nodded once and disappeared into shadows.

He stood waiting, the prickling at his nape telling him it wasn't over yet. Out of the blot of darkness at the statue's feet a deeper darkness stirred. A sliver of light and inky darkness spread, flowed like water from the statue. Another entry point, another demonkin escapee. The flow rose, stretched and shivered to become a man in a long coat, a hat pulled down over his eyes. The figure paused, then looked up at the window. Rue caught only the flash of sharp white teeth in the moonlight before it slithered off into the city. Quivering with rage, his hands pressed flat to the window, wishing he could blast the demonkin to ashes, Rue slipped to the floor, eyes trained on the deep darkness of the demon door. He would wait. Dawn's light should close the door. If it didn't, there was a much larger problem than the decisions roiling in one judge's heart.

* * * *

She woke to a cold bed. Serafina sighed, snuggling deeper into the pillows. Rue was gone. Part of her knew he would be. With a resigned sigh, she slid out of bed reveling in the aches that told her the night before hadn't been a dream. She slipped into her robe and wandered out into the kitchen thinking coffee might clear away some of the cobwebs left behind by a sleepless night.

He stood at the window silent as a statue. He was dressed, though his feet were bare. Warmth spread through her. She had been all ready to face the morning without him and here he was. She stepped up behind him to wrap her arms around him, pressing herself against his solid warmth. On tiptoe, she kissed him behind his ear, feeling him shiver against her. "Penny for your thoughts?"

"Why didn't you tell me?" His voice was low, broken.

Puzzled, she pulled away, tugging on him until he turned around. "What are you...." She trailed off when she saw the oversized envelope in his hand. She must have left the X-rays on the coffee table the day before. She'd remembered to stash the pills in her underwear drawer, but the X-ray hadn't fit. She'd tossed it on the table before crawling into bed.

"Why?" His free hand caressed her face. She leaned into the touch, closing her eyes, not wanting to see the fear and sorrow in his eyes.

"I just found out yesterday," she whispered. "I hadn't even thought it all through myself. I couldn't...." Her voice broke.

She heard the envelope hit the floor as he pulled her into his arms. She held him tight, not wanting to let him go. "Serafina," His words tickled her ear. "Tell me what you want. Tell me how I can help. I don't have much, but all I have is yours if you need it."

She pulled back and saw relief on his face that she was dry-eyed. "Rue, all I need from you is this." She squeezed him. "I just need you to love me or at least pretend."

He shook his head. "It wouldn't be a lie." His hands pressed her to him. "I should have said it yesterday, but I didn't want you to think I was just saying the words. I thought I should wait until the light of day." She couldn't take her gaze off him. He looked so serious, so intense, sunlight shining through his hair, haloing him from behind. "I love you, Serafina Kinnock." He tightened his hold on her. "I love you with everything I was, everything I am and everything I will become."

She swallowed around the sudden lump in her throat. "I —"

The front door swung open. Dan, whistling, a pink bakery box tucked up in one arm, froze in the doorway, eyes narrowing.

The box hit the floor and Dan moved. Fina found herself pushed behind Rue, pressed against the window at his back. "Dan!" she shouted in horror as her cousin rushed forward.

"You son of a bitch!" Dan fist connected with Rue's chin, snapping the taller man's head back.

She shoved between them, though she noted Rue hadn't made a move to defend himself. "Jeez, Dan! Knock it off!" She shoved her cousin back.

"Fina, if you think…."

"Back off! Rue's here because I want him to be here. It has nothing to do with you."

"Serafina," Rue's quiet voice stopped her. She turned. He reached out, catching her hands in his. "I think you should talk to your cousin." He looked behind him, giving the fallen envelope a pointed glance as he shoved into his shoes. "You shouldn't burn any bridges right now." He looked over her head to Dan. "I'm quite certain I'll speak to you later, Daniel."

"You can be damn sure of that," Dan muttered.

Serafina tried not to blush as Rue brushed a kiss over her mouth. "Come by after closing." She smiled, knowing her cousin was growing fangs behind her. "I still owe you my lasagna."

He nodded, kissed her again and swung his coat up around his shoulders.

After the door shut behind him, Dan turned his glare onto her. "What was that all about?" He flung one hand out toward the door. "You tell me yesterday you're too tired to talk to me after your doctor's appointment, have me worried out of my mind that there's something bad wrong with you, only to come here this morning and find you playing tonsil hockey with that guy?" He pulled at his hair. "Jesus, Fina, you don't even know his last name! No one does. I talked to Joss about him and all he knows is that he goes by Rue." She shook his head. "Do you know where he lives? Do you know what he does for a living? Does he even have a job?"

"Dan," she pressed one hand to her head. She could feel the beginnings of a headache. She had a handful of pills she was scheduled to take and her cousin was shouting at her so much she could hardly think straight. "Dan, listen to me...."

He didn't seem to hear her. "He could have killed you and robbed you blind. He could have a wife. Hell! He could have two wives. He...."

"Loves me!" Serafina shouted, cutting off his tirade. "He loves me." She could feel tears press against the backs of her eyes. "Is that so hard to believe?" She whirled away from Dan to stare down at the street and bridge before the tears could fall. Mackey sat there as always, the bright red scarf she'd given him a cheerful beacon against the cold day that didn't even hint that spring was supposed to be around the corner. Fear made her hands shake as she pressed them against the glass. Her head gave a frightful pound. Would she even be here in the spring?

She heard him shuffle his feet behind her. "What a mess," he whispered. "I'm sorry, Fina. I'm sorry." She turned back. He gave her a helpless shrug. "He just weirds me out." He grinned. "Of course you're loveable." He slung an arm across her shoulders. "I love you, cuz." He gave her a one armed squeeze. "To prove it, I'll let you make the coffee." He turned to pick up the bakery box he'd dropped in his zeal to punch out Rue. Checking inside, he shot her a grin. "Not too bad."

She bent to pick up the X-ray envelope. "Dan, I need to show you something."

The grin fell off his face. "That bad?"

She took a deep breath and gestured to the box. "Bring the sugar. We're going to need it."

CHAPTER EIGHT

Rue pushed his hands deep into his coat pockets, feeling them curve into fists as he stared at the huge bronze gothic doors at the front of the cathedral. They were metal, though fashioned to look like heavily carved planks of wood.

"They weigh more than a thousand pounds each, but are able to be moved by a single finger." He stiffened at the creature's words. "Humans are so clever." A sharp crunch, the sweet scent of fruit. Asmoday quirked one blond brow at him, gestured with the apple in his hand. "Want a bite?"

Rue returned the demon's smile with a stony glare of his own. "I suppose not." The demon blended beautifully with the lunchtime crowds. He nodded to the church. "You going in?"

"You are not welcome here, creature," the fallen angel growled. His fingertips tingled with remembered power. When he'd had his wings, he'd have been able to blast the Deciever back to the pit from whence he came.

"Can it, Ruvan." Asmoday finished the apple, tossing the core over his shoulder. "You don't have the juice anymore." He sat on the steps of the church, patting the cold stone next to him. "Pop a squat, mortal. I have a proposition for you."

"I have nothing to say to the likes of you," he insisted, though he sat. He knew Asmoday could make him very uncomfortable just for fun.

"Wise." The demon tipped his sunglasses down his nose. "Now, I know what you're going to say. Get thee back, demon, and all that other nonsense, but at least hear me out." He rolled angel blue eyes. "If the boss says to talk to you, Ruvan, I talk to you." His smile turned knowing. "Word in the realms has it you're finding being human to your taste." He leered at a young woman walking a trio of dogs on long leashes.

"Get on with it," Rue growled.

"In a moment," Asmoday's gaze followed the girl until she and her charges strolled out of sight. "I mean, who could blame you? Those holier-than-thou types upstairs don't know the benefits of a good roll in the hay." He looked knowingly at Rue's crotch.

He forced himself to stay still. "The purest forms of love are beyond the physical."

Asmoday stared at him in silence for a moment as if tasting the truth of the words. "You still truly believe that, despite rolling around all night with the redhead." He shook his head in admiration. "Man, you judges are made of some stern stuff. I told Luke you're not going to go for this, but...."

"Say what you need to say and be done with it. I have business of my own to conduct." He looked back over his shoulder to the bronze doors of Holy Name.

"Yeah, yeah, you've got some business to take care of before going back to bounce on the redhead some more." He leaned back on his elbows, tipping his head up to the wan sunlight. "I don't blame you. She's a fine piece of ass."

He longed to grab Asmoday by the throat and throw him down the church steps, but he knew the demon was braced for just such a thing so he buckled down on the violent urge. Even so, his voice was strained when he spoke. "You will not speak of Serafina in such disrespectful tones."

The demon's eyes sparked, with anger or amusement, he couldn't tell. He leaned forward, his smile too much teeth for comfort. "Damn me, Ruvan, and you already have, but you *do* love her." Rue remained silent. "Isn't your next line supposed to be, 'more than anything I've ever loved before,' or something equally maudlin?"

Conflict stirred in his soul.

Asmoday fired up a large stinking cigar. He blew the smoke at the next baby stroller that happened by. With a cruel snicker, he turned back to Rue. "It almost hurts me to hear the back and forth inside you." He stuck the cigar between his teeth and held out both hands, palms up like scales. "I love her so much I feel like I'm flying apart every time I'm in her arms." His right hand went down part way. "The judges need me to balance them, so humanity isn't unfairly punished for their crimes." The left hand dipped. "If I leave her, she dies." Down went the right. "She's so good she'll go to heaven and it's really for the greater good." The left dropped more. "It's sad, isn't it?" He jerked his head to the church behind him flicking ash toward a squirrel foraging nearby. "Going to pray for guidance?"

"What would you know of prayer, demon?" He choked on the smoke, smelling tobacco and brimstone.

"I've answered more prayers than you have, Ruvan." Asmoday's smile was pure evil. He *was* the deceiver and claimed to his credit a little trick with a snake and an apple back in the infancy of humankind. Rue could very well imagine Asmoday answering prayers in his own diabolic fashion. "Here I am," he said, throwing the still-smoking cigar into the gutter, "to answer one of yours."

"I have not prayed to you and yours, Asmoday."

"And yet here I am." He spread his hands. "I know what you're going to ask. I can see it in your heart. Save her. Are you willing to bargain? Save her and you'll return to the ranks of the heavenly hosts? Will you return to the Gate and please Nathanial by teaching his judges compassion and snatching souls from my master's hands?"

The demon's words hit him like pebbles.

"I have something better." He snapped his fingers. "Semiazas has given me this." The liquid in the phial gleamed moonlight white. "It can save her. You can stay here on earth with her. Live out your life, redeem this one small fall into temptation and be seated with the redhead among the heavenly hosts after death." He tossed it. Rue instinctively made the grab, snatching the miracle out of mid-air.

Semiazas, he thought, chieftain of the dark angels; king of those who had turned their backs on the light of heaven and found a haven in the heart of Hell. He turned to ask a question of Asmoday, but when he looked over, the demon was gone.

The phial felt warm in his hand and heavier than it should be. Cold wind snaked around the corner, making the tips of his ears tingle. The restaurant across the street was doing a roaring lunch business; the scent of roasting meat wafted over, making his stomach clench. Sharp hunger pains, the nip of cold, the hard stone under his backside— all sensations Asmoday, Naya'il, Azrael and the others would never feel, have never felt. His stomach churned, a greasy roil that had him thankful he hadn't eaten anything.

He wanted to throw the glass bottle, watch it shatter on the stone steps, the miracle potion falling like tears. He wanted to shout defiance to Asmoday and his lords. His hand tightened on the phial, desire warring with duty.

In the end, he shoved the little bottle in his pocket. With determined step he marched into the church at his back. The huge bronze doors slid shut behind him. He stood, eyes closed, breathing in the scents and silence. The weight of ritual settled on him, comforting as a pair of hands on his shoulders. He loved the old churches, ornamented, detailed, colored glass and carved stone. The old churches of Europe were lovely. He'd visited many of them when he'd had wings—from the famed churches of France to the decorated mosques of Saudi Arabia and the temples of the Holy Land. No matter the statues, the symbols, the languages… he'd felt the same light.

He wandered up the nave, eyes on the carved crucifix suspended over the altar. Despite the agony of the pose, the face that looked back at him was serene. He struggled to find his own serenity. His own peace. The phial seemed to grow heavier in his pocket.

He knelt at the altar steps, head bowed. He knew that to pray one needed only a prayerful heart, not the trappings of religion, but right now.... He shook his head. Right now, he felt he needed the extra comfort, the scent of candle wax, the play of sunlight through stained glass.

His mind spun. What to pray? Save her? He squeezed shut his eyes, feeling the prickle of tears at their backs. Save her? He had the means in his pocket. A temptation from the devil. What if she was meant to die? Meant, in the grand scheme of the universe, to be a light to shine for her little neighborhood, a light made brighter by its brevity?

Perhaps her medical science would yet save her? She'd told him she was receiving the best care available. The finest doctors... the thoughts wound to a halt. He'd seen Azrael outside her window. He knew, more than most, what that meant.

What, too, of his own destiny? Rue looked up at the golden altar cloth. The silver chalice placed just so. Nathanial needed him. Needed him to share his own compassion; his own loves with the other judges. He knew why he'd been sent, now. Understood what Nathanial had wanted him to understand and knew, beyond a shadow of a doubt, that he would be a much truer judge for loving Serafina.

But what of the demonkin? The two doorways he'd found, right in front of his face. Those he couldn't ignore. But what to do about them? Stay a human watchman, bring the demonkin to the attention of Michael and Gabriel? He shook his head. Heaven's princes wouldn't interfere. They're agreed eons ago to leave the humans to their free will. The light always honored the convenent. The demonkin, by their very nature, did not. But if he had his wings, what could he do? He was bound to Hell's Gate and couldn't hunt the demonkin on his own. The idea of leaving those creatures to trail after Serafina and the mortal friends he'd made had the blood running cold in his veins.

Too many questions and not nearly enough answers.

"So much conflict," the quiet voice barely broke the silence.

He turned, knowing before he did, Nathanial would be sitting beside him. "I wondered if you would come to me." He kept his own voice low.

"How frustrating it must be for most mortals to never truly know if their prayers were being answered." Nathanial sighed deeply. "I could have had your memories wiped clean. I could have insisted that Michael and Gabriel send you here with no recollection of who you were and from whence you came." The Archangel's voice was low, gravelly, the sound of stone scraping against stone.

"I think I know why you did not." Rue replied still not turning.

"Then you know the choices you must make." He always thought the weariness, the drag of the evil on the souls of the judged, made Nathanial sound so weary. Now, he could hear sadness.

"Naya'il told me." There was no need to explain. He would know.

"And?"

He turned finally to face the Archangel. Nathanial sat, his hands resting on his knees, his one good eye, black as Rue's own, on the crucifix over the altar. The other eye was gone, had been gone as long as Rue had known him, in a face marred by thick white scar tissue that sealed the eye shut and ripped down into the cheek below, to stop right at the corner of the angel's mouth. He had never asked. Never wondered. Nathanial's long fingers traced the scar, a gesture he'd made a million times. "How?" Rue asked at last.

The angel nodded, long blond hair falling forward to shield the scarred eye. "A reminder and a penance."

He felt his back tighten. Nathanial nodded.

"I lived, Rue. I lived, I loved and I lost her." He touched the mark. "I tried to save her. I had already decided to tell Michael and Gabriel to go to Hell." He tossed back his hair and smiled. "I know exactly what's going on in that head of yours."

The vial in his pocket felt heavy.

"I was tired of standing in judgment, of seeing only the worst of what humanity had to offer." He twisted the gold ring on his hand. "I knew there had to be more to mortality so I left to walk among the humans. Shed my wings and made my way as one of them." Gold winked as the ring once more twisted. Rue had seen that band for centuries as well and never wondered at its meaning, thinking it no more than an ornament. "Iya was a pagan priestess dancing a ritual to the moon, when I first met her." He gave Rue a sad smile. "You know what that hit to the gut feels like. I couldn't breathe." Shaking his head, he continued. "She became my wife."

Silence stretched between therm. Rue snapped it up, closed it. "How?"

"Ignorance. Fear." Nathanial gestured to the crucifix. "What has killed humans since time immemorial? They came for her, a faction of the priesthood not aligned with her beliefs." He shook his head. "After all these years I still don't know why they hated her so. She was a light and maybe that was why. She was a light they didn't control. They took her. I fought them, but they overwhelmed me. Left me for dead." His hand smoothed over the scar once more. "They killed her."

"Did you return to judge them?" He felt sympathetic anger bubble in his own gut.

Nathanial shook his head. "No. I returned because Michael told me I was needed." He tapped his heart. "I understood what drove men. I understood the true weight of humanity. Judges who understand are always needed." That single black eye pinned him. "Will always be needed."

Nathanial's presence felt comforting. So much more so than the others who had visited him. He had felt so uneasy in their presence. So unworthy. "Did you –" he choked, " –did you go back right away?"

He wondered if the angel would answer. After a few long moments of quiet, his voice finally broke the silence. "No. Not right away. I had some very human vengeance to wreak." Fury, even centuries old, shivered up Rue's spine. "I hunted those false priests down one by one and sent them to the Maker." One side of the angel's mouth winged up in a humorless smile. "So, I suppose I did judge them in a way."

"Then how...?"

His hand rested warm on his shoulder. "Penance and reminder." With a nod, the Archangel stood. "I understand, Rue." He fisted the hand with the wedding ring. "Remember, though, I need you. Humanity needs you." He tugged his long dark wool coat closed, snugged a hat down over his head. "Add that to your thoughts." His eye seemed to zero in on Rue's pocket, then up to his face. "Remember too, no matter what you decide, I won't blame you." With those final words, he turned and walked back down the nave. A blast of cold air from the closing door signaled his departure. No flashy exit for Nathanial. He'd never been one for theatrics.

One more look at the crucifix and Rue left. He had all the questions, all the answers. He just needed to start sorting them out.

CHAPTER NINE

He began to hunt. He needed more time and while he thought, while he lived, he decided to try and track the demonkin. Were they all coming from the same place? Were they all the same kind?

He left the SRO, rented a tiny efficiency apartment in a questionable neighborhood and spent many of the nights without Serafina walking the streets, peering into the shadows. He'd taken a blade, a long wicked number that flipped around and around before folding into its own handle, from the young man who had tried to mug him on the first night. He'd left the tough out cold in the doorway of a club on Clark Street. He would wake on his own and crawl away under his own power, or someone would find him and call the police. Either way, he was finished with his nefarious deeds for the night.

Rue drew in a deep breath. The cold air burned his nose and lungs, bringing him the scents of the city. Garbage, gasoline, oil, and the sharp, almost pine, scent of fear. He hadn't lost all of his resources with his wings, he'd come to discover. The memories he retained came with some abilities.

He found that he moved faster than most mortals. He also had sharper senses. He grinned in the darkness. That was a true benefit when wrapped around Serafina.

Shadows slithered and chattered at the mouth of an alley, pulling him from his musing. A cat screamed and bolted, a tawny streak across his feet. Slipping a hand into his pocket, he wrapped his fingers around the hilt of his blade as he made his way toward that chittering. They looked like men. Boys really, crouched in the shadows of a shattered streetlamp, a lump stretched out beneath their hands. The cat's companion lay still, dark fur glistening with blood in the moonlight.

Preternatural hearing caught his very human feet scuff. The three of them whipped around, eyes glowing unholy green. The tallest hissed, its fangs dripping blood. The other two stalked forward. The leader returned to its meal, trusting its minions to take care of the interruption.

Rue flipped the blade, small now in the face of three demonkin. He might be faster than the average man, but they were faster still. One of them leaped up the wall, skittering like a huge spider across the bricks. The other crawled forward, knees bending in ways that would break a human, reminding him that these forms were only illusions and not possessed humans, making his job easier and infinitely harder at the same time.

They hissed at each other. He recognized the liquid syllables of their infernal language, but his human ears couldn't understand the words. Their intent was clear. They were planning to feast on the foolish human who had stumbled across their hunting. The cats had been a poor meal for creatures who had been hunting human flesh, and here dinner had delivered itself.

Rue's other hand went to another pocket, palming a vial of holy water. He had only two vials, so he had to make his shots count and hope one of them fled. With a spin, he hurled one vial at the creature clinging to the wall above him. The vial detonated like an explosive against its head. It shrieked, the sound of brakes on the freeway, and clawed its now steaming eyes. It fell with a sickening crunch to the pavement, dissolving into a sticky puddle. Rue stumbled back from the advancing demon goo and right into the other creature's path. It launched itself at him.

Rue took the tackle, rolled with it, tossing the demonkin over him. It twisted midair to land with feline grace on its feet. He would have sworn if he'd been that kind of man. As it was, he brought the knife up in defense just as the bloody-fanged leader crashed into him from behind. The blade clattered down the alleyway. Clammy demon hands clawed at his back, digging at the leather coat, unable to tear through. Rue sent up thanks for that.

The creature crawled off, took a punishing kick that would have broken the ribs of a mortal, and grabbed the fallen angel to flip him over. The acid green eyes narrowed and it snuffled all over him, drawing in his scent. It sneezed. "Angel stink," it grated in a mortal tongue and spat, blasting a tiny hole in the alleyway. "What are you?" It asked, holding Rue's face in one scabrous hand. The sickly green eyes peered close. Its companion whined at the alley mouth.

The leader looked up with a snarl, then exploded into a rain of sticky demon muck. Rue rolled, gagging, spitting the stuff out of his mouth, got to his feet. A shadow detached itself from the walls, a cold wind hissing past him. Rue looked up into the amber eyes.

"You're a fool." Azrael swung his great scythe through the air once more before putting it up. The chill scent of graveyard dirt filled Rue's nose for a moment before the stench of the demon goo all over him rose to cover it. The angel looked at the trio of oily black pools for a moment before remarking, "Didn't know they exploded. I always thought demonkin just sort of melted away."

Rue spat again, retrieved his blade and gestured to the first demon pool. "That one did."

"Hmmm...." Azrael bent, touched one faintly glowing hand to the stained pavement. The pools flowed together, gleamed with silver light for a moment, then faded. Even the hole made by the demonkin's spit looked like a newly-patched piece of asphalt.

"Handy," Rue smiled. "The city of Chicago could use you."

Azrael snorted. "What do you think you were doing?" He gestured to the city sprawl behind him. "You're lucky I was attending a crossing right over there when I smelled the demonkin and came to investigate." He shook his head. "Are you trying to get yourself killed?"

"I'm trying to make some sort of difference." He slipped the switchblade back into his coat pocket. "I'm one of the few people who can see them. That's got to mean something. It's got to mean that I should take care of them."

Azrael reached out to poke him in the shoulder. Rue stumbled back two paces. "You're mortal. Did that little fact slip your brain? You can see them because the princes didn't take your memory." He rolled his golden eyes up to the heavens as if requesting patience. "I don't know why. Usually, they drop the fallen with no memory, but it's not my place to question them." He turned back to the street, saying over his shoulder, "If you really want to make a difference, think about where you can do the most good. Here or at the Gate?" With one more nod, Azrael stepped onto the deserted street and disappeared as if he'd never been.

Rue looked around the grungy little alleyway. Nothing but a dead cat and the lingering sweet stench of the demonkin. He hunched his shoulders against a sudden blast of wind, and started on his way home. Maybe Azrael was right. He was a fool. Maybe he did have a death wish. Watching Fina fade these last few weeks, it was all he could do to keep from slipping the vial of miracles into her tea. Part of him really wished to do it, really wanted to slip her the potion and sit back as the doctors claimed a miracle.

Maybe that's why he'd found himself not at her side every night, but out prowling the streets, looking for demonkin. It was his good luck that he'd found nothing but wholly human predators so far, and that Azrael had been nearby when he'd run into his first true threat.

Maybe he didn't have all the pieces of the puzzle yet, as he'd thought. A glance at the sky showed the brightening gray streaks of dawn creeping closer. Time to get home. Time to think.

* * * *

"Thank you, Azrael," Michael nodded to the Angel of Death. "I knew he would need help tonight."

Azrael bowed. "He's my friend too, Michael." He turned to press on to the next appointment on his list. "There's more going on here, isn't there, than simply Rue finding his compassion." It wasn't a question.

Michael stood silent as a statue, his silver eyes unfathomable. "We cannot interfere. We cannot violate the covenant."

Silence stretched between them. Azrael weighed the Archangel's words, heard what he said and what he very carefully hadn't said. With another bow and a slight smile he turned back to his own business. Though he would keep a closer eye on Rue.

* * * *

"Do we need to speak to him?" Gabriel eyed the portal through which the Angel of Death had disappeared.

Michael shook his head. "Azrael knows the covenant as well as you and I. He won't jeopardize what we already have in play."

"And what do you have in play?" Sim's acid question popped into existence before he did. "Ruvan nearly got himself killed tonight. Azrael's intervention was providential." He glared at Michael, as if knowing exactly where that interference had truly originated. "You nearly crossed a line."

Michael nodded, acknowledging the scold. "Ruvan is a special case, is he not? Of the humans, yet angel-touched as well?"

"He needs more," Gabriel put in.

Sim sputtered as Michael nodded. "Indeed. Trying to take on three demonkin with nothing, but a butterknife."

"I believe it was a switchblade, but an unhallowed one."

Silver and gold eyes met agreement in their depths. "Very well," Gabriel bowed to his fellow princes. "I will take care of it before dawn breaks." A shining shower of gold and he was gone.

"Well, Sim," Michael nodded to the waking world beyond their veil, "have you lost your doubts?"

Humans woke, stirred themselves to prayers even though they themselves did not know they prayed: prayers for safety, something for an empty belly, a job, a day with no pain. The heart prayers swirled around the two Archangels.

Sim gestured, letting the prayers gather in his hands like snow. "If *they* can still have hope, then I would be remiss to doubt." He gathered the prayers to him, lifted them to his mouth and blew. They flew like dandelion fluff. "Take comfort," he whispered, "take hope, see your fellowmen as brothers."

Michael breathed deep. The scent of the demonkin and their oppression began to lift. Hope, like spring dandelion weeds, began to crawl up through the cracks in the city. He clapped his brother angel on the shoulder. "To our work, then."

Sim nodded. They disappeared in a flash of light like the sunlight sparking off a lake.

* * * *

Rue let himself into his tiny studio apartment. Exhaustion dragged at him. He kicked off his shoes, stripped off his shirt and wanted nothing more than an hour or two of sleep before he had to go to work, but he knew that he needed to shower. He could feel the sticky demonkin goo on his skin, permeating his pores and pulling his thoughts in directions he didn't want them to go. Resentment bubbled and he took a deep breath, pushing it away. He'd scrub away the taint, take a nap and then go work. Good physical labor would drive the last of the demonkin poison from his system.

Then he'd see Serafina. She was a balm that could soothe any poison.

With a smile for the thought, he tugged off his shirt, dropping it on the floor next to the bed. The gleam of light caught his eye first. He froze, his very breath backing up in his lungs at the sight of the gleaming silver and gold sword that lay on the bed, its crosspiece on the pillow.

It was the twin of the celestial blade he had been able to conjure when he'd had his wings. He could feel the warmth of the blessed blade from where he stood and it went a long way toward driving away the lingering effects of the demonkin taint.

His hand reached out as if of its own volition to touch the hilt. It molded to his hand as though it had been made for him. A blast of warmth and light and wind, and he stood clean as if he'd just stepped from the shower and as awake as if he'd just woken from a good night's rest. The blessed blade shivered and twisted, shrinking itself down to the size of the switchblade he'd been using. Only then did he see the note. Written on a thick piece of white vellum in a strong hand were the words, "Use wisely."

The note exploded into a shower of silver ashes that melted away to nothing before they hit the floor. He raised his head to the ceiling, murmuring, "Thanks, Gabriel."

* * * *

This was much more the thing, Rue decided two nights later, swinging the celestial blade through the quivering mass of demonkin at his feet. They melted, the pool sucking in on itself before dissipating. He knew not even a stain would be left for the dawn sun to burn away.

"New toy?" Asmoday stepped from the darkness, an unlit cigarette twirling in his fingers. He circled Rue, keeping out of the reach of the weapon. "That's got Gabriel's fingerprints all over it." He shook his head. "Sure, it'll take out a few demonkin." He spat, the spittle sizzling on the shining silver blade. "Don't think it's got enough juice to take on a full demon, though."

Rue shifted the blade, catching the light in the darkness. "Care to try me?"

The demon chuckled. "I'm not one for pure confrontation. I prefer subtler methods."

"Trickery."

He shrugged. "Whatever works." He tapped a finger to the outstretched blade, the sizzle of burning flesh rising to Rue's nose. Asmoday closed his eyes for a moment, as if savoring the sensation. He lifted his burning finger to his cigarette. Sour smoke curled to the dark sky. His eyes, red as rubies, pinned the mortal. "Whatever works seems to be a common theme. You seem to be what works right now."

"What are you...."

"Are you actually asking me questions?" He shook his head, laughed. "You must be desperate." He cocked his head to the side as though weighing a few options. "Tell you what, Rue, I'll give you some answers, but I want something in exchange, just a little favor." He put the cigarette to his lips breathing deep, making the tip glow like a coal in the night. "Just a little tit for tat."

Rue snarled. "I don't need any help from you, demonspawn."

"See," he said, crushing the butt under his foot, "that's where you're wrong. You need to see if this is the right thing for you and the best way to do that is, well...." He snapped his fingers, opening a large hole in the fabric between the worlds. "All you have to do is survive. If you don't," he grinned, "say 'Hello' to your brothers at the Gate." With a wicked chuckle, he disappeared.

A tentacle slipped out of the portal, followed by another and another. A full sized demon, one of the creatures from the Greek Hells that he recognized, oozed out into the alleyway. A creature of Kaos, once worshipped as a Titan, but in truth a demon of the deepest degree, rose to its full height of ten feet, its twelve tentacle limbs twitching in anticipation of the first fresh meal it'd had in centuries.

Rue rolled and sprang to his feet, the barbed limb slamming down where he'd been standing. The creature was large, but slow. He slashed and stabbed, the celestial blade slicing great gashes into the thing's flesh. Purple-black blood flowed. The street grew slippery. A tentacle slipped through his guard, slamming into him and driving him to his knees. Azrael would not appear out of the shadows to save him this time. He was going to die, smashed and digested slowly in the deepest pits of the Greek Hells by this monster.

Another tentacle wrapped around his ankle and began pulling him, with awful slowness, toward the snapping beak buried in the nest of tentacles at the base of the thing's bulbous head.

Serafina, Joss, Fina's annoying cousin Dan and his sweet girlfriend Chloe, even Herm, Mackey and Locust swam in front of vision. If he gave up and died, what would happen to them? Would demonkin keep creeping out of the shadows? Would one of them be dragged next into the Abyss by one of the creatures? A sudden vision of Locust or Herm dragged by greasy black tentacles into darkness spurred him to action and sent a renewed strength through him.

Strength fueled by fear for them flowed from the heavenly sword. He had to succeed, and would, for them. He twisted, lopped off the tentacle dragging him backward. Leaped to his feet and turned, willing all his strength, all his hope and all his heart into his strike. It was not only skill, but conviction that lent strength to the bearer of an angelic sword. It came to him with sudden clarity and time seemed to slow. He could see just where to strike. With a murmured prayer, he whirled one last time.

Big demons apparently melted into huge puddles of evil sludge that slipped back through the portal. Rue hoped the goo rained down on Asmoday's head. He could feel dawn approaching now. He used the blade to will himself clean and refreshed, then shrunk it to fit in his pocket. What had Asmoday been trying to accomplish with that little trick? Had he been trying to kill him just for fun, or was there something more sinister behind the test and the demon's taunting words?

CHAPTER TEN

It's amazing, Serafina mused, *how we can adapt to almost anything*. She tied the shimmering silk scarf around her head and headed downstairs to open the shop.

Minutes had turned into hours. Hours to days and days to weeks. The weeks had flown by since she'd first seen the shadows smudging the edges of her X-ray. March had roared out like a lion leaving April to slink into the city, hardly lifting its head. Harsh winds had howled in the tunnels created by the skyscrapers ripping the heads off the tulips brave enough to peek above the tops of the huge cement planters along the streets. Eventually, though, spring tiptoed in from the west, softening the winds into mild breezes, coaxing hyacinths and crocuses into dancing gently in place. Sunlight danced on the building spires and glittered on the lake. Buckingham Fountain sparkled like a thousand diamonds in the spring light.

Propping open the door to the shop, she paused on the doorstep to take a deep breath. The sharp scents of the city, grease and gasoline mixed with the smell of earth and green growing things. The large planter Dan and Rue had put together as soon as the weather had broken made her smile as it always did. She brushed fingertips over the top of a parrot tulip, noting the miniature rose beside it was starting to swell at the tips. A tiny seasonal garden. For as many seasons as she had left.

She watered the plants and wandered back into the shop, flicking on display lights as she went. She knew she had about an hour before the meds kicked in and she was on her knees in the bathroom, so it was best to get as much done as she could before that happened. She shook her head again at her blasé acceptance now. It hadn't been that easy a few weeks ago.

To please herself, she scanned the auction sites in London. She'd never been, but it had always been a dream of hers to fly over and score some European treasures for her Trove. She'd always thought, "Later." On impulse, she hit a few buttons. Within in ten minutes she had two tickets to London on hold and reservations at the Strand Palace Hotel near Covent Garden. She felt her heart hammer in her chest. Would Rue go with her? Shaking her head, feeling her stomach give a slow roll to the left, she figured she'd worry about it later.

As if on cue, Chloe wandered in. She heard her cheery, "Morning, Fina!" as she bolted back up the steps to be sick in the comfort of her own bathroom.

Twenty minutes later, she sprawled on the couch a cool damp cloth over her eyes and concentrated on breathing. Chloe would be fine downstairs for the next hour or so. Fina knew she'd be able to eat in a little while. Then she'd been good to go until the next round of meds. Repeat process. She groaned. Was she crazy? How could she even think about traveling out of the country when she couldn't even get to the grocery store half the time? She pressed her hand to the rag. The last thing she needed to do is worry about ralphing all over a seat mate at thirty thousand feet. Snorting a weak laugh, she sat up and froze.

Rue stood in the doorway shadow silent, his dark eyes shattered. "What is it?" she asked, feeling a lump lodge in her throat in sympathy.

He shook his head. "I just hate seeing you hurting." His low, liquid voice sent a shiver race down her spine. Vaguely, she wondered if she'd ever get used to it.

"Well, there's nothing anyone can do about it." She shoved herself to her feet, heading toward the kitchen.

"I'll make you something to eat. Why don't you go rest?" He reached out, ran his hands from her shoulders to her wrists.

A little spark of resentment flared. "I'm tired of resting."

"Let me, Fina," he whispered, tugging her closer, his lips a breath away from hers.

She tightened her mouth, ignoring the flutter in her heart. "I'm not an invalid yet!" she hissed, yanked away. She felt his hands tighten momentarily on her wrists, but he let her go. He'd been so gentle, so understanding, so kind... and she was sick of it. "I am not going to fall apart any second."

"Serafina …." Rue approached her, hands open, eyes bewildered.

She slashed one hand down in scathing negation. "No, Rue. Not this time. You're not going to soothe me out of this mood." She shook her head, feeling the exhilaration of temper spiking through her pulse. "You, Dan, Chloe... everyone, you've all been treating me like I'm going to shatter if you say two cross words to me." She waved toward the stairs. "Hell, Rue, you and Dan were ready to tear into each other a couple of weeks ago and now you won't even look cross-eyed at each other because you're afraid you're going to upset poor little Fina." Her voice rose. "I'm sick of it! You're all going to stop it right now! Right now you're going to knock off all the touchy feely crap and go back to the way it was before."

Footsteps pounded up the stairs. Dan burst in, a scowl marring his thin face. "Fina, are you –?"

"Get out!" she shouted.

Dan skidded to a halt, narrowed blue eyes flicking from Fina to Rue. The frown deepened and he glared at the man standing silently in front of his cousin. "Did you hurt her?"

"I –"

"That's exactly what I'm talking about!" She grabbed a pillow from the couch and whipped it at her cousin. "Everyone's afraid of hurting Fina." Another cushion flew, whapping Rue on the side of the head. "Called my uncle to pay all the bills, huh, Dan? Don't worry Fina about running her own business." He started to explain, but a pillow across the mouth shut him up quick enough. "Unh-uh. I don't care if you thought you were being nice having your dad deal with all that stuff. It was my problem – not yours. You called my mom! My mom!" Her voice rose to a shriek. She knew deep down she was being ridiculous, a shrieking harpy, but it felt so wonderful to let loose. She couldn't rein it in if she wanted to and she didn't want to. "It took me three days to get rid of her and did she ask how I was feeling the whole time she was here? No. All she was worried about what telling me how I was never going to make the store a success and trying to get Rue's last name out of him while she had her own migraines." Her head throbbed at the memory of her mother lying on her couch fingers pressed to her temples as she wondered if she should be going to the hospital to have *her* head X-rayed while she peppered Rue with questions.

She whirled on him them. He'd been too quiet. "And that's another thing, Rue Ahren, Why did it take my mother two days to pry your name out of you?" Whap! Another pillow slammed into the side of his head. She noticed Dan taking her turned attention as an opportunity to beat a hasty retreat.

She heard him call to Chloe at the foot of the stairs. "Just leave it alone, Chloe, she's on a tear."

She turned her attention back to Rue. "Well?" she demanded.

He spread his hands in surrender. "I don't know what to tell you."

She felt tears burn her eyes. They were just there, spilling down her cheeks. "The truth, Rue. I just want the truth."

The energy from anger drained as suddenly as it had appeared. She dropped to the naked couch, the springs hard under her. She wiped her eyes with shaking fingers and looked around, truly looked around for the first time in the last several minutes. Cushions, from the small decorative pillows she'd kept on the couch to the big seat cushions, lay scattered. One of the big ones blocked the doorway. She vaguely remembered heaving one at her cousin as he retreated. Rue stood bewildered in the midst of the chaos, his sun-browned face puzzled and his scarred hands spread in supplication.

"I'm sorry." Horror and not the meds made her stomach tremble. "I'm so sorry. I don't know what got into me."

A slow smile spread across Rue's face. A dimple he denied having, winked in his left cheek. "I think it's about time it happened." He glanced over his shoulder, then bent to pick up the cushions. "You're right," he admitted, helping her put the room back together. "You're right about it all. I should have given you a last name the first time we met." He paused, hands twisting a decorative pillow out of shape. "I don't have an excuse other than I was new here and trust –" he shrugged throwing the pillow where it belonged " –didn't come easy."

Laughter suddenly bubbled up, spilling out of her. "Oh, God." She pressed a hand to her mouth. "I must have looked like a loony."

"Moderately." He sat down, patting the newly restored seat next to him. "Now, what set that off?"

She sank beside him, closing her eyes and just enjoying the warmth of the long line of his body beside her. "I was thinking that I'd never been to London and I'd always dreamed of going." She opened one eye to peer at him. "I actually put a hold on two tickets to London for the end of the week. I was wondering if you'd go with me when I realized that there's no way I can go now." She shook her head, soft sorrow winging through her. "I suppose I wonder if I'll ever make it there now."

The smile dropped off his face, replaced by a troubled frown. Rue's eyes left her to go the large glass window that overlooked the street. He sometimes looked out there, a troubled expression on his face, his eyes moving as he searched the shadows for something only he could see.

"What is it?" she demanded, sitting up to break his line of sight.

The look he gave her was more than troubled; it was guilty. He shook his head, "Nothing." He rose, breaking her grip on his arm.

She wanted to grab at him, demand that he tell her what was on his mind. Something was going on in there and in the weeks she'd known him, loved him; she knew that she was no closer to learning all of his secrets though her life was an open book. Resentment bubbled cold in her stomach. She dropped his arm. "I'm heading downstairs to relieve Chloe. She's got a class at ten and needs to get going to make it on time."

He nodded. "I've got to get to the job too." He reached out to trail his fingers through her hair. "Stay safe," he whispered over her cheek, his breath warming her. "I'll be back later on."

Serafina nodded, not trusting herself to speak at the moment. She didn't know what she'd say. Scream imprecations at him, demand to know everything about him, or melt in his arms with words of love. She needed to decide. And, she thought, locking the back door behind him, wandering out into the store to cancel two tickets to London, she needed to get back to work.

* * * *

Rue had found a job. Much to his surprise and delight, he'd discovered a talent for working with his hands. When Martha had told the men one evening in the TV room that a local construction company was hiring, he'd taken her up on the idea. It had afforded a way for him to move out from under Martha's watchful eye and into his own place. She'd looked at him too closely the few times he'd crept in at dawn when he'd been demon hunting back then. That was one woman, he'd decided, who saw too much. Some humans did, he'd learned, even without the grace of the angels.

He found, to his surprise that he liked the very physical labor involved in building one of the huge skyscrapers that towered like manmade mountains over the city jungle. Actually, they were working on a shorter building, an annex of sorts for the Ronald McDonald House attached to Children's Memorial Hospital. He liked the intent of the place—a home away from home for the families of children stricken with illness.

His home was a short train ride away, but he spent quite a few nights now at Serafina's. It was a brief walk through the urban streets teeming with life to the work site. He slapped his hard hat on his head and got to work, helping to guide the huge steel I-beams that formed the skeleton of the building into place.

The work kept him busy and kept his mind off the vial so carefully stowed in his lunch box. He took it with him everywhere—even on his hunts in the lonely hours of the night. Afraid to leave it behind. Terrified to throw it away. He should bury it in the walls of the building. A treasure for a family in need to find.

Even as such thoughts crossed his mind, they faded, replaced by Azrael's gleaming golden gaze and the sight of Serafina's red hair more in her brush than on her head. He still visited Holy Name on occasion. Still sat in the warm tinted sunshine, his head and heart so full of conflict he couldn't form a prayer if his life depended on it.

He paused, taking a long drink from the water bottle hooked onto his belt. He swiped his sleeve across his damp forehead.

"I just love sweaty men," the throaty feminine voice purred next to his ear and his crewmates whistled catcalls from their positions.

Rue felt his body tighten in response and knew without turning what he'd see. "I have no time for the likes of you," he murmured, freezing in place. He ran his thumb over his fingertips remembering once more the nip of a power that had once been his. His thoughts turned briefly, longingly to the blessed blade hidden away.

"I told you he wouldn't bite, Lilith." Asmoday's voice sounded more weary than amused. "Still toting around the little present I gave you, Rue?"

He turned. Lilith, in a screaming red halter top and skirt that covered just what the law demanded, released him. She oozed in a classic hip swaying fashion to wrap herself around Asmoday. She played with his perfectly knotted tie and ignored the whistles from the men on the job.

Asmoday's brow furrowed in annoyance and he snapped his fingers. Everything around them, the men on the site, the businessmen and women walking by, even the birds and breeze froze. "I just can't abide all these interruptions." Lilith had taken the opportunity of the freeze to loosen the demon's tie and wiggle free a few of his shirt buttons. He smiled, "Now, now, my dear, don't distract me from the business at hand." His blue eyes narrowed and simmered red for just a moment.

She snapped her sharp teeth at him, like a dog whose treat had been yanked away. He twisted her wrist in his and Rue smelled burning flesh. The demoness yelped and scurried away, hissing, cradling her injured wrist to her impressive breasts. Asmoday shook his hand, ashes falling to the pavement.

"She'll make me pay for that later," came the demon's laconic response. He turned and smiled at Rue. "I'm rather looking forward to it."

The man scowled. "What do you want?"

Asmoday straightened his appearance. "Just checking up on you, Rue. Just checking up." He blew at kiss over his shoulder at Lilith, who snarled at him. "How's your redhead?" He smirked. "Though there's not much red hair left now, is there?"

Rue felt his hands curl into fists, but said nothing.

Asmoday's mouth quirked up at one side. "Just a little reminder." He flicked a look to where Rue's lunch had been stored, just within the fallen angel's line of sight. "There's no expiration date on the vial, but there's an expiration date on the redhead." He crooked a finger at Lilith, who sashayed over to wrap herself around him again. The demon turned, taking the succubus' mouth in a deep kiss, one hand dipping into her shirt to squeeze her breast. The demoness moaned in pleasure.

With one more chuckle, he snapped his fingers again, restarting the scene, and disappeared in a stinking cloud of bus exhaust.

CHAPTER ELEVEN

The vial of miracles once again rested in Rue's pocket. It felt heavy and warm, seeming to slow his steps as he pushed through the crowds of after shift workers and commuters. The sun set in the west, setting the lake ablaze. The mild spring temperatures had brought suburbanites to the city in droves and Michigan Avenue, his usual route, teemed with people hailing cabs, zipping in and out of stores, chattering about dinner plans.

He swerved around a trio of women examining a menu in a window and slapped the hand of the young man who reached for the shortest woman's purse. The young man's eyes widened and caught Rue's gaze. The fallen angel glared and shook his head. The street thief slinked off, disappearing into the crowd. He most likely had already found another victim, but Rue had done what he could. The three women had moved on into the restaurant, oblivious.

Serafina was expecting him, but he just couldn't go there yet. He knew, deep down, that if he walked into the store now, saw her tired eyes and shaking hands, his hands would move of their own accord to give her the vial. Was he being selfish? Selfless? He shook his head. He'd intended to walk to the shore, watch the sun set and stain the water orange and crimson. Wait until he knew he would be able to think clearly, tell Serafina everything and let her choose her fate. Help him decide his fate—maybe their fate. A smile curved his lips. If she didn't shove him out the window or call the cops to have him taken away to a rubber room, she'd be able to decide for herself if she wanted to risk the demon's gift.

The acrid scent of smoke on the wind brought him back to his senses. Instead of the shore, his feet had carried him by habit to Fina's block. He looked up and froze in horror.

Billowing black smoke poured out of the shattered front window of the Spider's Den. Flames licked at the roof. The scream of fire engines and ambulances howled in the distance. The frantic honking and squealing of brakes heralded the daily traffic snarl and the staccato blast of a jackhammer told him some new construction project had begun. Passers-by on the street ran from the heat, cellphones glued to their ears as they shouted over the traffic and roar of the flames to 9-1-1.

The door glass shattered and Herm stumbled out, shaking and coughing, to collapse on the sidewalk. Two men in soot-smeared business suits, messenger bags slung crosswise over their chests, dashed in to grab the fallen man and drag him to the curb.

Herm coughed and rolled, eyes streaming, searching the faces around him. When that desperate gaze landed on Rue, it seemed to break his stasis. The younger man barreled through the crowd to Herm's side. "Lay back, Herm." He pressed a hand to the struggling man's chest.

Herm choked again, gesturing behind him to the building. Flame writhed across the magazines Herm always kept spread across the front window counter. "Joss," the rotund owner gasped out, his hand clawing at Rue's arm.

Rue's heart hammered, his eyes widening in horror as realization dawned. "There?" He jerked his head behind him.

Herm nodded, dragging the fallen angel down so he could whisper. "The back door. Don't know if he made it." The hand dropped as the shop owner curled over wracked with coughing. An ambulance slammed over the curb, brakes screeching as paramedics leapt out before it came to a complete stop. The fire truck roared up a moment behind.

Rue ran.

He slammed through the Trove two doors down, ignored Serafina's shout. "Keep her here!" He ordered Dan as he crashed through the break room into the alley.

He bolted down to the back of the Den. Quick hands felt warmth, not heat, through the back door. Backing up Rue kicked in the door. Black smoke billowed out making his eyes sting, his breath catch. Dropping to cleaner air he crawled in. Joss lay just to the right of the door, one arm outstretched. Gasping, lungs burning, fireflies of burning ash dancing on the updrafts near his head, Rue grabbed Joss's outflung hand and dragged him out into the alley. Above them something snapped and groaned. He glanced up. Dancing in the fire he caught a glimpse of a sly grin wreathed in flames and two eyes as blue as pilot lights. One eye winked, then disappeared with the snapping of another beam.

Rue slung Joss over his shoulder. The ceiling of the back room gave way. Burning debris spewed into the alley and Rue ran. Serafina stood in the back door of the Trove, Dan's hand hard on her shoulder.

"In here!" She gestured to the front showroom. Dan bolted out the front door for the paramedics.

Rue lay Joss down as gently as he could, coughing. Joss's chest didn't move. Serafina pressed her fingers to his throat. Rue could feel his own pulse leaping in his veins. He'd been singed. Hot stinging pellets of ash smarted against his hands and cheeks, but he felt none of it as he eyes met Serafina's over Joss's recumbent form. Her lips trembled. "It's there," she whispered, "but faint." Tears spilled over. "He's not breathing."

His hand closed over the vial in his pocket of its own volition. He heard his voice tell Serafina, "Get the door, help the paramedics." She nodded and rose.

He knew what he had to do. Knew it with a clarity he hadn't felt since he'd been dropped on earth in this human form. As soon as Serafina's back was turned, he pried the unconscious man's mouth open, yanked the stopper from the vial with his teeth and poured the moonlight potion down Joss's throat. His dark eyes flew open as the miracle coursed through him. He sucked in a gasping breath, his wheeling gaze locking on Rue.

The paramedics hit the door, the gurney they shoved through nearly toppling a rack of vintage dresses.

Rue backed away as the professionals swarmed Joss and broke their eye contact. "Wait!" Joss yelled and Serafina gasped, tears streaming down her cheeks.

"Sir, please calm down." The medic tried to string and oxygen mask over the artist's head. He batted it away.

"Don't need that." He struggled to get up, off the gurney. "Rue!" He called. "Hey, Rue, man!"

Serafina leaned in pressing him back. "Relax, Joss. They just need to look at you." She looked up, smiled at Rue who could see relief in her swimming green eyes. "Rue's not going anywhere." She slanted a questioning look at Rue, who nodded. Serafina turned back to Joss. "I'll ride with you to the hospital. Dan will give Aisha a call to meet us there."

Rue felt so detached, as though he was sliding away from them all. He couldn't feel his pulse anymore or the sharp sting of his burns. He wondered vaguely, if it were shock. They were always talking about shock on the TV medical shows. The paramedics were chattering away into various communicators, not even noticing his ash-smeared clothing. They bundled Joss out, Serafina calling instructions to her cousin over her shoulder as she trotted after.

A cold wind blew through the shop. Dan shivered and ducked into the back room after locking the front door. Rue knew he should be cold, but he wasn't. Shouldn't that worry him?

"It depends on your point of view." The gravelly voice should have startled him, but didn't. Azrael leaned in the shadows, his lean face impassive.

"What...?" he began, but knew the answer.

Azrael nodded. "I came for him."

"Should I apologize?" Rue kept his voice neutral.

Azrael's hand landed on his shoulder. The cold of his touch should have burned through to flesh, but felt like nothing more than a comforting pressure. "Welcome back, Ruvan." With a final pat, the Angel of Death turned to the shadowed corner of the store and disappeared.

His final words lanced through Rue like lightning from the celestial blade.

* * * *

He walked.

Darkness had fallen on the city, though not silence. It was never quiet. Traffic still hummed and honked on Lake Shore Drive behind him. A band tuned up at the Petrillo Band Shell in nearby Grant Park and the lake whispered at the shoreline. Sand crunched under his bare feet. He'd felt the cold slide of sand through his toes during the first really warm spring weekend when Serafina had taken him for a walk on the beach.

He felt nothing now but the pressure of his feet against the ground and a growing panic in his heart.

He knelt, sifting sugar soft sand through his hands. It whispered from palm to palm. Water lapped nearby. He rose and strode into the lake. Even in early May, the water should have been cold enough to wring a gasp from any but the most hardened of the Polar Bear Plunge group. It should have made his ankles ache, jabbed him with a chill that shot straight through to the bone. It soaked into his jeans at the ankle, the knee, the thigh. No sharp stab, no numb toes, just the swirl of the water around him. His throat burned and his back itched. He longed to scratch, rub himself against a tree like a bear as the itching grew worse.

A needle-like pain began at the small of his back and he welcomed the sensation. It reminded him of being human. The pain spread, deepened, soon wracking him with shuddering agony. He stumbled toward the shore, dropped to his knees with water still churning around him.

Hands dug into the wet sand; pain like a line of fire lanced across his shoulder blades making his muscles twist and cramp. A horrid tearing sound and another blast of searing agony wrung a gasp from him as his shirt ripped across the back. The wings Joss had painstakingly tattooed onto his skin and colored like a hawk's wings at dawn down to the last few inches, unfurled. Bone popped, muscle twisted and the pain blinded him for a few moments. When the transformation stopped, Rue still knelt in the surf, a few feathers floating in the water. Two of them were the amber and brown of a hawk's on the wing. One was black and pale gray—one of the unfinished feathers from his lower back.

"Rise, Ruvan," the ringing voice echoed chorally in his chest, "and rejoin your brothers and sisters." A large hand reached out helping him to his feet.

Michael, Simeon and Gabriel stood before him, their sandal shod feet hovering an inch or two above the water. The trio of heaven's princes were not trying to blend, he mused. He was mildly surprised that a pedestrian hadn't yet wandered over to see what was glowing by the lake. He flexed his shoulders and his wings shivered.

His wings.

He closed his eyes for a moment, reveling in the feel of his wings. He'd never thought to have them again. Never thought to see his brethren again.

"You've proven your compassion, Ruvan." Gabriel's voice always had that trumpet-like note. His golden eyes glowed like twin suns. "You've resisted temptation and acted selflessly."

Michael, with one side of his mouth tipped up in a smile, said, "I still know what you're thinking, Rue. Minor slips, is all. None of them really matter in the grand scheme of things." He nudged Simeon, who frowned.

Sim admitted. "Truly minor in regards to your greater actions." He snapped his fingers and a beam of pure white starlight shimmered on the surface of the lake. "Nathanial has need of you, brother." He gestured to the light.

Rue looked past the angels to the shore. The city crouched at the shore line. He could hear the rumble of the El in the distance, the bass from the concert. He thought of the warm glow of lamplight through a window and the comforting weight of a head on his shoulder.

"Not a good idea," Michael warned.

"But do as you like." Sim scowled, stalking to the white light. "Free will is ever our gift." He stepped into the glow. "And curse." With a flash was gone.

Gabriel said nothing for a moment, though Rue felt himself being measured. After a moment, the Archangel nodded toward the light. "I think perhaps it's been too long since Simeon has walked amid mortals."

One of Michael's golden brows rose and Rue smothered a laugh with his hand, turning it into a rather unconvincing cough. "That would be interesting." Michael gestured Gabriel ahead of him. He nodded to Rue and disappeared in his own flash. "I'm sure you can find your own way home." Michael patted him on the shoulder and disappeared.

Alone at the shore, he flexed his wings again watching their shadows dance on the water. With a thought, he clothed himself, power surging through him in a warm ribbon. His fingers tingled and he knew if he were to see Asmoday again their conversation would turn out very differently.

Serafina.

His elation slipped away like the sand through his fingers. The only sensations he could feel now were the ones he'd always known: the warmth of heaven's light, the tingle of power, the tickle of his feathers and the pull of his wings. Could he remember the silk of Serafina's hair, the heat of her skin, the surge of his own desire? Would...?

He shoved his hands into his pockets, fingers curling around the empty bottle Asmoday had given him. There was only one way to find out.

CHAPTER TWELVE

It had been a long day. Serafina glanced at the cable box. Later than she thought it would be. Why did hospitals seem to be time warps? They sucked you in and spit you out hours later. She needed to take her meds and eat something – not necessarily in that order, though. She shook her head, remembering Aisha barreling through the doors, knocking orderlies over like bowling pins in her haste to get to Joss. And that, Serafina tossed her purse on the coffee table, had been miraculous.

Joss told the doctors that while he remembered running toward the back door, it had been closer then. He didn't remember making it. The smoke had overwhelmed him, filled his lungs, driving him to his knees. He'd tried to crawl, tried to call out, but the heat had sucked the breath from him. He'd remembered nothing until the paramedics had tried hoisting him on the gurney. That's what he told the doctors. The story he told Serafina after he'd sent Aisha down to the café for some food went a little further.

He'd felt something like lightning sizzle through him, Joss recalled. Every nerve ending had tingled like it was coming awake, his lungs burning as though he'd been thrown into the fire, then clearing. When he'd opened his eyes he'd seen Rue, but it wasn't the Rue he knew. "Fina, sweetie," he said, his large brown hand clutching hers, "you're going to think I'm loco, 'cause I'm thinking I'm a little loco."

She patted his arm. "You've been through a lot."

The hand on hers tightened almost painfully. "Rue had wings." His voice dropped as a nurse bustled past the open door.

She smiled. "Yes, he does. Beautiful wings you'll finish as soon as you can."

He shook his head, the singed dreadlocks bouncing. "Nah, girl, I mean real wings. I could see 'em. Big huge hawk wings like a shadow behind him." He moistened his lips. She gave him the water cup, deftly sliding the straw between his lips. "And someone else. Did you see anyone else with him?"

"Dan was there. Remember he was holding open the door for the EMTs?"

Joss shook his head. "No, a tall brother in a black suit. Looked like a lawyer or a funeral director or something."

She thought about it, wondering if he were really as healthy as the doctors had proclaimed. They were only keeping him overnight for observation. Overall, he was remarkably uninjured for someone who'd been dragged unconscious out of a burning building. "No... no one else was there. Just Dan, Rue and me." He looked like he was going to say something else, but Aisha swept in, followed by a nurse declaring she needed to check his vitals. Fina took the opportunity to retreat. She hugged Aisha. "Let me know if you need anything," she whispered, then turned to Joss.

He should have looked pitiful in the hospital bed, the thin blankets up to his waist and the indignity of the blue hospital gown, but he just looked irritated. She bent to kiss his cheek. "Take it easy." She smiled. "Looks like they'll spring you tomorrow."

He grabbed her hand. "Tell Rue I want to talk to him tomorrow."

Aisha shook her head, "Na-unh, you don't." She declared, "You're staying at home tomorrow if I have to tie your sorry black ass to the bed." She turned to Serafina, "Bring your Rue over tomorrow night. I want to thank him for saving...." She trailed off, her eyes filling with tears.

She nodded. "I'll call you tomorrow." She left Aisha fussing over Joss.

She'd expected him to be at her place when she'd returned from the hospital and had felt her temper hitch when he hadn't been there. Maybe he hadn't felt comfortable without her there? Dan had left a note on the counter, "Cell's on. Call me when you have news."

She dialed her cousin. Music blared in the background and she couldn't hear anything other than his shouted, "Hold on!" for a minute.

The music became muffled. "So?" Dan's voice was threaded through with anxiety.

"He's fine. They're keeping him overnight for observation, but there's nothing wrong. All the tests came back good."

Dan's sigh buzzed in her ear. "Good. God, Fina, that could have been bad. Really bad."

She leaned against the kitchen counter, replaying the day in her head. "I know." Memory sparked. "Hey, Dan, did you see anyone with Rue when the paramedics came in?"

A long pause, during which she heard a bang and flush.

"Geez, Dan, are you in the bathroom?" She made a gagging noise. "Gross!"

He laughed. "It was the only place I could hear you. Chloe wanted to check out this new club. What was that? Someone with Rue?" She could almost hear the wheels turning in Dan's head. "No. In fact, I don't even remember seeing Rue."

"Dan, Rue's the one who pulled Joss out of the building, don't you remember?"

She heard nothing but another flush and muffled music. "Fina, it was a crazy kind of day. I'm lucky I remember my own name right now."

"You're right." She sighed, feeling the familiar pain start to build behind her left eye. "I'm going to let you go. I need to take my meds and seriously, I hear one more flush I'm going to throw up without the medication helping." He laughed again. "The bathroom, Dan? You need to think that through a little better next time."

"Go rest. I'll see you tomorrow."

She took her meds and lay on the couch, trying to keep her stomach under control. She always tried to last a little longer each time. Later, when she felt wrung out and a little sorry for herself, she curled up in bed. She shivered and debated getting the down comforter out of the closet. In the end she decided to stay where she was. She missed Rue. Like Dan had said it had been a crazy day and all she wanted to do was curl up against his warmth, his heartbeat steady under her ear.

Something thumped outside her window. She froze, ears straining. A light tap, tap, tap on the window in the living room. What in God's name could be out there? The apartment stood a full floor above the street level and the ledge outside the window wasn't even wide enough for an herb pot. She knew because she'd tried a few years ago and nearly brained a commuter when it had fallen. So, it had to be nothing. Satisfied with her sophistry, Serafina snuggled in her pillows.

Tap, tap, tap... louder this time. Lines from "The Raven" skittered through her memory as she slipped out of bed and tugged on her robe. She grabbed the baseball bat she kept next to the dresser and inched open the bedroom door. Moonlight and streetlight usually made the living room bright enough to walk through without needing to turn on a light. A large shadow blocked most of the light and made her freeze with her hand on the doorknob. Tap, tap, tap... Serafina saw the shadow raise a hand and tap on the window pane. Grabbing her courage in both hands, she reached out and flipped on the light switch.

The baseball bat fell from nerveless fingers. Rue stood on the tiny window ledge, large hawk-colored wings beating behind him, helping him keep his balance. She didn't even know she'd crossed the room and unlatched the large side window until he was standing in front of her, those huge wings stirring the strands of hair that curled over her throat.

She knew her mouth hung open. Knew she looked like an idiot, but... Joss's words came back to her. One of her hands lifted, not to touch the wings, though that would make sense, but to touch his face. Warmth, the scratch of whiskers and the same dark eyes. Sadness and longing swam in them. "Is it still you?" It was so hard to shove that strangled sound past her tight throat.

One side of his mouth tipped up, the same ironic half-smile she'd seen on his face for months. His dimple winked. "It's me," he said, his voice echoing strangely in her head. Still his voice, but oddly choral. He closed his eyes and with a groan gathered her into his arms, the wings sweeping warm and soft around her.

She closed her eyes, inhaling the scent of him. The arms around her, the body against her felt the same, but he smelled wrong, not like the man she knew. "What...?" She pulled back enough to see his face, feeling his arms tighten as though he were afraid she'd bolt. The brief question danced through her brain: why wasn't she bolting?

"This is me." He cleared his throat, his voice settling into its normal cadence. "It's what I really am." His eyes drifted to the city outside her windows. "I was sent here to find my compassion."

She smiled, though her stomach trembled with something other than medication. "I take it you found it?" She forced her voice light.

He returned her shaky grin. "I found more than that." His hands moved over her back into her hair. "I found you." His dark eyes were serious now. "When I first came here, I couldn't wait to get home. There was nothing out here that I could see worth saving. I saw greed, selfishness, cruelty." His fingers stroked through her hair, smoothing it away from her face. "Then I saw you." He brushed a butterfly- soft kiss over her lips. "I saw you and you restored my faith in humanity." He kissed her cheeks, her eyes. "You showed me how wonderful it was to be human. You love life. You care genuinely for people and bring out the best of everyone you encounter. You –" his eyes seemed to glow " –showed me how to love."

Serafina knew what he was going to say. Knew what she had to say. "You chose to go back," she whispered. She framed his face in her hands, willed her heart to stop breaking. "It was the only choice you could have made, Rue."

He shook his head, "No, I'd decided to stay here with you. To live out whatever time I had been given with you." He cast his eyes heavenward. "The Powers that be had other ideas."

He led her to the couch, settling her on the cushions. He sat on the coffee table, his wings moving slightly behind him, sending shadows to dance on the floor. "What happens now?"

The silence stretched long and thick between them. He shook his head, dropping his forehead to her lap. Long shuddering breaths shivered the wings.

"Please, Rue," she whispered, "just tell me. I think I already know."

He lifted his head. Tears glittered in his eyes. "I have to go back." Her breath caught. "They need me."

She needed him. She wanted to scream, to cry, beg him to stay with her for as long as she had left. She knew better, though. So, she swallowed past the tears that lodged in a hard ball in her throat and nodded. "I thought…. Her lips trembled. "I mean, Rue, could you just imagine the tailoring bills?" She reached out to brush her fingers over the wings. They were so warm and soft.

He closed his eyes, his breath trembling out of him. "I wish I could feel that."

Her hand froze. "What do you mean?"

"I can't feel that." He gave her a lost look. "I feel only the press of your hands, a slight pressure." He shook his head. "That's all." He caught her hand, pressing a kiss to her palm. "I wish, more than anything, Serafina, to feel you—really feel you in my arms one more time." He pressed her hand to his cheek. "I will carry the feel of you with me for the rest of my days, and believe me, there will be many of them."

"How long?"

He frowned.

"How long do you have left?" she clarified.

His gaze went to the windows. Gray pre-dawn light was filling the sky over the lake. She knew if she walked over there, she would see the water look like a rolling sheet of lead under the pearling sky. "Until dawn only."

* * * *

Dream or reality?

She tapped her pen on the desk. It had seemed so unreal, but Rue had assured her it was all true. She lifted the long feather in her free hand, trailing the tip of the pinion under her chin.

She could see it all without closing her eyes. She knew she'd see it for the rest of her life. Her heart sped up a little, making her breath catch in her throat, for however long that would be.

He'd wept as dawn stained the horizon, signaling that he had to leave. So had she, she admitted. Tears filled her eyes at the memory.

He'd felt the same to her. The same wide scarred hands. The same mouth. The same shattered dark eyes. But he'd felt nothing but the pressure of her against him. Angels didn't feel. Couldn't feel, he'd whispered against her hair, making her heart break a little more.

She wrote down a few more details. She didn't know yet what she'd tell Dan when he asked. Or Joss or Herm, Mackey... the list of those Rue'd touched kept

getting longer and longer. Without the wings that he'd
wrapped around her she didn't think she'd have believed it
herself.

Well. She closed the journal and leaned back,
certain she couldn't tell them the truth. Closing her eyes,
she took a deep breath. The open windows at her back
brought in a breeze and the scents of the city, flowers and
water. The wind made the scarf she'd tied around her head
to hide her increasingly bare scalp tickle her neck.

A timer in the kitchen beeped. It was time to take
another round of meds. With a deep sigh, she pulled herself
to her feet and wandered over to the counter where she
poured a handful of pills into her palm. She knew they were
supposed to make her better, but they made her feel so
awful. She dreaded the hour after they kicked in. She hated
the nausea, the shakes, the helplessness. She stared at the
colorful pills as if they'd jump up and dance.

A hard gust of wind kicked through the room,
blowing a pile of mail off the coffee table. She glanced at
the clock over the stove. Dan would be over in a little
while. Chloe would open the shop and he would wander up
to check on her as he had every day since the morning after
he'd found Rue in her bed. She clutched the pills, feeling
them bite into her palm.

Rue.

He wouldn't wander in before work to check up,
stop by at lunch to raid her fridge or come after work to
curl up with her on the couch and watch TV. He'd liked
mixed martial arts and Jackie Chan films, something that
had helped him bond with Dan who had a love for cheesy
martial arts movies himself. She'd bought him a boxed set
of DVDs that she'd never be able to give him. Maybe she'd
give them to Dan instead.

Padding across the kitchen, she threw the pills in the
garbage can, tossing leftover cereal over them.

She didn't fear dying anymore. Not after Rue. She was going to live as much as she could. She snapped on her computer. Time to book that trip to England.

"I knew you were brave." The silky voice froze her in her tracks.

With her heart hammering in her chest, she turned. Framed in the sunlight streaming through the window, his golden hair glowed. He had bright blue eyes and a sad smile. "Are

you....?" Her voice failed her.

"The Angel of Death?" He crossed toward her. "It's not your time yet, my dear." He gestured to the computer. "Make your plans. Book your trip." His hands were warm as he directed her to her seat. "I just wanted a closer look at you. I've heard so much about you from Rue."

She folded her hands, trying to keep them from trembling. "Is he...."

The angel waved one hand. "Back at work." Those penetrating blue eyes pinned her. "He thinks of you still. Probably will for centuries."

"Centuries," she whispered.

The angel leaned forward. "I have a proposition for you, my dear." He gestured to the computer. "Take your trip. Life awaits you, but –" one slender finger stabbed toward the sky " –I'll come see you after the first snow falls. You'll come with me then."

Serafina felt her heart trip in her chest. "The first snow?" It was just May now. Snowfall wouldn't be here for months yet. Months. Not the years her family and doctor were hoping for.

Months.

She firmed her mouth, met his eyes. "All right." She stuck out her hand automatically to shake.

He took her hand in his, turning it to press a kiss to her wrist. Her skin crawled a little at his touch. Something she figured was normal when the Angel of Death came nearby. Part of her wanted to scream and run, but she knew better than most out there that she couldn't run from the inevitable.

* * * *

Asmoday smiled, wrapping shadows around himself, disappearing from Serafina's sight. He hadn't even had to lie, which had been a rather refreshing change. Humans were such wonderful creatures. He loved the way they jumped to conclusions. He'd never confirmed that he was the Angel of Death; she'd just assumed and he now had her promise to go with him after the first snow fell.

Now that he had the bait, it was time to set the trap. Time to talk to Rue.

CHAPTER THIRTEEN

Some things never change. Rue crossed his arms over his chest, looking down the line of souls stretching from the huge flaming iron gates at his back to as far as he could see. Glaring illumination from the gates flared and faded, filling the cavernous chamber with shifting crimson light. Huge stalactites reached from the distant ceiling and things with wings, things that not even Rue had ever seen clearly, fluttered and flapped just out of eye-shot. It was altogether a place to put the fear of holy retribution into the souls who waited for their own judging.

Rue remembered with a twinge his last conversation with Serafina. She'd wondered about what he did. "No," he'd told her, holding her as dawn painted a spring sky outside her windows. "Not all souls are judged, just those in doubt and those who doubt." He'd brushed a hand over her hair, wishing he could once more feel the silk of it tangle in his fingers. "Good souls float like balloons and truly evil souls sink like lead. It's only those who are in doubt who need personal attention."

She'd distracted him them, pressing her mouth against his throat, stirring all sorts of regrets.

With a deep sigh, he turned his mind back to his duty. Nathaniel needed him. Needed him to stay focused and be the balancing stone for the other judges who did not have the knowledge of the human heart that he did.

The man in front of him hung his head, light from the flaming gate at Rue's back flickering through him. He read the man's sins as clearly as they'd been words on a printed page. Theft, greed, and envy... the angel pushed deeper beyond the surface of the sins to their root. A lost job, a sick wife, a rival who cheated his way into a job the man before him had thought he'd deserved... sins, yes, but not worth eternal damnation. Glancing behind him at the flaming gates, the infernal guards with glowing swords, he shook his head.

"Penitence and service," he decided. The soul before him flickered once as if surprised, then faded out, destined for the fields of Purgatory.

So it went. Soul after soul after soul... he wondered how much time would have passed if they marked time here on the borders of Hell.

"Heard you were on walkabout, Ruvan." Deimos, one of the gate guards, leaned against the fire gate, the leaping flames making his hairy, squashed nosed, tusked face even more grotesque.

"For a while, yes." He waved Yariel into his position and walked to the gate.

"Noticed you and the others been sendin' fewer over here." He licked the edge of his white hot blade. A thick bead of black blood slipped down the length of the weapon. "I haven't been able to jab a soul in a dog's age." He jerked his head to his goat-footed counterpart on the other side of the gate. "We're getting a little itchy here, Ruvan."

He shrugged, "Times change, Deimos."

The demon's harsh laughter scraped across his nerves. "We'll see."

He turned away, letting the endless line of souls, the twisted flaming gates, and the dark cavernous judging chamber fade. Once more he was on Michigan Avenue. He walked unnoticed through the crowds. A thought faded his wings back into the tattoos Joss had inked over all those weeks. His armor transformed into jeans and a Cubs t-shirt.

The planters were a riot of blooms now. When he'd left, they'd been budding with tulips and crocuses. Now, summer geraniums and marigolds burst in tangled bunches. The bronze angel at the foot of the bridge didn't look so much like an angel to his eyes anymore. Vines trailed up her skirts around the long flowing hair, making her look more like a being rising from the earth than a fallen envoy of heaven.

Sunshine glared down to bounce in dazzling splinters of light off the buildings. Women jogged in tiny shorts and tank tops, sunglasses and hats pulled low. Men in sweat-stained shirts muscled pieces of steel and poured concrete at a construction site in the center of the street. Cabs wove crazily around the construction avoiding suicidal bicycle messengers and distracted pedestrians.

Rue couldn't feel the heat of the sun, couldn't smell the breeze that blew off the lake at his back bringing with it the scent of the water, couldn't feel the warmth of the pavement under his feet. His eyes sought the corners, the tiny pockets of shadow where building met pavement or building met building. He hunted for deeper shadows. He sniffed the air trying to smell the sickly sweet stench of demonkin or the sharper scent of their full-blooded brethren. Shaking his head, he moved on. Nothing. A stray thought percolated through. Perhaps he had been drawing them out of their little hidey holes? Perhaps he had been the lure, the scent of the angel touched, and now that he was gone they too had slithered back to wherever it is they had come from. Some of the worry that had been gnawing at him since his abrupt return to the heavens lifted.

His feet directed him, dragging his body with him, to Serafina's glittery front display.

Closed.

He pressed one hand to the glass over the sign. Closed. Where was she? If he'd still been human, his heart would have started pounding, panic threading through his veins.

"Hey, dude, they're closed." The voice drifted over the traffic and construction noise from two doors down. "Owner's on vacay."

He nodded, not wanting to turn, not wanting Joss to recognize him. Regretting that it was summer and he couldn't shove his hands deep into pockets and hide his face in the shadows of a hood, he turned wandering toward the Artist's Café.

Footsteps pounded the pavement behind him. He braced himself a moment before the pressure of a hand landed on his shoulder. "Rue?" Joss' voice trembled, though he couldn't identify the emotion behind it.

Bracing himself, he turned.

Joss' dark eyes widened, his mouth dropping open. "Dude, I don't know if I should hug you or punch you in the face."

He felt his mouth twist into a crooked smile. "Your choice, but –" he looked around as a woman teetering on three inch heels, barking orders into a cellphone elbowed past him, " –you might want privacy for both of those."

Joss' face split into a slow smile. He clapped Rue on the back and gestured with his other towards the Den. "Come on. It's just me today. Herm's got the drunk flu and the first appointment is at three."

He nodded, following the artist.

"Where's...?"

"Fina?" He unlocked the Den, gesturing Rue through. "On vacation. She, Chloe and Dan went to England for ten days." He gestured to the newly refurbished shop. "What do you think?" It was sleek and modern, cool silver and black counters and shiny mirrors. Brilliant red leather chairs and modern art with wild slashes of color adorned the walls.

"It looks like a new shop."

Joss nodded, dropped into one of the red leather chairs. "Better than what Herm originally bought. The old bastard paid a premium for his insurance and this part of the Loop's gone bugnuts in value since he bought here." He grinned. "It's like working in one of those fancy places you see on TV. Herm's been playing around with the idea of changing our name to Chicago Ink. I told him he better look into the copyright laws there."

Rue perched on one of the red leather chairs. His wings were just ink and skin at the moment, but old habits died hard. "Why don't you ask me what's really on your mind?"

Joss fell silent, and leaned forward, his hands folded on his knees. "Why don't you ask me what's really on *your* mind?"

Man and angel fell silent.

Joss stared at his arms, rubbing the long fingers of one hand over the seraph on his left arm. Rue remained quiet and still. He had to remind himself to breathe. Finally, the man looked up. "Am I crazy?"

He didn't ask for clarification. He knew what he meant. After a brief internal debate, he shook his head. "No, Joss, you're not crazy."

"So, I did see wings?" He shook his head, forestalling any excuses, "I don't mean the wings I gave you. Real wings?"

Rue smiled, nodded. "Real wings. Though the ones you gave me come in handy at times."

Joss frowned in puzzlement.

He stood and pulled off his shirt, turning to show the inked wings covering his back – as perfect as they'd been when he'd first had drawn them. "You gave me back my wings in more ways than you know." He thought not only of the art etched into his skin, but the fact that the act of saving Joss' life was the selfless action that caught the attention of heaven's princes.

A tugging sensation, the copper scent of blood, though none fell, the sound of tearing cloth and the wings pulled free. His fourteen-foot wingspan crowded the shop. He glanced back over his shoulder, catching sight of Joss' hand outstretched as if to touch the feathers. The tattoo artist paused, dropped the hand back to his lap, and leaned back in a casual pose, though, judging from the leap of the pulse in his throat, he wasn't causal at all.

"That's something," he murmured. One hand scrubbed over his face.

Rue felt his mouth twist up into a smile, the first real smile he'd felt since returning to Hell's gate. "Well, they certainly impress the locals." With a careful turn, he closed his eyes for a moment, willing the wings to fold back into the delicately colored artwork.

After another moment of silence, "She said she sent you away," Joss told him, his eyes grim. "She said you didn't want to go, but that she sent you away. She couldn't stand you watching her fade minute by minute."

Rue bent his head. "I didn't have a choice."

"I see that now." His face twisted into an ironic smile. "I wasn't the only one who wanted to take you apart for abandoning her, brother."

Rue sat back down. "I don't blame you. There have been times in the last several weeks I've wanted to throw myself into the fires for abandoning her." Silence fell, thick between them. "How is she?" The words crept across the quiet.

Joss didn't respond right away. He gnawed his bottom lip as though chewing his words. "She's weaker by the day." He shook his head and rose wandering over to the tall locked glass cabinet behind the register. He unlocked one of the drawers in the bottom and started to pull out bottles of paints and other sealed bits and bobs. "She won't say, but I don't think she's takin' all the meds the doctors want her to." He lined the little bottles up on the counter. "She –" he broke off as the door open, the bell above it jangling.

A tall thin young black man, his denim shorts sagging low and a tight white sleeveless tee clinging with perspiration, let the door close behind him. "You take walk-ins?" A blue bandana wrapped around his head didn't stop the line of sweat from sliding down the back of his neck.

"Yeah," Joss smiled. "I don't have an appointment for another few hours, so we can maybe get started." He gestured to the short bookshelf on the wall nearest the counter. "Do you have an idea or do you want to look at the portfolios?" Thick black binders – some with Joss' name, some with Herm's name – sat on the shelf next to several other ink magazines.

A shivery prickle skated down Rue's spine. Fear and guilt poured off the young man in waves and another bead of sweat slipped down his cheek. Without a word, he stood, shifting to look at some of the framed pictures behind the counter. "Joss, you did some of Kane's art?" Kane, a local body builder and new Hollywood action legend, beamed from behind the glass.

Joss grinned as the kid shifted his feet. "Yeah, Celtic cross on the dude's right pec." He shook his head, tossing a look over his shoulder at the kid. "So, you got an idea?"

The kid shuffled back, keeping both men in his line of sight. "Yeah, I want this," he shoved a hand in one sagging pocket and came out with a gun. The weapon glinted in the sunlight-washed shop as it wavered in the kid's hand. "Just gimme what's in the register and no one gets hurt." He swiped his sweating brow with his free hand.

Joss froze, his hands coming up in that universal, "I'm unarmed" move. "Whoa, kid." His voice lowered, slowed. "You don't want to do this." He shook his head, his dreadlocks bouncing against his cheeks. "Seriously, man, you don't wanna do this. I gotta brother doing a dime down in Cook right now...."

"Shut up and jus' do what I say!" The kid's hand shook more.

Rue unfocused his eyes, letting himself see past the flesh to the spirit. The kid was a glowing coal of resentment, anger and fear. He could see the promises made, fueled by anger, vengeance and alcohol. He saw the gun pressed into the kid's hand by a much older man with a shaved head, a tribal tattoo over one side of his pate, and a cruel scar under one eye. He saw other men smile and laugh when the kid swore he'd be back with the money or die trying. He also saw the young man's mother, a rail-thin woman with tired eyes and the picture of one dead child already on the wall. Rue shifted, breaking with their reality for a moment, stepping into the space between worlds to close the distance between himself and the boy. To the boy and Joss he knew it would look like he'd simply disappeared and reappeared in the blink of an eye. Willing himself beside the kid, he reached a hand out and in, grasping the boy's soul. The gun clattered with the ground when the young man gave out a painful gasp. Joss jumped on the weapon, snatching it up, flicking something on the side. Rue pulled the soul, stretching it out from the young man's body. Some part of his mind wondered if it hurt.

"Greed, fear, vengeance…." He looked at the boy, capturing the kid's dark gaze with his own. "If I were to judge you now, I would send you to the fires for punishment, for cleansing." He released the soul, letting it snap like a rubber band back into the boy who dropped shivering to the tiles of the store. "Your mother's already lost one child. Do not let her lose another." He pointed out toward the street, allowed his voice to echo chorally. "Go. Repent. Save yourself." The boy scrambled to his feet and all but dove out the door.

"Damn." Joss' curse was a long drawn-out sigh. "Damn, Rue, you're one scary dude." He shook his head. "I swear, man, when you were talking to that punk, I could almost see the shadow of your wings behind you."

Rue shrugged.

The bell over the door rang again. Rue sank back into a red upholstered chair when he recognized the tall dark man in the rather severe looking suit. "Ruvan," he nodded.

He nodded back. "Azrael," he acknowledged.

Azrael looked over at Joss. "Sir," he said admiringly, one side of his mouth tipping up in a smile that didn't reach his golden eyes as he spoke. "We never do seem to meet." He slanted another look over at Rue. "Someone always keeps interfering."

Rue lifted one shoulder in a negligent shrug. "You can't expect me to apologize, Azrael."

Joss backed up until his back pressed up against the glass cabinets behind him. "Do I know you?" he finally asked, after studying Azrael's face for a long, silent minute.

The angel nodded. "All men know me." He stepped forward offering his hand. Joss took the proffered hand automatically. "Allow me to introduce myself. I am Azrael, Angel of Death."

Joss gasped, dropping his hand.

"Ah, well." Azrael sighed, turning to Rue. "No one ever seems happy to meet us, Ruvan." The angel dropped into a seat beside him. "We need to talk." He gestured and Joss froze. The traffic behind them and even the fly bopping itself against the plate glass window at their backs halted mid-air as Azrael slipped them between the worlds. "I think you should see this." He tossed Rue his iPhone open to the calendar.

He frowned down at the list of appointments Azrael had in four months' time. "It's November, what about it?" He scrolled down through the list.

"There's supposed to be an early snowstorm before Thanksgiving this year. Several of those are homeless who don't make it through the first night." He nodded. "Keep looking."

"A lot to attend to personally here, aren't there?" Rue asked.

Azrael sighed. "I'm thinking of taking on an apprentice this winter." He gestured, the silver ring on his hand glinting in the frozen sunlight. "It's always the busy season." He fell silent.

He continued to scroll, to scan the names. They meant nothing to him. Nothing. He hadn't been with humanity long enough to really form any... then he saw it. Serafina. He knew that if he still needed breath it would have stopped up in his throat. His gaze flew up to Azrael's. He nodded and waggled his fingers for the phone. Rue looked again, just to make certain.

November 10th Serafina was slated for departure.

"I made sure that she'd be on my list when her time came. I wanted to tell you, let you come along and ease her through." Azrael tucked the phone back in his pocket. "When I saw how soon it would be I thought you should know." He snapped his fingers again and rose fluidly, nothing in his manner indicating that more than a fleeting second had gone by. He nodded to Joss, giving him almost a small bow. "I will see you again, though," his chuckle sounded like the dry scrape of leaves over the pavement. "Just not for a very long time. You have an interfering guardian angel."

"Thank God for that," Joss muttered, then bit his lips when he realized what he'd said.

"Yes," Azrael nodded, "thank God for that indeed." He nodded to Rue, "Ruvan, I'm sure we'll speak again."

"Yes," he managed. "Soon."

Azrael ducked out of the door, the bell jangling.

Joss let out a pent-up breath. "Well, man, I don't know about you, but I need a drink." He went over the first station and rummaged through the bottom drawer. "Herm keeps a fifth of tequila here for a bad day, and seriously, this is one of those bad days." He held up the bottle sloshing the three inches or so of golden liquid inside it in invitation. "You want?"

Rue shook his head. "No, I should be going." He stood and flexed his shoulders, feeling his wings. "Who knows how many souls have piled up in my absence?"

Joss shook his head, tilting the bottle back. "I seriously think I might cancel that three o'clock, go home and get piss-faced." Rue laughed and reached out to clap his friend on the shoulder.

"Well," he smiled, "it isn't every day a man meets the Angel of Death and lives to talk about it."

"Amen to that, brother, amen to that."

CHAPTER FOURTEEN

"Excellent." Lucivar stroked long fingers over his chin. Asmoday knelt on the gray stones before the iron throne and bowed his blond head in supplication. A small dragon-like creature with stubby leathery wings, sharp teeth and protruding yellow eyes crept from behind the Lord's throne, its claws clicking on the flagstones. "You've pleased me, Asmoday." The demon looked up, a small smile hovering on his lips. "She'll go with you when the time comes and the snows will fall early this year." The Lord of Hell shook his head, his long black hair brushing against his shoulders. "All these centuries and I'm still amazed by the gullibility of these mortals."

He reached down to stroke the dragonet's wedge-shaped head. The yellow eyes slitted in pleasure. "Shall I have Lilith prepare her a room in the newest wing, Master?" Asmoday settled back on his heels. "She will upset the balance of Hell if she's allowed to mingle with the lost souls."

Lucivar nodded, his eyes glowing like red coals. "That's for the best. Tell Cethan that she's to be housed...."

Terik, a huge demon with the traditional goat's hooves, red skin and black horns, tapped on the hall's great door. Lucivar's eyes flared at the interruption. "Semiazas is here, Lord, as you asked."

Lucivar nodded and settled back on his throne. "Semiazas," he acknowledged, waving the dark angel forward. Sem's gray and black wings cast long shadows behind him and his arrogance matched the Lord of Hell's own.

"You called for me?" His voice was not at all gracious.

"Semiazas," Lucivar began, his voice a low thrum that could slice through human bone, "you and your brothers and sisters enjoy your sanctuary here in the darkness, do you not?" A wealth of threat hung in the air.

Asmoday's eyes flicked from one being to the other, then froze on the stones. He didn't want to draw either the dark angel's attention or the Lord of Hell's notice. *Best to just fade into the stones.* The little dragon must have had the same thought, for it scuttled below the Lord's throne. All he could see were its bright little eyes shining from the darkness. He kind of wished he could wedge himself into a hole as well.

He knew Semiazas was seeing his adopted home in his head. Seeing the sun-washed fields of the Fallen Isles, the sugar sand beaches, glistening water and white marble hall where they were attended by air spirits, kept in much better state than they'd ever seen in the halls of heaven. In all honesty, if he were ever honest even with himself, Asmoday had to admit the dark angels had it pretty good. If he could stand all that white marble and angelic posturing, he'd visit the Fallen Isles a little more often himself.

Semiazas bowed his head momentarily in acknowledgement, resentment burning in his eyes. "Your commands, my Lord?"

Lucivar smiled, tenting his hands on his lap. "Not so onerous a duty as you're thinking, my dear Semiazas. I wish you only to take a brother of yours on a little tour of your haven. Show him the wonders I have given you, the pleasures you can have that those who are still slaving in heaven cannot." He waved one slender hand vaguely in the direction of the Fallen Isles. "Your little Eden in the midst of Hell." A chuckle escaped the devil at the phrase.

"Who?" Semiazas frowned.

"Ruvan."

He nodded. "I understand, my Lord. I had heard that he'd returned to Hell's Gate." The dark angel shook his head, long red hair brushing the shoulders of his golden garments. "I can see how you would not wish to have a compassionate judge cluttering up the works." He looked around the nearly empty throne room. "I have noticed that the construction in the newest of the halls has slowed."

Lucivar nodded. "It disturbs me. I wish to tempt him to join you." He waved Semiazas away.

Sem bobbed a bow that was barely civil. "How, my Lord, did you wish me to lure him here?"

Lucivar nodded to Asmoday, who rose. "Don't worry your pretty little head about that, Semiazas. Rue will come to you." Asmoday smiled at his Lord. He did have an ace up his sleeve there.

After a moment, Sem nodded once more, then left.

"He doubts you, my lord," Asmoday warned.

"Then he's not a complete idiot." Lucivar replied and shook his head. His longer hair retracted back into his head and slicked back to a wicked widow's peak. His teeth elongated until his eye teeth were fangs fit for the best B-movie vampire and his skin darkened, deepening from the sallow olive complexion it had been when Asmoday'd entered the throne room to a deep red. The tailored suit disappeared, revealing red musculature and goat's legs with sharp black hooves. A whiplike tail slashed the air behind him. "I've a need to talk to Hathorn, Asmoday. He's been fomenting a rebellion in the 8th circle. Perhaps, it's time to move him down a level?"

Satan, as he'd now adorned himself, stalked out of the hall, his black hooves striking sparks from the stones.

Asmoday shook his head and finally pushed to his feet. Hathorn had better watch it, he mused. He remembered whispering in the councilman's ear back in Salem, reinforcing the foolish girls' story of witchcraft. Hathorn had been personally responsible for the deaths of seven of Salem's victims. "Good times," Asmoday murmured, smiling. "Good times." Too bad humanity wasn't quite that gullible any more. No matter that the Lord of Hell still thought them nothing more than foolish sheep; the demon knew better. He'd been out in the world. With the exception of a few forays, it had been centuries since the Lord had walked for any length of time among humanity. "Damn science," he muttered and wandered out of the hall. Maybe he'd take a field trip to Hell's gate and see what Rue was up to.

* * * *

Regret.
Fear.
Selfishness.
Greed.
Lust.

The sins of mankind hadn't changed in centuries. Simply the means, Rue mused. He sentenced the woman in front of him to the pits. She deserved a century of punishment for the corruption of over a hundred children – children lured into drugs and prostitution because of her and her compatriot. He frowned for a moment, searching for her partner's soul and nodded with satisfaction. He'd dropped straight as stone through water into Hell. Vaguely, he wondered what sort of Hell these humans believed in. Were they still caught in the Dantean fire and brimstone? Or had humanity evolved to some new tortures?

A flash of gold beyond the gates caught his eye. Asmoday grinned from behind the flaming iron bars. He turned to ignore the demon, bent his concentration on the next soul in line. The familiar face rocked him back on his heels. "Mackey?" He reached out to grab the soul by the shoulder. His fingers passed through.

Mackey wheezed out a laugh. "Hell's bells, Rue, you dead too?" The spirit's hollow eyes widened, his mouth dropped into an "o" of astonishment at the sight of the wings framed in the flames behind him. "Guess not," he murmured.

Yariel glared when Rue focused his will to grab Mackey from the line, ushering him to an alcove off to the side. Mackey's eyes rounded as they traveled around Hell's

Gate taking it all in. Reaching out again, Rue shook him. "Mackey, focus!"

Those wheeling eyes settled back on the angel. "I died, right? The tall black dude come and got me. Never seen wind like that in October, Rue." The spirit shuddered, rubbing his shoulders in memory of the cold, "It's goin' to be one early nasty winter." He nodded to himself then sighed, squared his shoulders and tipped his face up to the angel. "I done bad. I know I did." He smacked his lips. "Lost my Mary, lost my house and business to booze and bad decisions. I hated my no-good thieving nephew, woulda tossed him off the pier with cement shoes on could I've gotten away with it." He shook his head. "Intent, the priests say, they say if the intent's there, the sin's there." He looked back over his shoulders at the shimmering black gates. "I was just wondering if I could see my Mary one more time before I got to go down and grab a shovel and pick for the demons and devils to start savin' my soul."

Rue frowned, reached out to snag Mackey's soul, weighing it, reading it. Greed and anger, yes, but the deepest stains were despair and a loss of faith. Doubt stained this soul. "You are weighed," Rue intoned, "you are judged." He tightened his grip on the spirit so it wouldn't flit from his grasp in response to his will. "Fina?"

Mackey focused on him on that whispered, desperate word. "In a bad way." The spirit hung his head as sorrow weighed him down. "I gotta tell you." He pressed a hand to his chest. "I am happy this old soul went before her. She's wasting away in front of our eyes." His anguished eyes filled with phantom tears. "I don't think she'll make Christmas."

She wouldn't, Rue knew. The numbers on Azrael's calendar loomed in his mind's eye. "What date was it there?"

The spirit began to fade, the weight of the judgment pulling toward his eternal reward. Rue firmed his will, the soul stretching like rubber. Mackey's face thinned, the mouth opened, "November 1st," he whispered, then with a pop disappeared bound for the fields of Purgatory. Rue hoped he'd find his Mary soon.

* * * *

It took all her willpower to stay on her feet. She swayed, checked herself, and grabbed the front of the pew. Dan stiffened beside her, but didn't reach out. Old Mackey's casket lay draped in orange lilies and white carnations in front of the altar at St. Sophia's. Mackey's no-good-dirty- rotten nephew had come through in the end, claiming his uncle's body and arranging the funeral. Mackey hadn't been quite so alone in the world as they'd all thought.

She looked around the small church. Pews halfway back were filled, mourners dabbing their eyes and exchanging whispered confidences. Why would Mackey have been happier on the streets of Chicago than in the residential facility his nephew had found for him after Aunt Mary had died? Why had he died on the streets, where Dan had stumbled across the old man's body curled under the fire escape behind the buildings? Tears, warm and salty, slipped down her cheeks across her lips. Her insides quivered at the memory of her cousin, white faced and shaking, running in the back door to grope for the phone. She'd demanded to know what was wrong. He could do nothing but shake his head and shiver, his hand white-knuckled on the phone as he dialed 9-1-1.

The tickle of smoke and incense stirred in her heart and mind. Memories from a childhood thought long forgotten; her father taking her to church while her mother "suffered" in bed from a migraine. The dim colored light, the scents of wax and dust, the comfort of a routine she'd left behind so many years before. Rubbing a hand on the worn wood of the pew in front of her, as the priest intoned the final phrases of the requiem mass at the front, she wondered if everyone returned when they saw the end of the their own roads?

Mass ended. "Do you want to go to the cemetery?" Dan's raw voice brought her out of her reveries.

She shook her head. "I'm going to take a little walk, head back to the shop." She ran her hand down his arm. His eyes still looked desolate. Chloe clung to his other arm, her look more worried than sad. She saw the command in his eyes, beat him to it. "I promise I won't open the shop, just go upstairs and take a nap."

He nodded, then turned with Chloe to follow the mourners out to their cars. She stayed put. Silence fell after the organist and cantor left. She sank to her knees, rested her head on her folded hands and prayed that she could find the words to pray. Her heart hammered in her chest, her pulse leapt. She could almost feel her blood running a frantic race in her veins as if every part of her knew that her time was growing shorter. Clocks had been turned back two days ago. She wished it was that easy to gain time. She tipped her tear- stained face up to the crucifix above the altar. Was this how it felt to know that your breaths were numbered? The statue stayed silent.

Chill wind blew down from the Canadian border, withering mums and icicle pansies. Frost painted delicate patterns on windshields around the city and every white-puffed breath reminded her of the promise she'd made to the Angel of Death all those months ago in her spring-scented living room.

After the first snow.

Possibly any moment now. Chicago had boasted Thanksgiving weather fit for both basketball and bobsledding in the past, so that first snow could happen tomorrow or in another few weeks, though it was inevitable.

With a shake, she stood, tugged her coat closed around her. She would face what needed to be faced when it needed to be faced. Shoving hands in her pockets, she pushed out of the church to squint in the bright sunlight that flooded the parking lot. She'd walk to the shop. It really wasn't all that far away; take that nap she'd promised her cousin. She'd take each day as it came—for however many she had left.

Settling sunglasses on her nose she headed off towards the Loop. She just wished she'd be able to see Rue one more time before she went.

* * * *

Frail. The first word that sprang to mind when he saw her. Invisible to mortals, still in the world between worlds, he watched her. He longed to reach out, take her in his arms assure her that all would be well even though he knew the words would be a lie.

Unless....

He faded from the mortal world, back to the antechamber at Hell's Gate. He settled into the line and with an absent look weighed the next three souls in line. Two for purgatory, one for the fires.

"November 1st." His eyes traveled blindly along the long line of souls stretching from the flaming gate to the smoke-smeared horizon. Asmoday leaned against the bars, impervious to the fire, a smirk on his perfect face. Power sparked from Rue's fingertips to dance and spatter on the rough stones.

He strode to the gate, reached through the bars to snag Asmoday's perfect tie—grinning white skulls on black silk. With a jerk he dragged the demon to the gate, catching his head between two flaming bars. "We need to talk," the angel grated. "Now." He dropped the demon, who stepped back, smoothing his clothing.

"Well, since you ask so nicely." He snapped his fingers. Deimos rolled his ruby eyes, but opened the gates causing the souls still standing in line to shriek in terror. A trio of dogs black as night with coal-red eyes leapt from the portal. They ran and snapped at the souls, nipping heels and clawing unsubstantial flesh. Their growls echoed like the demonic laughter in Rue's ears.

"Call them off," he instructed.

Asmoday shrugged, his eyes still on the scattered souls and the hounds. Two of them had caught one soul in their teeth, engaging in a game of a terrible tug of war, the soul stretched impossibly between them. The third had chased a soul up the nearest stalagmite. It perched at the top, balanced on the very point while the dog snarled and jumped. "Deimos," Asmoday jerked his chin in the dogs' direction, "Let them play for another ten, then call them off. We wouldn't want to make the judges feel sorry for the souls and let them off easy. The Master hasn't been happy that construction in the new section's slowed. We need the labor." Deimos grunted in assent.

Rue followed Asmoday's beckoning hand. "Let me give you a tour." He grinned around at the grim antechamber to Hell. "It's been about two centuries since the last of your kind came over."

"I'm not here for a tour, but for answers."

The demon nodded. "I know, but indulge me." He kicked a few souls scrubbing tiles out of the way. "I know things don't change all that much on the other side –" he rolled his eyes " –being perfect and all, but things are always changing around here." He scratched his chin. "Wish the new construction was finished. It's turning out beautiful, looks just like the Senate gallery." He shook his head. "I love humans. They have such wonderful imaginations. Every few centuries it's time to rip up pavement and lay out a new Hell. Though, we've had this whole Judeo-Christian thing for a few too many centuries. The boss is getting a little tired of being red with horns and hooves."

They passed through the stark antechamber of Hell. The paved black walk opened up to a huge cavern, the ceiling lost in low scudding gray clouds. A black river wound through the cracked landscape, rapids roiled into a white froth around the jagged teeth of rocks protruding from the water. A long low barge, the bargeman's skeletal hands chained to his pole, bumped to the shore. Asmoday gestured Rue aboard. "I remember when there were souls six deep all clawing at my hem trying to get free passage on Charon's barge." He hopped aboard, making the shallow boat dip. He slanted a look up at the bargeman. Rue could see the empty hollows of its eyes glow a sickly yellow in the wan light. "Freeloaders, huh, Charon, buddy?"

The bargeman ignored the demon, his pole cutting through the surging river.

"I need to see Semiazas," Rue said, his eyes fastened on the far shore of the Greek Hell. In the distance he could see the silhouette of Sisyphus rolling his boulder up his hill. He recalled these halls, remembered the Greek and Roman souls in line begging for mercy, gold coins clutched in their hands. Fare for the ferryman.

"Sem, huh?" Asmoday clucked his tongue. "That's pretty far in." Rue looked over. The demon seemed to come to a decision. He shrugged. "Up to you." He smoothed his wrinkled tie. "The boss asked me to show you around anyroad. So, no skin off mine."

He wanted to ask why, but knowing Asmoday, he wouldn't get a truthful answer. Or he'd get a truthful answer and not believe it anyway. If he'd had a heartbeat still, he knew that it would have galloped at the thought of being in Hell. He'd never walked its slimy halls, but had known those who had. Very few of them had ever returned.

They passed through the darker halls of Tartarus. Kronos, once worshipped as a god, then feared as a titan, roared his displeasure and hatred to the stony limits. The unholy shriek would strip the flesh from a mortal, drive them insane if they did survive and make them wish for death. Immune as he was, Rue felt his skin shiver as they skirted the edge of his ice-rimed hole. He recalled fighting one of the Greek Kaos' minions in an alley in Chicago before he'd regained his wings. A minion Asmoday had summoned to test him or kill him. Rue had never been able to figure out which. He looked over at the demon strolling along at his side as though he were strolling through a lovely meadow. As if feeling eyes on him, he turned. His angel black eyes flashed red when they met Rue's gaze as though daring him to ask. He remained silent.

They left the Grecian Hells behind them. Tantalus cursed them from his pool, weeping as he bent for water. The path wove downward along a thick wooden walk, twisting until it was clear they no longer walked a road, but rather the twisting roots of a great tree, a tree so huge its roots rested in Hel and its highest branches supported the furthest vaults of heaven.

Water gurgled and splashed. Rue looked around. Water flowed from between two huge roots to pool into a shallow gray basin. Something gleamed in the water. Asmoday shrugged when the angel cocked his head at him in question. "The well of knowledge." He bent, picked something off the ground, tossed it to the angel. Rue snagged it out of the air. He stared at the tiny seed for a moment before recognition set it. An apple seed. "It's where I got the idea."

A scrabbling in the shadows at the edge of the pool had Rue bracing for an encounter. He willed his sword into being. The silver light from the blade penetrated the darkness. Three women, grey, twisted and bent with age, their long hair lying in tangled hanks around withered faces, hissed at the sudden light. Their eyes, dark pits in their faces turned in his direction. The one to the left, the one most twisted, reached into the tattered rags over her breast. She keened, one long low moan, as she pressed her hands to her face. When her hands dropped, she looked at Rue with one bright blue eye. Silver lightning shattered the blue iris and pinned the angel in place. "The Nordic Hel," he whispered.

"We are the Norns," the crone intoned, as her sisters trailed skeletal fingers through the silvery water pouring into the fountain. "We tend the fountain of knowledge. We see all." Her sisters crooned in awful counterpoint behind her. "We know all. Ask."

Asmoday tossed a rock in the pool. The harridans hissed, narrowed their hollow eyes at the demon. "They're frauds." He flicked an apple seed. It landed with a little *splish*. "You can go ahead and ask anything, but you'll get as much truth from a Magic 8-ball."

"Ask!" she shrieked.

He felt torn. It had to be a lie. Demons always lied. Would they know about the vial of miracles? Did it exist anywhere other than in the hands of the king of the dark angels?

"Time has passed." She turned, tucking the lightning shot eye – Odin's eye if he recalled his legends— into her rags and turned back to her sisters.

"Let's go. Leave these crazy broads," Asmoday reached out as if to take Rue's elbow, paused. Rightly so. Confusion and fear met in Rue, ignited angry sparks from his fingertips. The Norns disappeared amid the Yggsdrasil roots, fleeing his wrath. He fisted his hands at his sides. Struggled to pull in all the rogue emotions he'd been feeling ever since he'd had his wings returned. He hadn't felt all these things before. He'd felt disgust, anger and brief flashes of joy. This welter of feelings, tugging, yearnings made him long to wheel on the demon and blast him into atoms.

He took a deep breath, drew on the light in his heart. The deeper he walked into Hell, the easier it was to fall prey to his own fears, the darkness that dwelled in every soul. He needed to get to Semiazas, ask his questions and get back as soon as possible. He closed his eyes, tipped his head up. He knew, unlike the mortals that walked the earth, that heaven wasn't "up" but everywhere at once. He knew that, but like the mortals, he felt right now, in the depths of the darkness, that he needed that reminder. He asked for blessings, for strength, for wisdom. He turned back to the demon, gestured him to lead on wondering how many prayed here in Hell?

Long fingers groped at bars, empty eyes followed him as he walked on. How many souls prayed in Hell? Probably most of them.

They twisted through the edges of the Nordic Hel, past the vast battlefield of those who died peacefully in their beds doomed for eternity to fight the battles they lost or avoided. Despair floated thick on the fetid wind, coating his throat. The wooden roots of Yggsdrasil faded and pale sandstone took its place.

A dry breeze replaced the sea salt wind of the Nordic Hel. Smoothly fitted bricks lined the walls. Hieroglyphics carved themselves into the stones as they walked. He could read hieroglyphics, even though he had never judged the Egyptians. Asmoday paused in the judgment hall to scratch Ammit's hippopotamus ears.

They left the Egyptian Hell behind, a strange place, Rue thought—nothing more than the judgment hall with the odd little hippo-crocodile creature that tore into the souls, not, Rue admitted, that many souls had passed through the hall in eons. He'd actually felt a little sorry for the little creature. It had run to Asmoday, wagging its hippo tail so hard its chubby hindquarters shook with excitement, its crocodile mouth agape in almost dog-like joy. He couldn't object when the demon decided to throw a battered rubber ball for the animal a few times. "I try to come by at least once or twice a decade," he'd explained, whipping the ball down the narrow tomb corridor. "I've been busy the last thirty years or so." He picked up the slimy ball Ammit dropped at his feet and threw it again, ricocheting it off the hieroglyph grafitti'd walls. "Poor little guy doesn't get any attention since Anubis left. Bastard decided to take off a couple centuries after the boss let go of his Osiris gig, thought he'd have some fun in the mortal world scaring the natives." He snorted, whipping the ball again. "Idiot got himself cursed into a sarcophagus. Still there for all I know." After another throw, he pulled a huge rawhide out of a pocket it could never have fit in, rubbed the hippo's ears, and stood. "Let's go. It's getting late." He held out the rawhide—Ammit took it eagerly, and ran off to a corner to enjoy his treat, his tail swishing happily.

The angel nodded, following the demon out of the sandstone corridors into more of a traditional black marble hall veined through with all the colors of the rainbow. The beauty stopped him for a moment before he picked up his pace, following the demon deeper into Hell.

The monotony of the black marble halls were interrupted by random pits from which moans, curses or pleas emerged as the inhabitants sensed someone passing by. Asmoday primarily ignored the sounds, gesturing every now and again to the imps and demons attending to the tortures. A huge stone arch rose just past another huge crater, pale smoke rising from the depths. They passed through the archway and Rue stumbled as bright sunshine hit him like a blow to the brain. He reeled at the threshold of the cavern, shielding his eyes, feeling his wings beat in confusion at his back.

Asmoday gave an oily little chuckle and one last acid comment, "I can't stand all the smarminess here." He clapped Rue on the shoulder. "You can find your way back to the Gate, right?" A puff of acrid black smoke and the demon vanished.

CHAPTER FIFTEEN

"Be welcome, brother," the voice emanated out of the light. Rue shook his head, squinting. The being came into focus: a slender female angel, her golden hair like a fall of sunlight down the back of her silver garments.

"I am no brother of yours," he grated, then wanted to bite his tongue. He was there to beg a favor. He would need to remember his manners. Old habits died hard. He bowed his head, "My apologies. I came to see Semiazas."

Her eyes glittered though with temper or anticipation he couldn't tell. "Are you Ruvan, Guard of the Gate?"

He wished for a moment that he could lie. "Yes. I am Rue."

She nodded, then gestured for him to follow. "This way. Semazias is waiting for you."

He longed to ask her how Sem knew he was coming, then frowned at his own foolishness. The original vial of miracles had come from this shining island, if Asmoday could be believed. Gossip spread through Hell quicker than through an all girls' high school, he knew. Sem would know that he had used the vial not on Serafina, but on another.

He pulled himself out of his thoughts to look around. Very few had ever seen the Fallen Isles. He couldn't quite believe that such beauty existed here in Hell. Tall slender trees with feathery leaves and white bark carpeted the hills to the left. To the right, the tide of a silvery sea lapped at a shore of sugar white sand. Gray peaks rose before him, the road spiraling around and around the outer edge of the tallest of the peaks. A golden sunset glowed perpetually in the west.

And angels.

Everywhere he looked he could see angels. Two with dove gray wings leapt playfully from tree to tree. A handful of others, their wings and hair pastel shimmers, cavorted in the surf, pale slender limbs tangled together in wild abandon. He halted. Shock rocked him on his heels for a moment.

"The answer is yes." The deep voice startled him and he swung around. Semiazas. He recognized the king of the dark angels: wings of grey and black, deep red hair and golden eyes. He was a legend among the judges having been one of the first of them, one of the best of them before he'd walked away from the judges and through the Gates of Hell. He'd never returned. He'd struck a bargain with Lucivar, the original fallen one, and he'd established these Isles. The Isles had stood for a millennium as both haven and temptation.

He continued, "Yes, you would feel as you did on earth here." He gestured to the sun-washed sky. "It is our own Eden here in the darkness." He flared his shadowy wings. "Yet you would not need to give up your wings to have it."

Rue's guide slid in close, wrapping her arms around his neck. Her lips brushed feather- light kisses against his jaw, making him stiffen. He should have felt nothing more than the faint pressure of her against him. Her caress should have roused in him no reaction other than annoyance, yet desire spiraled through him, weighing down his body, catching in his throat. "You could choose from amongst us a mate worthy of you," she breathed, flicking her tongue over his lips. "You would learn delights not known on the earth." She wrapped around him like a clinging vine, her wings blocking the king of the fallen from his view.

The last time he'd felt his body tighten came back to him. A vision of red hair, green eyes and a small smile flashed into his mind's eye chilling him. He shoved the female away. She stumbled, batting her wings to keep from falling over the edge of the path, a grin on her face. "Or those instincts and pleasures as well can be indulged." She laughed and swooped away.

"Forgive Varisily," Sem gestured to where the female had disappeared. "She's only been here a century or so. She hasn't gotten to the end of her indulgences yet and settled down."

"And do they?" he asked, following Sem into a high-ceilinged cave.

"They do, usually." He offered Rue a seat on a plush low couch before a dancing fire.
"Can I interest you in something to drink? Eat?" A small white lizard with silver eyes scuttled from the corner to stand at attention at the table side.

He shook his head. He was too well-versed in the legendry of Hell and had no intention of eating or drinking anything and risking being trapped for any amount of time.

Sem dismissed the lizard with a wave of his hand. "Well, you're no fool no matter what Asmoday might think." He leaned forward to steeple his hands on his knees. His wings folded gracefully at his back to drape on the silver-flecked gray stone floor. "You'd be welcome here, Rue." He waved to the plush cave and to the door beyond. "You've tasted the gifts of the flesh. Here, you could have that all back and keep your wings too."

Rue shook his head. "It's not just the pleasure, my lord. It's the love that comes with it. I don't know if I could ever make you understand."

"The woman is doomed." Those golden eyes, so like the eyes of Simeon, the dark angel's brother, pinned him. "Doomed by your hand, I believe." He leaned back. "Noble, sacrificing and foolish." He reached out and took a handful of purple grapes from a crystal bowl on the low stone table.

Fear clutched Rue's insides. "Then you have no more vials of miracles?"

Semiazas snorted, popped a grape in his mouth. "You should know as well as I that miracles are difficult to come by." He shook his head. "No, I have no vial of miracles left to give to you." Scorn tinged his tone. "What would you do with it anyway? Leave it on her table with a 'drink me' note on it like something out of *Alice in Wonderland*? Or would you personally deliver it, save her life, then fade out of that life to leave her for an eternity facing the depraved souls at Hell's Gate? Knowing the entire time that the woman you loved, the woman who gave you back the compassion you needed for your duty, was in another man's arms? Holding another man's child?" Another grape was crushed between his teeth.

Despair and a deep sadness welled in Rue. Here he could feel so much. At Hell's Gate, when he was at the edges of the Realms, he felt nothing but the palest imitations of the emotions he'd reveled in on Earth. Here, though, in the cursed golden light of the fallen ones' realm every feeling cut like steel.

Sem pressed relentlessly on. "How much better would it be to let her die? Let Azrael take her to her eternal reward. Let her bask in Heaven's light and lose yourself here?" He accepted a delicate glass goblet from another lizard creature that scuttled back in the room. He sipped. "Pleasures abound here. Here you will forget the mortal, yet still enjoy those lessons she taught you."

A small cough sounded at the door. They turned. Another angel, his wings the color of burnished copper, stood looking faintly embarrassed. "Semiazas," he began and bowed. "I crave your indulgence, but we have an issue in the lower forests." He glanced over his shoulder and Rue heard and felt an explosion rock the mountain. Pebbles and rocks fell and bounced from the ceiling.

Sem rolled his golden eyes. "I'll be right back." He gestured to the little lizard creature. "If you desire anything simply request it of Kiz here." He smiled. "If you require anything at all."

A rush of wings and Sem and the messenger took off. Rue sat, eyes on the dancing flames in the white marble hearth. Fina dead, not supportable. Fina alive, but with another. He shook his head. Sem was right. He was a fool. He wished he could go back in time... and what? Let Joss die? No. That wasn't an option either.

Impossible.

The sound of someone clearing their throat nearby had Rue dragging himself out of his despair to look around. "My lord," the lizard Kiz stood at his side, its wide gray eyes trained on his face. "Ask, my lord." It nodded, one paw gesturing. "The lord said ask for anything."

Realization dawned. "You mean... anything?"

Kiz's mouth dropped open in what he assumed was a smile. "Yes," it hissed, "*anything.*"

"Then you know about the vial of miracles?" The little creature nodded. He cast a look over his shoulder to the open door. It remained empty. Kiz waggled a claw, indicating for him to follow. "It really came from here? Asmoday didn't lie?"

It shook its head. "No, not about that. It came from here."

He followed Kiz down a smooth floored white hall, dancing silver lights lighting their way to a large brass bound door. A ring of keys appeared in the creature's hand. With a muffled jingle the door opened and Kiz waved Rue in. A huge glass fronted chest, lit from within, dominated the far wall of what appeared to be an office.

"It amuses the lord to play at being master here." Derision dripped from the little creature's words. He crossed to the chest, jingled out another key, reached in for a small golden vial. "Here, my lord. They are playing games and I have never approved of playing when all the players don't know the rules or the stakes." With no more explanation of those cryptic words, Kiz handed him the potion. The vial of miracles lay warm in Rue's hand. A few more moments had the chest and brass bound door locked.

Kiz walked him back to the main room. "And that, my lord, is what you could expect if you came to live here as well."

"So, all of the lodgings are similar?"

Kiz nodded, gestured him back into the room, bowing to Semiazas. "Yes, my lord, and all of your own as well. There is no need to share with others, as I have heard you must in the heavenly realms."

"I see Kiz has given you the tour?" Sem smiled at Rue, his golden eyes alight. "What do you think?" He gestured at the richly appointed living space. "It is a far cry from the accommodations at the Gate, isn't it?"

"That is the truth."

"Well," Sem clapped him on the shoulder, "think about it." He walked him to the doorway. "Just look, Ruvan, look at everything you could have." He snapped his fingers and Varisily appeared. "See him back to the borders."

"My pleasure, my lord." She dipped a low bow.

Rue shook his head. "No, I can make it there myself. Besides," he said, allowing his wonder at the Fallen Isles to echo in his voice, "I want to have a closer look at some things here."

Sem nodded. "Take your time." One side of his mouth tipped up in a small smile. "I understand that it can be overwhelming. Walk among your brothers and sisters. Talk to them. Ask them questions. Feel free to come back and ask me anything. Consider the Fallen Isles your home."

Rue bowed. "My thanks, Lord Semiazas. I will think long and hard on what you have said and what I have seen." He bowed again and backed down the twisting white trail, the vial of miracles heavy in the fold of his tunic next to his heart.

* * * *

"He took it, my lord." Kiz served up another glass of wine and a plate of delicate sparrow hearts.

"Excellent." Sem speared one of the hearts. "Ah, Kiz, just the way I like them—still beating."

"I am ever here to serve you, my lord." The creature bowed and began to withdraw, stopping when the dark angel raised a hand.

"You are happy here?"

"Yes, my lord. My brethren and I never quite fit with the others in the pits." He shrugged. "You have given us a home in the light. You allow us to serve the shining ones. We do not have to torture souls or deal with the abuse of the greater demons." He bowed. "You are kind, my lord, kind and wise."

"And just," Sem insisted. He swirled the wine in his glass, speared another still beating heart, bringing the meaty little morsel to his lips. "I have not fallen so far." The coppery burst of blood spilled over his tongue, settling a hunger far deeper than for mere food. "I may bow to the true Fallen One, but I myself have not fallen so far."

Kiz bowed, snagging the empty plate and glass in his claws. "It is as you say, my lord," he whispered, withdrawing.

"No," Sem insisted, "I am still what I once was." A tiny thread of doubt bloomed in his heart. Asmoday had wanted Rue stalled in the Fallen Isles, knowing that time moved differently in Hell than on earth or in heaven. Knowing the judge would have a difficult time finding his way back to the Gate. The Lord of Hell had asked that Rue be tempted and tempted he had been. Sem had seen many angels fall, their fortitude giving way to the seductions of the Fallen Isles. Hadn't he, himself, once one of the Archangels, one of heaven's princes, been tempted into leaving behind the warmth of heaven's light for the cold light of the Isles and the comfort of power?

A cold comfort right now. He closed his eyes, tipped back his head, the long forgotten feeling of the light of heaven's love warm in his memories. Even after all these centuries, he could still remember, ever so faintly, what it felt like to be in the circle of the true light.

* * * *

Rocks shifted and slipped under his feet. The corridor tilted under him, sliding him toward the pit. He batted his wings, lifted free from the pavement, hovered as the imps and prisoners snarled and clawed the air. He thought he and Asmoday had passed this way before, but he couldn't be sure. He pressed his hand to the cold slimy rainbow flecked stone. He remembered this shining stone. He remembered the creatures in the pits and the demons jabbing at them. But, he whirled in place, it hadn't gone on for this long, had it?

A nasty chuckle echoed, sounded behind him. Rue called his sword, the shining celestial blade cut through the imp's cloak of shadows. "Speak," he ordered.

The imp cringed away from the blade. "Lost, ain't ya?" it sneered, large protruding tusks dripping with slaver. "I could show you to the Gate." Two yellow moon eyes, one larger than the other, scanned Rue from halo to toe. "You're one of the judges, ain't ya?"

"Point the way to the Norse Hel. I can find my way from there."

The twisted little creature was shaking his head before Rue had even speaking. "The Hells move, you fool." He rolled those yellow eyes. "Didn't you see how they twisted round each other when you was being shown down here?" He shook his head. "You're all fools, but I'll show you the way out."

Rue narrowed his own eyes. "What do you want for it?"

The imp shook his head. "Nothin." He stumped along in front of the angel. "Asmoday told me to look for you. He said let you stumble along for a while, but to get you back to the Gate before you got into too much trouble." Rue seemed to have to choice but to follow the little creature. "You're too good," he sneered, "to wander around here. You creatures always get into trouble." He muttered, "Letting the souls out, telling the demons to lay off on the tortures…."

The stone changed under his feet to wood. He peered into the shadows of the Yggsdrasil tree searching for the Norns. This time he would ask, but he saw no one. If the hags were there, they stayed well out of sight. The Fields of Asphodel and the Pits of Tartarus came into view. The little imp stumped along before him, muttering, occasionally slapping at the hands that poked from between bars or up from pits in supplication.

The imp came to a halt, digging his horny little feet into the slimy soil at the edge of the River Styx. "This is as far as I can go," he said. "Asmoday only gave me leave to get you here." He pointed across the river. "The Gate's that way."

Rue nodded. "Thank –"

The imp bared his teeth. "Don't bother," he grated, turned and stalked away.

Charon's boat bumped to shore, his chains rattling with impatience. Rue stepped into the boat, allowing the ferryman to take him back to where he belonged. He reached into his tunic, wrapping his hand around the vial. It burned, hot against his hand. He would save Serafina. That much he knew. There was no future for him at the Gate, in the Fallen Isles, or on earth without her alive and well. He didn't care if Sem was right – if he were a fool for saving her and walking away. He would save her and then he would go somewhere for a while, somewhere to think. He remembered Nathanial telling him of his time on the earth. After he'd lost his love, he spent quite a while walking the earth, thinking. Rue had done too much reacting and certainly not enough thinking. He knew Nathanial wouldn't begrudge him the time.

The boat bumped against the far shore. The lonely stretch of black sand and stone wound through the antechamber of Hell to the flaming Gate. Even from here, Rue could see the flicker of fire in the distance. He nodded his thanks to Charon, who pushed away from the edge without a flicker of emotion.

Yes, Rue decided as he walked, he'd go away for a while to think. He'd seen the Fallen Isles now. He wanted to sit in the Hall of Heaven at the feet of the Lord's throne and bask in its healing light. He wanted the light of heaven to wash away the guilt and pain from his soul. He wanted to see the mountains again. He wanted to watch the sun rise over the sea and the Northern Lights dance on the ice. He wanted to weigh his options and sort everything out knowing that Nathanial understood and Serafina was safe.

The roil of emotions he'd been drowning in since arriving back at Hell's Gate finally settled. A smile tugged his lips and the warmth of the vial of miracles warmed his heart. The shining Gates rose before him. Deimos growled, but opened the gates without comment or complaint. He looked in the shadows, but didn't see Asmoday lurking anywhere nearby. He wanted to repay the demon for the little trick he'd played deep in the depths. Later, he decided, letting power spark off his fingers.

Yariel and Fesinth nodded to him from where they stood, judging the endless line of souls that stretched beyond Rue's sight. He's go see Nathanial, then Serafina.

"Rue!"

He jerked to a stop, frowning, searching for who called him. The souls nearest to him moaned, hands outstretched towards him. Fesinth reached out to judge the soul. It cringed away from the silver winged angel. Darkness poured out of it and Rue could see why it didn't want to be judged.

"Rue!" Azrael winged across the cavern, his dark wings lost in the shadows overhead.

"Azrael," he smiled, "you don't come down here very often."

The grim angel landed. The souls screamed and scattered away from him. Deimos and his fanged partner hissed, lashing out with their whips to get them back in line.

Yariel glared. "You're scaring them out of the shadows of the wits they have, Azrael," he complained. "They think you're here to take them again."

Azrael ignored the angel's griping. "Rue, where have you been?"

He gestured to the Gate behind him. "I went to see Semiazas. He had something I needed." He grinned. "I can't talk now, Az, I need to go see Serafina."

His hands tightened on Rue's shoulders. He knew had he still been mortal that touch would have chilled him to the bone. "It's Serafina."

Rue froze.

"She's gone." Azrael's golden eyes glowed in empathy. "I looked for you. For hours, I put off taking her soul. I knew you'd want to be there to ease her through, to say goodbye." He tightened his grip. "Where were you?" His anguished voice threatened to drop Rue to his knees. "I asked Yariel and Nathaniel. They told me that you'd disappeared behind the Gate days ago."

"Days?" Rue choked. "It's been hours. Only hours, I swear. I—"he broke off, the truth dawning on him. He knew all the legends of the Hells. Knew not to eat anything, not to bargain with any of the denizens, not to trust even what his eyes showed him, but he'd forgotten one fundamental rule of Lucivar's domain. Time ran at the Dark Lord's will. It had seemed like hours, should have been hours, but had been days. Days in which he could have seen Serafina, spoken to her and said goodbye or saved her.

He refocused on Azrael. "Gone?" He cleared his throat. "She's gone, then?"

Azrael dropped his hands, stepped away. "That's what else I need to tell you. I was going to collect her personally. She would have slipped right up to the light, but I had put in an order to be called on when she was ready to go."

Rue nodded. "I saw that."

He slipped his schedule out of his pocket, tossed it to Rue. "Look here."

The date was opened. Serafina had been highlighted on the calendar, a personal request. Her name was gone. "What does this mean?"

He slipped the phone back in his pocket. "There was a glitch. She was removed from my schedule."

"A glitch? Azrael, it's heaven. There are no glitches."

"Then it was sabotage."

"So, she went up by herself?"

Azrael was shaking his head before Rue had even finished the question. "I thought of that. Went up to see her, talk to her and assure her that I would get you through to her. She wasn't there."

"What do you mean she wasn't there?"

"Just what I said, Rue. She wasn't there. She should have been on my schedule. She was removed. She should have ascended on her own, she was good enough. She's not there. That tells me that there's more at work here than we know."

A cold spiral of fear lanced through even the numbing effects of being at the edge of the realms. "Sabotage, you said." Azrael nodded. Rue narrowed his eyes, peering beyond the bars, searching the shadows.

A flash of silver, a shift of light and Asmoday stepped up to the bars. He was dressed in funeral black, his shirt a shining silver, his tie decorated with grinning skulls.

Rue looked over, his gaze meeting Azrael's. "I think we need to have a little chat with the Deceiver," Rue whispered.

One corner of Azrael's mouth tipped up in a smile. He reached out, pulled a scythe from the air. The souls in the line screamed and scattered again. He gestured to the Gate. "You first."

CHAPTER SIXTEEN

Souls scattered, terrified by their advance. Deimos shouted out a warning. Asmoday's blue eyes flashed red as they widened and he dove for the safety of the deeper Hells. Rue and Azrael swept souls from their path. Yariel sprinted for the gate, but he was too slow for the two angels. Hell's Gate slammed shut behind them. Asmoday, of course, was nowhere to be found.

"Rue!" Yariel's voice reached from behind them, but Rue and Azrael completely ignored the judge and carried on.

Azrael grabbed Deimos by the throat, lifting the demon off his feet. He kicked, his eyes bugging out more than usual, ice riming the skin around the angel's fingers. "Where?" he grated and gave the creature a vicious shake.

Dark choking laughter squeezed from the demon's throat. "Gone. You'll never be able to follow."

With a growl, he threw Deimos against the Gate. The flames flared and flickered, dancing wild shadows around the judging chamber.

The red-veined black tiled antechamber of Hell echoed silent as a tomb. The quiet lap of water did nothing to cool the rage burning within Rue. "He was right there!" He gestured with his shining sword to a jut of stone just in sight of Hell's Gate.

Azrael's deep rumble did not sound amused. "It seems we were deceived." His hand landed on his friend's shoulder, a comforting pressure as opposed to the biting cold grip it had been on earth when he'd worn a man's flesh. "He's had centuries to perfect it."

Chill wind buffeted them. Cool fingers of mist trailed over his face. He jerked away with a frown at the unexpected sensation. "What?"

Azrael's hand shot out. "Hold," he ordered. "There's a wandering soul trying to get your attention." He reached out, the hand with the skull ring disappearing into the mist that had appeared in front of them. "Speak." The choral resonance of the Angel of Death's voice shook a few stalactites loose from the unseen ceiling. They crashed nearby. "Be seen," he ordered again.

The white mist coalesced. A woman – no, Rue corrected – a girl, long flowing skirt, billowing sleeved blouse, hair loose and straight to her hips, appeared before them. She shook her head and he heard the musical clash of a trio of large metal hoops at her ears. "Whoa," she staggered, fetching up against the outcropping of stone to catch herself. "Been a while since I had some weight to me." She offered them a smile.

"Speak," Azrael ordered. The spirit shuddered in response.

"You're looking for Asmoday, right?" She went on, not waiting for their nods of ascent. "You're never going to find him if you just blunder on into Hell." She waved one hand at the River Styx. Charon's black barge bumped to shore. "You can get across here, but the halls all twist if you don't have a guide."

Rage and despair twisted inside Rue. Resolve hardened into a hot ball in his belly. Who knew how long he'd blunder about this time when Asmoday truly didn't want to be found. And with Azrael at his side, how much would tangle in the mortal realms with the Angel of Death otherwise occupied? A thread of understanding started to spin through his thoughts.

Azrael chuckled beside him, drawing his attention back to the problem at hand. He turned to see the Angel of Death's golden eyes twinkle in amusement at the shade before them. "Do you want freedom then, ghost girl?"

She stuck her chin out in defiance. "I've been hiding from the demons since the sixties when I was brought down here and sentenced to Hell." Her gaze raked Rue from toe to head. "Wasn't you." She gestured back toward the blazing gates. "One of the others thought I had enough sin by association to deserve the fires." She lifted one shoulder in a negligent shrug. "I get it in some ways. I was part of Manson's group for a while, but I got out before the Tate murders and all."

Rue reached out, reached through the girl, snagging her soul, ignoring her indignant little shriek. He sifted through her sins: indulgence, drugs, lust, greed, theft... then a realization that she was sinking so much deeper than she truly wanted. He saw a man with wild eyes and a silver tongue, a group of people nodding in a haze of smoke and drink to a plan that would end in death. Cold fear threaded through her heart driving her to slip out of an abandoned house where they were squatting. Nowhere to go, turning to the only life she knew selling her soul and her body on the streets where she met an untimely end at the hands of a man who wanted more than she was willing to give.

He released her. Her eyes opened pale blue in the dim light of Hell, the color discernible only in Azrael's presence. She cocked a brow at him. "You know how much that hurts?" She shook her head. "I'm sure you agree with the other judge." She shrugged again, her earrings jangling. "Doesn't matter."

"So, what do you want?" Azrael tossed his scythe in the air letting it disappear. "If not freedom, then what?"

"I didn't say I didn't want freedom," she countered.

Rue growled, his sword still glowing silver bright in his hand. Time was wasting. The longer they lingered, the longer it would take to find Serafina, the longer she'd be forced to endure horrors of Hell. "We don't have time.... "

"You'd better make time," the ghost snapped. "I've been watching Asmoday for the last little while. He's up to something."

"What else is new?" Azrael snorted. "He's the Deceiver. He's always up to something."

She shook her head. "No, there's something a lot bigger going on. I've been around for a couple of decades and I've learned to figure out when something big is going down." She gestured to the Greek Underworld across the river. "Asmoday's had the little guys poking holes into the real world." Her mouth twisted. "I tried to get through. I thought being a spirit out there would be better than dodging demons down here." She shook her head before they were even able to ask. "Works only for demonkin. I got zapped into smoke when I tried. Took me most of a day to re-form. I saw a handful of them go through not an hour or so ago. Of course, time's a little wonky around here."

"Demonkin?" Rue frowned. "Az, when I was mortal, I kept seeing demonkin. I thought they were drawn to me because I was angel-touched. The princes left me my memories and those memories came with more abilities that a normal human would have. I thought they were just drawn to me. I got a sword from the princes. I was –" Realization dawned. "They were let loose on purpose."

"To kill you or to test you?" Azrael pondered.

Rue shook his head. "No idea. Maybe they weren't there for me at all." He turned to the ghost girl. "Can you lead us to Serafina?"

"My name's Elli," she muttered.

He dipped into an apologetic bow. "Can you lead us to Serafina, Elli?"

She pursed her lips. "I can lead you to the Labyrinth." She waved one arm crowded with bracelets past the Greek Hell. "I know she was being taken to the maze, but that's it. I can't lead you through the maze, but I'll help you." As if she knew what he was about to ask she continued, "There isn't any way through the maze. Well, there is, but everyone has to find their own way through. It's complicated. You'll see if you're really serious about going there."

"I ask again," Azrael's deep voice echoed, a choral command to the spirit before them, "what do you want? We make no bargains with the denizens of Hell."

"What I want...." she trailed off, glancing at the flickering gates of Hell. "I want to serve. I want to have a chance to earn my way out of here." She waved a hand, encompassing all of Hell in her gesture. "You all think we're here for punishment or to work out our sins, but it's not what's happening. All that's happening is punishment. I've been here more than forty years and I haven't heard or seen one soul who was let loose. They all talk a great game about serving the greater purpose, but I haven't ever seen anyone let go. What's the point then?"

Azrael stroked his chin, then nodded. "Very well." He snapped his fingers, his scythe appearing in his hand. "Allow me to touch you with this, ghost girl, and you'll be bound to my purpose." He shrugged. "I've been meaning to take on more help."

She skipped away from the shining weapon. "You can't. Not yet." She gestured around them. "If I'm bound to you then I'm not a creature of Hell anymore and I can't make the halls move." She pursed her lips. At their uncomprehending stares, she gestured to the solid looking stone wall at her side and explained, "The halls move. They shift and only those of us who reside here can force them to our wills." She shrugged. "I'm not very good at it, but I'd be a damn sight better than the two of you. We might have to grab an imp to help us."

Rue smiled. "I'm up for that."

She grinned, "I knew I liked you. You're not like all the other judges, are you?"

"Definitely not," he agreed.

Azrael gestured her toward Charon's boat. "Then lead the way. We will bargain when the woman is safely where she belongs."

They boarded the barge. Charon poled, unconcerned that he seemed to be letting enemies into his master's territory. Or was it his master's territory anymore? Rue wondered. The ferryman's master had been Hades. Had his loyalty left when Hades had been abandoned for Abbaddon or Satan? As Hell changed, so did its master. Black water slid by. Sharp-toothed fish broached the surface as if scenting flesh. The barge bumped the ebon sand shore of the Grecian Hell.

"My thanks," Rue said to the ferryman who raised his head to nod in return, the first such gesture he'd ever gotten from the creature.

"Let's go!" Elli's voice rang from the twisted path. "The last time I went to the labyrinth it was past the Norse Hel and right next to one of the African ones." She squinted across the large low plan that stretched before them. The Fields of Asphodel with its hordes of ancient Grecian dead milling about amid pale white flowers, stood now at their feet. Definitely different from when he'd come through Hell the last time. They'd skirted the Field, heading right toward the heart of Tartarus. "I know that it's usually on the far side of the Greek Hell." She flitted down the twisting smoke gray road that wound down to the Field. "The ancient Hells don't move around so much as the more modern halls, though they do move. They're usually just always up against each other. I just hope we don't need to go through all of them." She shuddered. "Some of them are really, really weird."

"Lead on," Azrael gestured.

She nodded and floated down another dozen yards leading the way into Hell.

The Fields looked like nothing more than a vast rolling expanse of flower fields. White flowers, pale as corpse fingers waved in a non-existent wind. The souls of the Grecian dead who had not been particularly remarkable in life milled about, jabbering to each other in high screechy voices, unable to be understood by one another or visitors. Since they did nothing remarkable in life, they were doomed to do nothing in death. Truly, Rue thought, one of the more diabolical tortures of Hell. He paused before a woman. She ignored him, continued to stare straight ahead with no sign in her washed-out blue eyes that she even saw him. Perhaps, they didn't mind?

Rue remembered the lines of Grecian dead at Hell's Gate, though he and his brothers had never judged these souls. They fell of their own accord onto the Fields knowing that they had not lead remarkable, heroic lives. In the Greek afterlifes, only those who were heroes or who were shining paragons of virtue were ever allowed paradise. Everyone else wound up in the Fields—of Asphodel or of Punishment. He had once visited the Isle of the Blessed, a beautiful sun-filled city of white marble crowded with athletes, philosophers and those who performed deeds of honor and glory.

The Fields of Asphodel went on and on. The dreariness of the scenery started to drag down his eyelids. His feet stumbled over clumps of white asphodel flowers. Their scent, heavy and sweet, spiraled up to surround him, clouded his mind. He looked up. Instead of the lowering ceiling of a cavern he saw a gray sky painted with scudding white clouds. It would be nice to lay down his burdens for just a moment... his shining silver sword slipped from his grip to tumble amid the asphodels. A flash of white light and the celestial blade scorched a circle about six feet in diameter at his feet. The harsh stench of the burning flowers jerked him back to reality.

Shaking himself, Rue picked up his sword and the pace, jogging through the ashes of asphodel to catch up with Azrael and Elli. They walked on, unconcerned and unaffected, through the Field. He could hear her voice happily chattering away to the Angel of Death, bombarding him with question after question. Why had it affected him? Why had he been the only one drawn in by the curious lassitude of the flowers? Did some lingering weaknesses from his brush with humanity still linger on him? Perhaps, Rue thought, just as he'd been able to tap into some of his angelic strengths as a human he was hindered by some of his former human weaknesses as an angel. Only time would tell.

The fields gave way to a broad wooden avenue— the pathway to the Nordic Hel, Elli told them, and he was only too happy to leave them behind. One glance backward showed the white flowers waving in that ghostly breeze as if beckoning his return.

The pathway narrowed, twisted back on itself, rose from the ground to become the gnarled branches of the Yggsdrasil Tree. Try though he might, he couldn't hear the tinkle of the fountain of wisdom at its roots. Apparently, Hell was twisting him through a different pathway this time. He patted his chest. The stolen vial of miracles pressed warm against his heart. He only hoped it would still be useful.

* * * *

Heaven was definitely not what she expected. Serafina had expected large broad avenues of marble or gold, lofty buildings, a gentle suffused light and... angels. Yes, even if all the rest of it had been childish dreaming, she'd still expected to see angels. After all, Rue stood before the gates of Hell itself and had wings. You'd think that those beings who served in heaven would definitely have them.

However, she hadn't seen even the flicker of a feather.

She'd awoken that morning, or maybe a hundred mornings ago for all she knew, to see a light dusting of snow coating the sidewalk in front of her shop. She shivered and knew, without turning around, who would be waiting for her. He'd been all solicitousness. He'd bowed formally to her, then stretched out one hot, dry hand. She'd always thought Death would be cold.

She'd expected a jerk, a feeling of disconnection as her soul left her body, but there had been none of that.

She'd felt, instead, pulled off her feet as though her entire person had been dragged through a hole. She'd seen the shining glitter of a star studded sky, heard the lap of water at a shore and smelled a hint of dirt and decay before her senses were overcome and she fainted in the angel's arms.

She woke, hours, days, years – who knew, later in a lushly appointed bedroom with walls carved from quartz flecked marble. Definitely lovely, but cold when she pressed her hand to the wall. Should she be feeling cold? Her head throbbed a little, distant as if a memory. Maybe such human feelings faded with time.

She waited.

And waited some more.

Was heaven supposed to be so boring?

She tried the door and found it locked. A tiny niggle of fear began to scurry around her brain. Something felt terribly off about all of this. Perhaps Rue had been wrong and this was Purgatory and not heaven? Maybe she was being sentenced to sit around in boredom for a century or two before actually making it to heaven. No. That just didn't sound right. Besides, did the church even acknowledge purgatory anymore? She nibbled on her thumbnail. Then again, which church?

With an exasperated groan she strode back to the door, tugged on its heavy iron handle. Nope. Nothing. She pounded on the dark wood. "Hey!" she yelled. "Anyone else out there?"

Tired, she sank to the floor, leaning against the door, her nightgown pooling around her, her bare toes cold on the stone floor. Several things started to fall into place. She shouldn't be feeling cold or weariness or, her stomach gave a growl, hunger. Everyone agreed that you left those problems behind when you died. Therefore, she shoved herself to her feet, tugged down her nightgown, and was positive she wasn't dead. That blue-eyed blond guy who'd taken her hand earlier that morning, and she was almost certain it was just that morning now, had not been the Angel of Death. She'd been tricked. She was being held somewhere and she was certain deep down in her frantically beating heart, that she was bait for a trap.

And Rue was the prey.

She wandered over the tall wardrobe across from the luxuriously appointed bed. Well, they were going to get more than they'd bargained for. She whipped open the doors. If she was going to try and get to the bottom of this she wasn't going to do it in bare feet in her nightgown. Clothes burst from the wardrobe – a little too over the top, she noticed. Silver lace, golden silk, sparkling stones and detailed embroidery spilled over her hands. It was like a scene out of "Beauty and the Beast." She snorted, digging down a little deeper. There had to be something practical in here. While she didn't find jeans, she did find a rather simple dress—silvery in color with very little adornment and the shoes were comfortable as slippers, but with a much more substantial sole. "Well, it'll have to do." With a quick look behind the curtains – they covered more rock, not windows – just to make sure nothing was lurking, she dressed.

She picked a book at random from the tall bookcase and settled into a deep cushioned chair to wait. They'd have to come and feed her eventually. She needed to find out where she was. She needed to find out what they wanted, why they'd taken her and how she could get home.

A terrible bloom of hope rose in her mind. One thing, bright and shiny, floated in front of her. She wasn't dead. And with that thought, her adrenaline surged.

CHAPTER SEVENTEEN

The book fell from her hand to the stone floor with a thump. That thump woke her. Serafina sat up with a groan. Her neck stiff, her stomach empty and rumbling, her right arm asleep under her. Her head gave a sharp pound and empty stomach roiled. Yep, if she needed any more proof that she wasn't in heaven, her body was giving her plenty of clues. She sat up and whipped the book at the door which opened at just that second. The tiny woman ducked, but wasn't fast enough. The book, however, sailed right through her head. Serafina gulped.

"Beg pardon," the stranger giggled, a high pitched little sound that sounded slightly off to Serafina's ears. "I should have knocked, but bodies around here aren't known for their manners." She chuckled again and Serafina wondered how she could handle the tray in her hands and manage to kick the door closed behind her if books could sail right through her head.

"Where am I?" She decided to stick with a safe question since she was beginning to think that she knew the answer already.

That off-putting laugh again. "Where do you think you are?" She thunked the tray on the bedside table. "Here you go, dear, some nibbles for you." She gestured to the plates. "A little fruit and some bread. The bread's from above, so no worrying there."

So it was, she could see, a whole loaf of Wonder bread still in its classic red, white and blue packaging. "I'm in Hell, aren't I?"

The spirit nodded. "Aren't we all?" She cackled again, eyes wheeling a little wildly in her head. "Aren't we all!" She gestured to the tray. "Eat up, need your strength."

Not really wanting to, but knowing she needed to, Fina snagged the loaf of bread. The gluey mass stuck in her throat, but she didn't dare ask for water. She'd read her myths and just in case, she didn't want anything from down here to pass her lips.

"So," the spirit wandered around the room to finger the clothes still spilling out of the closet, "you must be pretty darn important to keep here."

Fina swallowed with difficulty. "I don't know about that." She ripped the corner off another piece of bread. The spirit ducked into the wardrobe to pull shoes off the bottom, making an appreciative humming noise deep in her throat. Fina reached out to grab the lamp on the bedside table, a heavy twisted wrought iron affair. A shoe sailed over the creature's shoulder as she continued to scrabble. "Where is here?" Fina asked.

The spirit snorted, head still in the wardrobe. "One of the newer halls—they just started building them a few decades ago or so." She sat back, still not looking at Serafina, tugged off a heavy work boot and began wiggling her large foot into a dainty golden stiletto. "Must need the room soon. Only thing I can figure is that the powers that be are going to start some mess and need the space." She held her shod foot up to be admired. Fina crept closer, lamp in hand.

"What do you think is going to happen?"

She shrugged and picked up the other shoe. "Last time we added on so much it was one of the world wars." She trailed off for a moment, her eyes glazing in memory. "Reminded me a little of when I came down here— Napoleon's still screaming down in one of the deep holes." She leaned back, both feet held up in front of her. She began to swivel. "Hey, you mind if I take .... " Serafina lunged and swung. The lamp hit with a satisfying *thunk* and the spirit's eyes rolled up into her skull and she crashed over to the side, golden shoes still glittering on her feet.

"Thank God," she murmured, dropping the lamp. She figured as long as the creature had been trying on shoes she'd be solid enough to hit. Good thing her speculation paid off. Now, to get out of here.

She grabbed the loaf of bread, tucked it under her arm, found a Silver Springs water bottle that had rolled sideways on the tray and hidden under a napkin. She headed out into a black stone hallway, threads of white and gold veining through the stone. She could only hope that the corridor could lead her somewhere helpful. Though how helpful could you get deep in the bowels of Hell?

* * * *

"We have a problem."

Asmoday didn't really need any more problems. One of his demon doors had just imploded, sending nasty little chunks of bloodsucking demonkin to splatter all over his new tie. Not to mention, he knew that Rue and Azrael were stalking around somewhere down here, looking to tie his neck in a knot. However, the boss needed a little extra time to put the finishing touches on the Labyrinth, so he'd sent a couple of imps to twist the paths a little and slow them down. One of the imps had come back already to tell them that something was helping them. It looked like Asmoday was going to have to take matters into his own hands.

He really didn't want to have his tongue tied around his throat, though, so he sent Bezaal and Semoath to slow the angels down. They'd be sliced to gooey little demon bits, but they'd buy the boss time to finish in the Labyrinth and give Asmoday enough time to change his tie.

He snarled at the spirit in front of him. She was one of the younger ones, somewhere between a hundred and two hundred years old, dressed in a homespun dress with ridiculous gold stilettos on her fat feet. "I said there's a problem, my lord, with the prisoner."

"The guest, Lally," he corrected, "the guest." He yanked off his soiled tie and snapped his fingers, letting it burn to ashes. "What's the problem? I made sure we had some food that wouldn't lock her in here." He pulled another tie, this one blood red, from the air. "Might not be fancy, but it's better than having her stuck around here for months on end meddling in things she should leave alone."

"The thing is, my lord," she said, starting to edge away, " she... well, the truth is, she got away from me."

He froze in the act of knotting his new tie. "She what?" He bit the words off.

She crept further back. "She got away. She's loose in the new halls."

He took a deep breath, drawing in the scent of brimstone and fear. It usually calmed him. Not this time. As quick as thought, he snagged her even as she tried to ghost away from him. A flex of his will forced her solid, his fingers burning into her throat. "Run that past me one more time," he grated.

Around the pressure of his hand, she gasped the story. Asmoday tightened his fingers, a flash of flame and the spirit disappeared, banished back to one of the deeper Hells to pay for her failure. A pair of glittering golden heels dropped to the ground before him. He kicked them out of his way. He did have problems. Serafina Kinnock was loose in Hell. Not only was that a disaster waiting to happen, he no longer had the bait he needed to tempt Ruvan. This was all falling apart around his ears. He needed to do some damage control. Find the girl, particularly before she got into one of the populated Hells and started wreaking havoc. He shuddered. A good soul in Hell – who knew what kind of trouble that could cause? The last time it had happened, over a hundred souls had been released. That would completely piss off the boss, particularly when he had something big in the works.

With a decisive nod and the fervent hope to deflect the inevitable wrath off of his neck he poked the last demon door into the mortal realm, shoved the first three demonkin through personally, then took off. He needed to get to the new halls before she got out.

* * * *

"Another one." Azrael pointed his scythe at the demon door and sealed it with blazing celestial light. Not only would the door be sealed on this side, but any demonkin trying to get back through from the other side would be fried to a crisp.

"That makes seven we've found." Seven connections between Hell and the mortal realm. Rue didn't know where they'd all lead to, and he knew for certain that they hadn't found them all. Elli was right. Asmoday and his brothers had been busy little bees. He looked up at the spirit flitting ahead. "Are we nearly there?"

She shook her head. "I think so, but the halls are moving so much." She gestured behind them. "I've never even seen that Hell before." She shuddered. "What culture came up with flesh eating sea serpents that ate you, spit you back out and ate you again for all eternity?"

He said what they were all thinking. "Someone's playing games."

She laughed. "Of course they are. This is Hell." With a roll of her eyes, she continued, "Seriously, are all you guys this naïve?"

Azrael reached out his scythe, a small arc of power leaping from it to her. She screeched at the zap and, rubbing her behind, whirled to glare at him.

"Mind your manners, ghost girl, if you want to get out of here."

Rue could see her chewing on a retort, and smiled when she swallowed it. "We just need to keep going forward." She gave herself a shake, fading out for a moment. "Maybe we need to refocus." She gestured them over to her, taking their hands in hers. "You might think it's all hippy woowoo, but I've found that taking a couple of minutes to really visualize my destination works pretty well." Rue stopped trying to pull away and she smiled. "All right, now just close your eyes." She jerked and Rue guessed that Azrael had tried to escape her clinging little fingers too. "Close your eyes, take a deep breath and just concentrate. Let your mind fill with what you want to find."

The feeling of foolishness faded and Rue settled, his wings drooping behind him, as he let Serafina's face fill his mind. Her dark eyes, the smattering of freckles you needed to be really close to see, the tangled riot of red hair. She was alone down here. Probably scared. He needed to find her and take her home where she belonged. The warmth from the vial of miracles spiraled through him. Take her home and save her.

"Well, well, well, are we getting in touch with our feminine sides?" The sneering voice made Rue's eyes flare open. He felt Elli's fingers freeze in his hand.

"They're already halfway there, Bezaal." The leering demon raked them over from head to foot. "They're in dresses, for Satan's sake."

Azrael growled deep in his throat, his scythe flaring diamond bright for a moment. Several things just out of eyeshot screamed and dove for cover. Puffs of greasy smoke marked places where those little things didn't get out of the way fast enough.

"Put the flashlight away, Az," Bezaal snarled. "We're not wussy demonkin to run away from some light."

Rue willed his own sword to the fore. "You will die nonetheless," he promised.

Semoath grinned, triple rows of needlelike fangs glinting, and rose to his full height, all seven slimy purple feet of it. "This is going to be fun. Haven't pulled the wings off a butterfly in an age, eh, Bezaal?"

Bezaal laughed, harsh scraping laughter that made Elli shudder in and out of visibility. "Been a while, Semoath, been a while." He flexed his huge shoulders, his knuckles dragging the ground.

Azrael swung. Bezaal ducked, losing only one sharp horn. "You're the ones gossiping like old women."

With a snarl, the demons attacked, wielding iron-studded clubs the length and width of a man's leg. Rue backwinged, lifting off the ground, gaining the advantage of height on Semoath. "Get back here!" the demon howled, dodging a shining bolt of celestial light. "I'm going to stuff my pillow with your feathers!" A painful shudder rippled through him. He remembered too well not having his wings and the demon's foul threat shot a bolt of pure anger through him.

Almost as though his body belonged to another, Rue dropped to the ground, furled his wings tight to his back, willing them back to ink and faced the demon on his own poisoned ground. He ducked, he whirled, felt the painful burn when Sem's nail-studded mace grazed him. He felt sweat or blood slide down his brow. He scored the demon in a dozen small places. A nick here, a swipe there. Ichor, thick and black in the shifting light of Hell, gleamed slipping into the demon's eyes.

He heard and saw Azrael out of the corner of his eye, driving Bezaal back. The scythe, gleaming silver in the uncertain light, made the demon flinch whenever it whirled too closely to his head.

Rue danced back, his feet slipping on the uncertain rock surface. Thin sticklike fingers, strong despite their seeming fragility, wrapped around his ankle. He stumbled. Semoath's glowing violet eyes widened in triumph. The club rose. Rue vanished his blade, wrapped his hand in pure power and grabbed the demon's throat, pouring all his righteous anger and fear into the figure. The demon's hands spasmed on the club's handle, his eyes gleaming, flashing from sickly purple to pure white. Light poured from his mouth and the creature's entire body began to pulse. He stumbled back, dropping his weapon, weeping tears of shining light. Willing his weapon back into his hand, Rue strode up to the writhing demon's body and drove the sword deep into its back. Semoath melted into a smelly pool that oozed through the cracks in the floor and disappeared.

"Speak!" Azrael ordered. Rue turned to see that he'd backed Bezaal against the wall, the shining scythe burning blisters into the demon's neck. "Show us the way to the Labyrinth."

Bezaal spat, his spittle striking a hole in front of Elli's floating feet. She ghosted up a little higher. "You'll scatter me anyway, Angel of Death, so do it now."

Rue could see Azrael calculating. He looked over and Rue knew, without hesitation, what he asked. He nodded.

"We will release you if you show us to the Labyrinth."

Bezaal laughed, that harsh sound, the scraping of tiny claws on bone. "You'll let me live? I show you the way and Asmoday pulls out my entrails with a hook." He shrugged. "Either way I die."

Rue stalked closer. "We can end you here and now. But you might be able to hide from Asmoday."

Speculation twisted the demon's face as he weighed the options. Certain doom now or a possibility of freedom.

"Who knows," Azrael's voice sounded like a low purr, "what the Dark Lord will do to Asmoday if we succeed and all his plans fail. Look at the opportunity."

A slow smile spread across Bezaal's face, visions of not only freedom but currying favor dancing in his evil little head. "Agreed."

Azrael stepped back, the scythe disappearing. He waved Elli forward. She drifted down to take his hand. "Will you complete our bargain now, ghost girl, that we have another guide?"

She shook her head. "Not until you're safely in the Labyrinth. No matter what, I don't trust it."

Bezaal laughed. "Safely in the Labyrinth."

Azrael nodded. "Very well."

Rue shot silver strands of power into the demon, a celestial leash to keep it from scurrying off into the darkness. "Now, bend the halls and lead on."

Bezaal bowed and closed his shining eyes. The halls twisted, rose, blurred. The harsh coppery stone hall they'd stood in shifted and changed without them stirring a foot, changing to smooth white veined black marble. The long corridor stretched to an unseen distance, punctuated by dark wooden doors. "This way."

With the demon in the lead, they continued deeper into Hell. Rue could feel the press of evil sliding along his bones.

* * * *

She heard whimpering. Soft little cries that pulled at her heart. With her pulse pounding in her throat, she tiptoed to the nearest doorway. A grill set high up in the wooden door let her see a body – woman or man, she couldn't tell – chained to the wall. It was this creature who wept.

Against her better judgment, knowing that nothing good could possibly be down here, yet unable to turn away from that pitiable crying, she tried the door, and was half-surprised when it opened under her hand.

The figure- – one of three figures now that she could see clearly – looked up, tears streaking her face. The other two men hung listless in their chains, no expressions on their wan faces. "Who...?" she began.

The woman shook her head, greasy dishwater blonde hair obscuring her vision. "It doesn't matter," she croaked. "We deserve it."

One of the men in chains beside her snorted, clanking against the clammy stone. Fina walked forward and shivered, noticing how the temperature dropped as she approached the wall. A table and a chair sat not to far away from the victims, as if set up for a comfortable show. She rested her hand on the back of the chair, not really daring to get any closer. "Can I help?" Her voice sounded breathless in her own ears.

The woman moaned a little. The man beside her snorted again and the third man said nothing, but stared with hungry eyes. "There is nothing," the woman rasped, "though..." Her tongue darted out to wet her lips. "I would kill for some water."

The man laughed, chains clinking. "Yeah," he added, "kill for some water."

Their hands were chained above them at a shoulder breaking stretch. Their feet were chained at the ankles with very little slack. "I have water." She pulled the water bottle out of a hidden pocket in her skirt. All three sets of eyes fastened on the bottle.

"Water," the woman whispered, her voice a pained plea.

Fina nodded, tiptoed up, unscrewing the cap. Her hands shook splashing water over her knuckles. It froze in white patches on the floor. Shivering, she raised the bottle to the woman's mouth. She sucked greedily at the bottle, eyes rolling, chains rattling. The man at her side moaned. The third man's eyes seemed to bore holes in her back. With cold seeping through her dress into the flesh beneath, she moved down the line. The sneering man guzzled from the bottle, the dripping water freezing on his skin. She approached the third man with the most apprehension. He'd said nothing, moved not a muscle, but his eyes hadn't left her since she'd first opened the door and they made her skin crawl and her head pound. With frozen fingers she raised the bottle to his mouth. He finally closed those hideously burning eyes and turned away.

"No," he said. She could barely hear his voice. "No, I deserve this."

She shook the bottle, making the water splash. "There's still some left." Her breath puffed winter white.

Another head shake. "No. It is my punishment."

With a nod, she backed away, replacing the cap on the bottle. "Then I will hope your punishment is over soon," she whispered.

He nodded, eyes still closed.

"I hope you will all be free soon." She tucked the water bottle away. "I wish I could free you."

The third man lifted his head, a tiny smile curving his lips. "You've already begun to free us."

Confused, Fina nodded and turned to go.

"Turn left," the woman called after her. "Turn left at the next corridor and you should be out of this hall."

She nodded, deciding then and there that she had to take the help on faith, that one good turn deserved another. "Thank you."

As the door closed behind her, she thought she heard one them reply, "No – thank you."

CHAPTER EIGHTEEN

"Shit." Asmoday ran his hand over the white veined black stone. The white vein was growing larger. Sure sign something was changing the halls. They'd been an unrelieved black a few days before. Serafina's very presence had altered the geography. He'd hoped to keep her influence to this out-of-the-way hall, but now she was wandering around, running amuck and getting into who knew how much trouble.

He sniffed. A faint trace of decaying humanity—like rot and roses—trailed down from her cell to a holding pit. Overflow prisoners who'd just arrived had been chained in this room. He edged the door open. Against the wall of ice still, the prisoners hung, heads bowed, chains slack, but... he breathed deeply and swore again. Instead of the rank, sour scent of despair and anger, the copper smell of terror, he breathed in the fresh water scent of hope. Another inhalation of air and Asmoday gagged, nearly vomiting onto the stones. Underlying the fresh water of hope another fragrance, once so rarely inhaled here in these halls that it turned his stomach. A scent like a blend of cinnamon and honey, warm sunshine and freshly mown grass—all those scents that spoke of home and homecoming to humanity—the scent of forgiveness.

He wished he had enough time to whip some more fear back into these prisoners, but he needed to find Serafina and drag her back to her cell. And find someone competent to watch her. He slammed the door shut behind him barking out an order to the demonkin who followed to get someone in there to cleanse the stench of forgiveness. Then his gaze trained on the ever widening trail of white threading through the black stone. He got back on the hunt. The boss wouldn't notice a few bruises, would he? Particularly if he were careful on where they were applied?

* * * *

"There it is. Now, fulfill your promise and release me." Bezaal waved one clawed hand in the direction of the huge statues guarding the entry to the Labyrinth.

"Based on the Greek mythos, I believe," Azrael nodded to the twenty foot tall stone minotaurs that guarded the entrance.

"Being a god was a power trip," Bezaal agreed. "We kept a lot of stuff from the old days. This one works good. Now, let me go."

Rue tightened the celestial leash one last time before snapping it, freeing the demon. "We keep our promises."

Bezaal snarled.

"Is that Asmoday?" Elli bounced up, waving. Bezaal froze mid-snarl and disappeared in a flash of flame and putrid stench. The ghost girl settled back to the ground. "Oh, I must have been mistaken."

Azrael laughed and summoned his scythe into existence. "Come, ghost girl, you said there was no true way through the labyrinth. I would not have you separated from us. Touch my blade and you will be bound to my purpose." His eyes glowed gold with the command.

She swallowed and floated forward to press one fingertip to the shining silver weapon. A flash of light, a thin scream and it was done. Elli didn't look any different. She ran her hands over her head and down her legs as if making sure she was all there.

"All right, that's done." He snapped the blade back into the ether and slanted a look over his shoulder at Rue. "Any idea on where to go?"

Remembering Elli's words, he closed his eyes and concentrated, bringing Serafina's face into focus. He wrapped one hand around the vial of miracle and prayed for one. Guidance? Help? "Something tells me we're on our own down here, Az. Heaven's princes probably aren't really happy with us right about now, so I think we're being left to our own devices."

Azrael shrugged and pointed onward. "Well, then, when in doubt go left."

"Go left? Why left?"

He shrugged as they passed beneath the gaze of the stone minotaurs. "Why not?"

"You two don't have the first idea on where you're going, do you?"

"We're open to suggestions, ghost girl."

"Never mind." She flitted ahead a few feet. "Left it is."

The broad avenue past the minotaur statues took a sharp left as if in accordance with their wishes, just ten feet into the labyrinth. The walls changed from red and brown sandstone to irregularly hewn gray building blocks. A fetid breeze blew down the hall bringing with it the scent of rust and water. Rue looked up. The ceiling of the cavern they'd been in had looked just like that—a cavern. Now, though the open sky loomed above dark clouds scudding across a slate gray sky.

"It must twist through multiple times and places," he murmured, the enormity of what he was attempting dawning on him.

"And all at the Lord of Hell's will," Elli added. She trailed one ghostly hand across the rough stones.

"Yippee." Azrael shook his head. "Lead on, MacDuff." He gave Rue a shove.

"Yippee?" Elli asked. "Yippee? Isn't that a little flip for the Angel of Death?"

He shrugged. "I spend a lot of time with humans. Some of it rubs off. I particularly like their humor."

She snorted a laugh. "I think we'll get along just fine."

"Provided we live."

"Yeah," she agreed. "There's that. Good thing I'm already dead."

Rue tuned them out, bent all his concentration on his need to find Serafina and return her to where she belonged. Nothing mattered to him anymore beyond this. She didn't deserve to be in Hell. She didn't deserve to be a pawn in a game meant to trap him. He'd beg Lord Lucivar to release her. He'd give the fallen lord anything he wanted in return.

The corridor narrowed, pressing in so tightly they needed to walk sideways, their wings scraping the walls. Three hallways shot out, branching in three directions. Which one? He pressed a hand to the vial making sure it was still safe as he peered down one dark hall. The vial cooled against his fingers. Concerned, he tightened his grasp and turned to the second hall. The vial flashed hot in his hand. With hope blooming inside him, he turned to the final corridor. The flask of miracles cooled perceptively. It only burned hot at the central corridor. He'd found a beacon to follow.

"This way." He plunged into the darkness ahead. The floor tipped beneath his feet, sending him sliding. Elli screamed behind him and he knew then that the ghost girl too had been caught up in a trap for both corporeal and incorporeal beings. He flung out his hands to stop the slide. Pain sheared across his palms. He skidded to a stop, teetering at the edge of a gaping chasm. Elli and Azrael slammed into him from behind. He lost his grip and they tumbled headlong into the pit before them. He snagged Elli as she plummeted past him, noticed Azrael beating his own coal black wings frantically. They landed on the far side of the pit. He cast a light into the darkness, only to have it swallowed.

"We'll have to go in blind as mortals."

Rue nodded. "Take hold of my belt," he ordered Elli. "Az, take her hand. I'll lead, but I need my hands free." His companions nodded. They pushed on. He trailed one hand out in front of him to trace along the cold wall. The other he kept fisted around the vial waiting for it to signal which way to go.

Heavy breathing assaulted his ears. The click of claws on stone. He smelled rotten meat as they turned another corner, led on in the darkness by the miraculous vial. Faint ruddy light gleamed at the base of the walls, a faint flickering glow like firelight. Sweat trailed between his wings. Details of the room became visible as the light slowly rose. They came to a huge metal chamber, the ceiling hung with chains, the floor slimy gray stone. A huge red creature slumbered and just beyond it they could see the dark eye of a portal.

"Are you sure this is the way?" Elli whispered.

He summoned his blade without a sound and nodded.

The creature shifted in its sleep, turning its head toward them. "A dragon," Azrael murmured.

"Sure looks that way." Elli's voice trembled in a breathy whisper. "We're not going to play sacrifice the damsel to the dragon, are we?"

Az snorted. "My dear girl, we're the good guys, remember."

"Sorry, old habits."

"Would you two zip it?" Rue snarled in an undertone. "We need to get past the beast and I really don't want to have to kill it."

"It really is a remarkable creature." Azrael nodded. "I haven't seen anything like it since they went extinct on earth more years ago than I care to remember."

"You can ooh and ah over it all you like when we're on the other side." Rue slid a foot into the room. "Now, hush."

Elli bit her lips as if to keep herself from saying anything as they eased across the slimy chamber, setting their feet with extreme care amid the detritus of the dragon's former meals. Rue wondered idly if it really were a dragon or merely a facsimile, alive only here at the dark lord's behest. It grew larger as they got closer. Its head was easily the size of a man. Its eyes, when open, must be as large as dinner plates and the teeth poking out of the mouth were the length of his forearm. Its huge gold-rimmed nostrils flared as they tiptoed past and it stirred as though it dreamed of angel flesh.

They almost made it. Three more steps would have seen them through the portal and out the door when Elli caught sight of the chain. A huge metal manacle that would fit easily around Rue's waist was clamped around its back leg and attached to a chain thicker than his wrist. It was locked to a heavy iron hoop high above their heads.

"It's a prisoner," she moaned.

A shudder and a snort, and one acid green dinner plate eye opened. The lips peeled back into a snarl that rumbled through the chamber. "You poor thing!" Elli rushed forward. Azrael snagged her, yanking her behind him, his scythe held low.

"Are you mad?" he snarled.

"It's trapped!" She strained against his hold. He shook her hard. "No!" She tore herself away. "No! I've been trapped before and I won't let anyone else be." Azrael froze, letting her go.

She ran to the dragon, crooning low in her throat. Rue waited for that snarling mouth to snap up the ghost girl, but the creature froze as if as stunned by her actions as the angels. She collapsed against the creature's head, stroking the long nose. "Poor baby," she murmured and worked her way behind the creature to the manacle. Her fingers ran over the pitted iron searching for some way to release it. "Help me," she commanded.

They glided forward, the dragon's eyes shifting to keep them in sight. "I don't think... "

She whirled on them. "Look, I know it sounds stupid to you, but let me tell you: I was just like him for a while. When I first got down here, I was chained to this ice cold wall and starved. They let the imps beat me and I couldn't put my arms down." Tears shimmered in her eyes, slipped over her cheeks. "They wouldn't let me sleep. All I could see for days on end, if it even was days, it could have been years for all I know, was everything I'd ever done wrong in my life and everyone that I'd ever disappointed." She tugged futilely at the huge manacle. "I swore when I got out of there and got away that I wasn't ever going to let anyone suffer like that again." She swiped a hand under her running nose. "I know that's just how they start on us now." She gestured beyond the Labyrinth to the whole of Hell itself. "I know that's just standard procedure now. Just like I know I need you guys to pop these locks." She sat back on her heels, the dragon's breath a warm, coppery whuffing over her shoulder. She patted him on the nose, pushing his head out of the light.

"What do you need?" Rue knelt the dragon's side. The manacle had no visible lock. No seam. No weld. It looked as if it had grown around the creature's leg.

"I can't get it open," Elli said. "Before the labyrinth, when I could go misty, I could slip my hand through the cuffs, but I still couldn't open them. I think one of you might be able to find the weak point."

"Hmmm...." Azrael dropped to the floor, hands running over the metal. "I have an idea, Rue. I'll freeze the metal. You strike it. Both of us might be able to shatter the bond."

Rue stood, turned to Elli who stood at the beast's head scrubbing her hands over its floppy ears and crooning to it. "You're sure you want to free it? It might be serving a sentence here too."

She narrowed her eyes. "If it was, then shouldn't that sentence be done by now? Didn't Azrael say it's been centuries since he'd seen one of these guys?"

The angels exchanged a look. The ghost and beast stared at them, their eyes pleading.-"Very well," Rue nodded to Azrael and stepped back, readying his blade. The Angel of Death grasped the chain. Frost immediately began to rime the iron.

"I think we should aim for one of the smaller links instead of the manacle itself."

Rue nodded and began to concentrate. He didn't judge the souls of beasts. He'd never seen one of them in either Heaven or Hell; knew of no judge who weighed the souls of creatures. In fact, he couldn't read the beast's sins, something he'd been able to do with every mortal he'd ever encountered. No matter. A soul trapped in Hell for so many centuries deserved freedom, deserved the right to redeem itself. He focused those righteous thoughts as Azrael's power ate at the iron chain. The Angel of Death stepped back, nodded, and still wrapped in his righteous anger, Rue struck. The sword hit with the ring of a bell that ricocheted around the massive chamber. A single crack snaked across the link. With the sound like a shotgun blast, the metal split, falling in two pieces. The dragon-opened its dinner plate eyes wide. It settled on its haunches, lifted its face to the chain shrouded ceiling and gave voice to an ear shattering shriek. Chains rained from the roof with chunks of masonry and brick. The angels and Elli dove for the safety of the doorway behind the beast.

When the roaring and crashing subsided, the ceiling was gone. A dark sky strewn with stars stretched above them, thin wisps of clouds sliding across the face of a gibbous moon. The beast turned, its snakelike neck whipping around to see them crouched in the shadows of the doorway. Elli, tears of joy streaming down her face, stepped out to rest a hand on one webby wing. "You're free," she choked. It dipped its head in a bow and crooned low in its throat. She patted it again. "Go," she said, her voice more insistent. "Go. You're free."

Once again its head shook and the wing dipped lower.

"I think he wants to give you a ride," Azrael's own golden eyes looked wide with wonder. He looked over at Rue.

"Maybe it wants to give us all a ride?" Rue suggested. He vanished his blade and walked toward the beast. "Is that it? Can you see us to the center of the Labyrinth?" One corner of the dragon's mouth tipped up in an unmistakable smile and its head dipped in a bow. "Well, I think that's clear enough."

Without another word he leapt on the dragon's long neck and reached a hand down to help Elli up behind him. The ghost girl squealed in delight. "I love this!" She gave Rue an appreciative little squeeze. "I read every dragon book I could get my hands on when I was a kid. I remember wishing that Gandalf would come take me away when I was a kid." Her arms tightened around him when the dragon launched. He felt himself clutch at the sharp neck ridges before him. The beast spiraled up in ever widening circles, showing a maze of corridors, pits and covered rooms below them. Eyes streaming in the cold wind, Rue peered ahead of them, hunting for the center of the Labyrinth. He could feel the vial of miracles ever warmer against him and he knew in his heart of hearts that he would find Serafina. Hope spiraled up with every beat of the dragon's wings.

* * * *

She crouched behind a stalagmite, pressed to the slimy surface as a troop of small horned creatures marched past under the direction of a huge goat-hoofed monster with glowing yellow eyes and jagged teeth. "This way," the yellow-eyed monster snarled. "It's through here." It peered into the shadows opposite Serafina's hiding place. Seeming to find what it was looking for, it reached down and grabbed the first two little creatures in reach and shoved them through the wall where, instead of smashing as she thought they would, they disappeared before ever hitting the stone. She stifled a gasp with her hand. Where? How? The larger demon just kept shoving the little ones though an unseen hole.

"How's it going, Hereg?" a cheerful voice called down the hall. Muttering and growling, the monster moved up the line of little creatures. Where they'd stood in ragged formation, they now smartened up, standing almost at attention. A shadow stalked down the hallway and formed into a man with blond hair and bright blue eyes dressed in a smart black suit, silver shirt and red tie. "Getting them through all right? Do I need to make it bigger?"

Unable to stop herself, she gasped and the man's nostrils flared. His blue eyes narrowed and flashed red for a moment. "No, no, no," she begged silently.

He turned and whirled diving behind the rock to fasten a hot hand on her wrist. "Where the Hell have you been?" he snarled, dragging her forward. "I've been all over these halls looking for you. Do you know the trouble you've caused?" She struggled to pull away from him, but his grip was firm as stone. A snicker from the line of imps behind him turned his attention from her for a moment. Without letting her go, he located the snickering creature and pinned him with a red-eyed glare. "Allow me to aid you on your journey to the mortal realm." He picked the creature up with his free hand and hurled it at the stone wall where it splattered into a pool of black goo. "Oops," he murmured, "I missed." He raked the line with a look. "Anyone else have a comment?" Silence greeted him. He turned to the creature in charge. "Get this group through, then move on to the next hole. Azrael and Ruvan are sealing them as quickly as I can open them. The boss wants as many through as possible. So get a move on."

The yellow-eyed creature snarled what could only have been an affirmative and began throwing the little creatures through as quickly as he could get his claws on them. Fina's heart stopped beating for a moment at the mention of Rue's name. She couldn't think and mindlessly allowed the beautiful creature to drag her away. All she could think of was the fact that Rue was down here. Looking for her. She let him drag at her, closing her eyes for a second on a prayer. Of thanks.

CHAPTER NINETEEN

It could have been worse, he decided as he dragged Serafina with him. There'd only been three souls given the hope of redemption. She'd only made two imps implode after stopping them from fighting and making them apologize to each other and one of his demon doors had sealed after she'd helped a demonkin who'd been stuck halfway through. Random acts of kindness closed those things faster than an angel's blade. All that mattered was that he'd found her and no real mischief had been done. He rubbed his free hand over his face. He didn't even want to think about what the boss would have done to him if he'd had to admit that he'd lost her.

"Where –?" She stopped after that one word.

Asmoday slowed his pace, loosened his grip. His anger had begun to fade. If he were ever honest, even with himself, he'd admit a grudging admiration for her spunk. He really didn't think she had it in her. "Where am I taking you?" He flicked a hand, twisting the halls to make the walk last a little longer. The white streaked black walls peeled away to reveal red sandstone covered in hieroglyphs. He seemed to be partial to the Egyptian hall lately. Ammit didn't come running to meet him. The little guy must be sleeping under Osiris' throne. He tugged her closer, tucking her hand in the crook of his elbow as if he were escorting her instead of dragging her. "I'm taking you to the Labyrinth. The boss is waiting for you there." He patted her hand. "Nothing personal, you know, just business."

"The boss?" He could hear fear waver in her voice, scent the air with its perfume.

"Satan, Lucivar, the Fallen One, yeah. Whatever you want to call Him. He wants to see you. Wants to meet someone who can tempt a judge."

Her voice went hard. "Rue was a man when I met him."

He snorted a laugh. "Yeah, well, he still wants to talk to you."

"Talk?" He could hear the doubt.

He stopped, turned her to face him. "Look. I'll level with you, sister. We don't want you around here anymore than you want to be here. Good souls just cause trouble." He gestured at the twisting path behind them. "Look at what you did in only an hour. Could you imagine the kind of trouble you'd get into if we let you roam around here for longer than that?" He rolled his eyes. "Nah. The boss just wants you to play bait. Then you can go wafting on up to heaven on your own when you have to."

He tugged her along the path. Sandstone shivered, becoming gray flagstone. He heard her gasp. "When I have to? You mean, I'm not...."

"Dead?" He grinned. "I'll let you figure that one out when I send you back." And that, he decided, was the last of the truth he was going to speak. What had come over him? He gave his head a sharp shake, like a dog coming out of a pool. She was insidious. Having the Deceiver spouting the truth like he was an oracle? The boss was going to fry his brains if he didn't get his head on straight.

The minotaurs' eyes glowed an eldritch green as he passed between them. A flash of green fire when those beams met sent them right into the heart of the maze where Lucivar waited.

* * * *

"Incredible." The tall man in the sharp dark suit with the long black hair tapped the huge crystal sphere held up by a trembling imp. "Just incredible. Asmoday, come here and look at what they've done." He moved away to wave the demon into his place. Asmoday dropped her hand and stepped forward.

Serafina felt nailed to the floor. Her limbs were heavy, her heart beat so quickly it felt as though it were going to leap from her chest any second. Her tongue stuck to the roof of her dry mouth. The man turned away from a chuckling Asmoday and she got her first look at the face of evil.

It was a handsome face. Long, lean, with sharp cheekbones and a strong nose. Lips that were almost a little too full curved into a welcoming smile, but it was his eyes that caught her, pinned her like a mouse in a hawk's gaze. His eyes gleamed silver as moonlight in the artificial light of the underworld. Gleaming streaks of gold spiraled through those moonbeam eyes and seemed to twist as she watched them, drawing her in. He blinked and she stumbled. He reached out, caught her with a strong warm hand. "My pardon, my dear." His voice sounded low and melodious. She could listen to it forever.

"What...." She swallowed and tried again. "What are you going to do to me?"

He led her to a low bench against the wall. She had no choice but to follow. "You are my guest, Serafina. I need you only to wait and watch." He gestured and the stone wall opposite her rippled, turning into silvered glass. "And say nothing." The bite of command in his tone shivered like ice water down her spine.

He turned back to Asmoday and the shining crystal globe. The room outside that shining window was a small stone chamber; round, made of rough-hewn stone with a pedestal in the center. A small stone statue of a minotaur stared back at her from its perch. She couldn't figure out what was so important about that little room.

"How the hell did they manage that?" Out of the corner of her eye she saw Asmoday lean closer to the sphere.

"Kindness, compassion, acceptance are always the tools of goodness."

The demon made a retching sound deep in his throat. The Dark Prince chuckled. "Yes, I know." He crossed to the window, ignoring Fina as if she weren't there. "They'll be here sooner than I'd thought, but –" he turned and shot her a sizzling smile, " –I'm ever ready to improvise." He snapped at Asmoday. "Get Lilith." The demon bowed and disappeared in a puff of acrid smoke. "Time to slip into something that Ruvan might be more comfortable with." He shrugged out of the suit coat, hanging it meticulously on the back of a chair. He unbuttoned his shirt. "You're wondering if this is what I really look like." It was a statement, not a question. "You've been raised on stories of the red skinned devil with black horns and hooves." He turned to her and Fina had to admit to herself that the devil was built. "I could change into that image if you would prefer, but this is what I truly look like." He flexed and shadows unfurled from his back. Cold slithered to embrace her and she shuddered in the bone deep chill. The shadows coalesced into wings, huge wings that began white as snow at the tops, then faded into ever-darkening shades of gray to finish as the deepest black at the tips. He glowed with a faint luminescence, and Fina remembered that once upon a time he was the shining one.

"What would you like, my dear?" His voice echoed in her rib cage, hovering on the edge of pain. "Anything you want, anything you wish." Those spiraled eyes of gold and silver seemed to catch her, drag her into their shining depths. "Do you wish health?" She felt her heart hammer in her chest at the words. Her pulse leapt like a frightened rabbit. "Do you wish to wake tomorrow in your own bed, hale and hearty, with no lingering shadows?" His wings spread, blocking even the uncertain light of the chamber. "Or does something else entirely whisper in your soul? Do you wish wings of your own? Would you like to shed this shell of yours and spend eternity flying at Ruvan's side?" He reached out, taking her hand in his, his skin warm and dry against hers. "I can make it happen." His words dropped to a sly whisper. "Speak the words and I will bend reality to my will. I can almost see your wings, a soft gold. You're lovely."

She could see them too: golden wings, glowing in the light of a perpetual down. A beach of pink sugar soft sand kissing the edges of a purple sea stretched below her. A rise of white mountains, trees with feathery leaves lining their slopes-touching a cloudless sky. A feeling of freedom, of weightlessness lifted her. A laugh and she turned. Rue coasted beside her, his own hawk wings outstretched. His eyes, no longer sad, held joy and love.

"You can have it all. Here, in my realm." That soft voice pulled at everything in her, made her yearn, made her unbearably sad. "Say the words, yield to my will, and I will reward you beyond measure."

"At what cost?" She forced the words out. She longed to say yes, to bow her head and beg him for the world he'd shown her. The vision faded and she saw the rough hewn stone chamber again. It took every ounce of willpower in her to pull her eyes away from his. Over his shoulder she saw Asmoday with a woman at his side. The demon quirked one brow and nodded as if impressed. "At what cost?" she repeated, not daring to look at the Lord of Evil again. "I will play the cards I've been dealt." She shrugged. "Thank you, though. It was a lovely dream."

The Dark Prince chuckled, dropped her hand and stepped away. "You cannot imagine the tortures I could put you to, Serafina, my dear. I could have you screaming in agony, your mind a shattered shell in a matter of seconds."

She swallowed the nausea that rose to the back of her throat. "I am quite certain that you could, sir. As they say, death's the end of all, and from what I understand, I wouldn't stay long in your hands after that."

A charged silence sizzled across the room. Then Lucivar burst out in harsh rasping laughter. "I admire you, Serafina. I truly do. I am beginning to see how Ruvan fell." He gestured the woman forward. "I admire defiance. I had enough of my own, so I will abide by my promise. You will come to no physical harm at my hands or the hands of any my minions."

She heard what he didn't say. "What about non-physical harm?"

He shoved the female forward. She had an odd, almost feline beauty with slitted catlike eyes in a piercing blue. "I make no promises there. Lilith, make it good."

The female bowed. "As you will, my Lord."

Those cat eyes studied her for a moment, then the woman's face began to shiver. Bones melted and merged, her hair shortened, straightened from a riotous mane of black curls to match Serafina's own sleek reddish gold style. She closed her eyes and when she opened them, Fina looked at her own face.

"Not bad." Asmoday paced around the two of them. "If I didn't know better, I wouldn't be able to tell you apart." He reached out, grabbed the demoness and hauled her in for a deep kiss. "I wish there were enough time to tell Ruvan I had his woman." He snickered. "After a fashion."

"You're...." the words dried in her throat.

"Evil?" the demon rolled his eyes. "Welcome to Hell." He gave the demoness a pat on the backside, directing her to follow the Devil. "Now, you sit here and behave." He pointed to the window. "Enjoy the show and – ," his eyes flared coal red, " –keep your mouth shut."

"Threats, Asmoday?" Lucivar sighed. "How childish of you." Those gilt eyes pinned her. "I'm quite certain that Miss Kinnock can understand the severity of the situation. He snapped his fingers and a heavily decorated golden goblet appeared in his hand. "However, prevention is one of the few virtues to which I ascribe." He handed her the cup. It was bitterly cold and heavy in her hands. "Drink, Serafina. It will not bind you here. You have my word."

The word of the Devil. What choice did she actually have? Asmoday stood nearby, cracking his knuckles as if to show her that he was perfectly willing to pour the concoction down her throat. With both hands she lifted the cup. Colder than ice water, yet burning at the same time, the liquid coursed through her. She was awake. She could see, hear, understand, but it was as if she were viewing everything outside of herself. She felt no pain, no weariness and yet a peculiar lassitude spread through her being. She could do nothing as Asmoday, the demoness Lilith who adjusted her clothing to match hers, and the devil arranged themselves in the small room beyond the window. At a gesture from Lucivar, the chamber flexed and shifted, becoming much larger. From where she lay, she could just make out a sliver of murky sky.

* * * *

The dragon banked. Elli whooped in joy, slapping the creature's side, encouraging it to go faster. "There!" Azrael's scythe pointed the way. "The center of the maze."

Elli yelled, "That way, George!"

"George?" The shock of the name momentarily pulled Rue out of his contemplation of what he'd do to Asmoday when he got his hands around his throat.

"Yeah, George," the ghost girl repeated. "You know those old Loony Tunes cartoons—'I will hold him and pet him and name him George?'"

"Not a clue," Azrael responded.

She shook her head. "Seriously, you guys are really deprived in heaven. Don't even know Bugs Bunny."

George banked right and pulled up, backwinging to hover over the huge circular chamber at the heart of the Labyrinth. Rue jumped off, unfurling his own wings to catch his fall, summoning his blade. Azrael landed at his side. George, with Elli still astride him, landed as far away from the figure leaning against the wall as possible.

Asmoday grinned. He flicked away his lit cigar. "Heard you been looking for me, Rue."

"We're on even ground now, demon," Rue growled, stalking forward. "Will you meet me?"

He snorted out a laugh. "Seriously? Do you guys have someone writing that crap? Is that Shakespeare's eternal reward? Write bad dialogue for the angels?" He shook his head. "You spent enough time with the redhead to learn how to talk like a modern man, Rue. I'd expect that out of Az, here, but not you."

"You might be surprised," Azrael flicked his wrist, calling his scythe into existence. "Care to dance with me, demon? Let's go a round and see who's still standing."

"See?" Asmoday asked gleefully. He reached out, pulling his own stygian black blade from a fold of shadow. "That's what I'm talking about!" His eyes glowed a hellish red as he crouched over the blade. "Come on, Az, it's been a long time since we've crossed blades."

"Showing your age there, old boy," Azrael drawled, spinning the scythe in a wicked arc.

"Enough!" Rue shouted, slapping both the blades up. He reached out, grabbing the demon by the throat. "Where's Serafina?" He shook him like a dog. "I know you took her." Another sharp shake. "Speak!"

"I think that's enough of that." The smooth, cultured tone pulled Rue's furious gaze away from Asmoday's sneering face. "He was doing my will, Ruvan."

Every cell in Rue's body froze, like ice water shivering through his veins as the Lord of Hell advanced, his wings outstretched behind him, his swirling silver and gold eyes demanding nothing but absolute obedience. He saw Azrael falter beside him, the scythe dropping from numbed fingers even as his own blade fell and disappeared. "Release him." Rue's hand opened automatically on the command. Asmoday stepped back, straightening his ruined tie.

"Where's Serafina?" Rue forced the words out past a tongue frozen by the Lord's sheer presence.

"In good time, Ruvan." The Lord nodded to Azrael. "It's been a while, Azrael. I hope you're doing well."

"I keep busy." The angel folded his arms over his chest. "Are you going to repeat your offer?"

The devil smiled. "Of course I am. However, I have an addition for Ruvan here."

"What offer?" Rue asked, bewildered.

"In due time, Ruvan." He turned to Asmoday, who conjured a chair. "Two more, please, Asmoday. We don't want our honored guests to become fatigued." The demon conjured two hard-backed wooden chairs, then looked at his master. "You may kneel," was the reply. Grumbling a bit, the demon dropped to his knees on the hard stone floor, head bowed. "Azrael, could you please tell Ruvan the offer I made you?"

No compulsion to obey laced the tone that Rue could feel, but Azrael nodded. "He offered me the Fallen Isles."

"Semiazas offered me the same," Rue commented.

"It was a little different for me. He offered me rule of the Fallen Isles. Sem would be nothing more than a supplicant to my throne."

Rue's thoughts bulleted around in his brain. "Is that what you want?" he asked without thinking. "To be served?"

Azrael shrunk in on himself a bit. "I've served my entire existence. You and the other judges have each other. You have brothers, Rue. I have only myself."

He'd never thought of it that way. Azrael had always been alone. There had ever been only one Angel of Death. It had been Azrael and Azrael alone who had flown through the tribes like a plague taking the first-born sons of Israel. It had been Azrael on the mountain with Abraham as he lifted his son in sacrifice. It had been Azrael who had gathered the dead of the plagues to him in droves. All feared him. All humanity bowed before him. How incredibly lonely. And sad. He reached out, laying his hand over Azrael's. "We are brothers, know that. You're not alone."

A flash of white. The chill of spirit fingers over his. Elli wrapped her arms around Azrael's shoulders. "You're not alone anymore." She grinned, earrings jangling. "You have me now."

"A spirit?" The devil's voice was lightly derisive. "I could vanish you in a heartbeat." The threat shivered her entire form. She faded for a moment.

"No," Azrael's voice firmed. "She is bound to me and my purpose now, my lord. You no longer can command her." She solidified at the angel's touch. Behind them, Rue heard George growl deep in his throat. The scent of brimstone floated on fetid dragon breath.

"You've corrupted two of my creatures, I see." He snapped his fingers. Asmoday jumped as if jabbed with a pin. "It seems I'm wasting my time with our good dark angel." Rue saw Azrael stiffen up at the address.

The strange gold and silver eyes turned to him. "However, you and I have much to discuss." He nodded to Asmoday, who scurried off, disappearing through a crevice in the rock. "What did you think of the Fallen Isles?"

"They are very beautiful, my lord. Certainly a temptation."

"Were you?" He leaned back, steepling his long fingers.

A small vicious battle waged within him. He wanted to shout defiance at the Dark Lord, throw anything he might offer into his teeth, but he knew somewhere Serafina waited for him to save her. "I was sorely tempted, my lord."

"But...."

"But Nathanial needed me."

"Ah, past tense." He conjured a wine glass; deep red liquid swirled within. He sipped. "Why past tense? Does my brother no longer need you? Have you taught the judges your compassion?" He gestured with the glass. "Should I stop construction on the new halls because you will no longer be sending me any souls? Humanity has been saved?"

"You mock me, my lord."

"Perhaps." He tossed back more wine. "Good has always existed to be mocked by evil. Tell me."

The command could not be ignored. "Serafina," he whispered. "Serafina needed me more than Nathanial did. I abandoned my post. Took Azrael with me to save Serafina. Asmoday took her. She was supposed to go to heaven and he stole her away before her time and hid her down here. She needs to be released, my lord."

Silence. Nothing but George's grumbling behind them.

"Please, my lord," Rue began. "I would offer myself in her stead. Take me, my lord. Let her go."

"An angel's soul for one tattered human soul?" The devil pursed his lips. "Are you sure? It seems to be a one-sided trade."

"She's worth more than ten of me." He looked over at Azrael. "She's bound straight for the light."

Lucivar nodded. "She shines."

"Yes, a trade. Please, free her."

The Devil leaned back, calculating. Rue and Azrael exchanged a look. He could see the questions in his friend's eyes. Could almost hear him shouting at him. "Very well. Give me a moment to fetch the woman." He rose, chair and wine glass disappearing.

As soon as the rock swallowed the demon lord, Azrael leapt up. "What maggot is in your brain? You know he can't keep her here. Why would you do something so... so...."

"Stupid?" Elli provided.

Azrael glared at her, would have snapped had Rue not reached out to grab him. "Promise me. Promise me you'll get her home." Az nodded. He reached into his robes pulling out the vial of miracles. "Give her this when you get her home."

"What th –?"

"Don't ask where it came from, just promise me."

"I promise." He tugged Rue in for a one-armed hug, secreting the vial with the other

hand.

Elli had silvery tears trailing down her cheeks. "You must really love her."

He nodded. "More than my existence."

The crack in the stone widened, letting out the demon. Asmoday dragged Serafina behind him. Tears scored tracks through the dust on her face. Her hair, once a long straight fall of gold-fired red fell in a tangled mess to just her shoulders. Hollows under her eyes and lines of pain around her mouth spoke volumes to him about her experiences. "You're still hurting," he murmured. Asmoday let her fall. Rue stepped forward, pulling her to her feet and to him. Her arms, thinner than they'd been before, wrapped around him. She wept, her tears pouring hot and bitter on his skin.

"I thought you'd never come." Her voice hitched and broke.

"I'd walk through more than hell to get to you."

She tipped her face up to his for a kiss.

* * * *

Fury burned through Serafina. She twisted in silent rage on the low bench. That imposter! That demoness! That bitch! She opened her mouth trying to scream. Nothing. Not a sound. She kicked out, falling with a painful thud to the stone floor. Wiggling, squirming, anger burning through the icy bonds that held her, she managed to crawl to the window. A one-way window she now realized. She'd watched and listened as the devil had taunted and tempted, confident that Rue would reject him just as Azrael had done. Admittedly, she hadn't expected either the ghost or the dragon, but in all honesty they weren't among the strangest things she'd seen the last couple of days.

She had to get to him. She had to let him know that woman was an imposter. He was going to sacrifice himself to save a demoness and probably doom them both in the process. She heaved, arms feeling as though they'd been asleep. A furious pins and needles sensation flooded her, nearly bringing her to tears. Didn't matter. She clawed her way up the wall, sharp pains slicing into her. Determination and anger, laced with a little bit of jealousy, flowed through her, lending her strength.

* * * *

Those thin arms tightened around him, making him want to deepen the kiss. Here, deep in the heart of Hell, he could feel as he hadn't been able to since the last time he'd stood as a human in Serafina's arms. He remembered the sensations that poured through him at the threshold of the Fallen Isles and recognized them as pale imitations of true feeling. He pulled away, smiling a little as her fingers dug into his shoulders. "It's time," he murmured against her hair.

She shook her head her hands digging in almost painfully. "No, I'm not leaving you."

"You have to." He pulled her hands away from his shoulders, nodded as Azrael came forward. "Az will take you home. Your cousin's probably frantic. I don't know how much time has passed there, but it's certain that he's frantic that you disappeared on him."

She shook her head. "I don't care." She grabbed his hands in here, her hazel eyes glimmering in the dim light. "I want to stay with you. I don't care if it's in Hell."

A tiny wiggle of suspicion spiraled through him. She didn't care? Didn't even mention her beloved cousin's name? Had Hell changed her?

"Is it a deal?" Lucivar drew his mind away. "You agree to stay here with me." He nodded to Asmoday. "I've been looking for another lieutenant. Asmoday's becoming a little too well known."

The demon chuckled. "Well, fame has its price."

"This woman goes," Lucivar repeated. "You stay and serve me."

* * * *

"No!" Serafina found her voice. It ripped her throat, pain nearly pulling all the air from her lungs. She swallowed, tasting blood, but she'd found her voice. "No!" she screamed again, dragging herself to her feet. Fingers dug at the rough stone sill. Blood stained the stones. "Rue! It's not me!" A sob caught in her battered throat.

She heard the devil's words. "*This* woman goes free." A trick, a trick to keep them both.

"Look this way," she begged, pressing her hands to the slick surface that separated them. "I'm right here." She closed her eyes, not wanting to see the moment it all fell apart. Concentrating, she poured all her love, her hope and her will into a prayer. "Please, please, let him see through this. Save him."

* * * *

Warmth.

A trickle of warmth, the faintest memory of the light from Heaven's throne made Rue pause. Lucivar stood patient as a stone before him, waiting for him to answer. Serafina, wrapped around him, felt cold in his arms. Heavy. *Wrong.* And then there was that tickle of warmth again like a beam of sunshine on a cloudy day.

"If I agree to serve you, you'll let Serafina free? Send her back home with Azrael?"

Lucivar rolled his eyes. "Of course, I swear it. The woman goes free. Azrael can have her."

Asmoday's mouth curved into a cruel smile. "Have her in more ways than one, if he so chooses."

Rue leveled a glare at him. "You will keep a civil tongue in your head when you speak of Serafina, demon."

Asmoday tugged at his mangled tie. "Geez, Rue, lighten up already. I just meant that she's grave bait as soon as she's up there." He winked at Fina tucked in the curve of Rue's arms. "Aren't you, sweetheart?"

Fina narrowed her eyes and hissed at the demon.

Rue stiffened. *Hissed?*

That tickle of warmth at the back of his neck became a searing blast of heat, cleansing the cobwebs from his brain. He thrust the woman away from him with one hand, called his seraph blade with the other. "What are you?" he demanded.

"Rue!" she whined, two more tears spilling down her cheeks. "It's me, Fina." Her bottom lip trembled. "What's wrong?"

The blade dropped.

* * * *

"Please!" Admittedly, her prayer was beginning to sound more like a demand, but she'd always been taught that God helps those who help themselves and damned if she were going to stand there and watch Rue be taken in by that cheap evil imitation. "Help me," she commanded. A blast of heat and light flooded the little room. The last of the chill vanished from her veins. Her limbs no longer sluggish, she scrambled to the crevice through which Asmoday had disappeared earlier. She needed to get to Rue now.

* * * *

"How can you treat me like this?" She whimpered, swiping her face, leaving smears of dirt high up on her cheeks. "Do you know what I've been through these last few days?" Her chest heaved with suppressed sobs. "What I've seen...?"

The blade dropped further. "It's all my fault," he murmured.

She smiled, one hand reaching out to touch his face. Before she made contact, she screamed as something tackled her from the side, driving her down.

"Fina!" The protests died in his throat. Two Serafinas sprawled on the floor.

"You keep your hands off of him, you bitch!" one Serafina swore, punching the other dead in the face. The struck Serafina's hands curled into claws that she raked down the first woman's face – claws that lengthened as he watched.

"Cat fight!" Asmoday nearly danced in delight. Azrael snagged him as he darted forward for a better look. Lucivar simply looked resigned, and summoned another glass of wine, sipping it.

"Explain." The Angel of Death gave the demon a sharp shake.

Dropped to his feet, Asmoday grimaced. "When are you two going to stop doing that to me? I'm not a cat."

Azrael feinted forward, making the demon stumble back. "All right, all right." Asmoday waded into the fight and pulled one woman out of the fray by her hair. She shrieked a high pitched keening that could peel flesh from bone. Her hair darkened, lengthened, her eyes, already narrowing in anger, narrowed further, revealing Lilith's cat-eyed glare. "The gig is up, sister. Knock it off." He twisted her hair around his fist, pulling her in for a vicious kiss. "Later," he promised, and threw her at their master's feet.

She bowed before the Dark Lord. "Ah, Lilith, you cannot change your nature." He snapped his fingers. The ground at his feet erupted. Hands reached out of the stone, seizing the demoness, pulling her down into the depths. She screamed, eyes wheeling in panic, clawing at the edges. "We will discuss your failings later." The ground closed with a violent crack. He strode to where Serafina had been thrown by Lilith. He extended a hand, pulling her to her feet. "My dear," he brushed a kiss over the back of her hand. The scratches on her face healed at his touch. "I could wish you and your damned faith to the depths for foiling my plans."

She tipped her chin up, meeting his eyes. "But you won't."

Silence stretched between them. Finally, he answered. "No, I won't." He passed her off to Rue. Her hand trembled in his. "Go." He shot a flash of red power at the sky, which cleared. "The way is clear straight through to the human realms."

"You're letting us go?" Serafina stuttered, pressing herself as tightly against Rue as she could.

He nodded. "Three trials are all I'm allowed. You've passed three. This time." He turned. The shadowy crevice stretched to accommodate his wings. Lucivar turned. "Leave before I decide that you've chosen to stay." The stone snapped shut behind him.

"You heard the boss. Clear out." Asmoday knotted another fresh tie around his throat. "Take the damned dragon too. He's not good for anything now. Besides," he snickered, "I can't wait to see the humans panic when they see that thing coming."

"It's not a thing," Elli bristled, stroking the dragon's snout. "His name is George."

Asmoday snorted. "George? That's the stupide –"

"We'll take George with us." Azrael interrupted. "I'll find somewhere safe for him and talk to Gabriel, Michael and Simeon." He bowed to Serafina. "It's a pleasure to meet you. I wish it were in better company." He flicked a glance over at the demon. "Here." He reached into his robes and handed the vial of miracles back to Rue.

"You can do the honors yourself. Though, I'd wait until I was back on earth under sky before trying it."

Rue nodded, tucking the vial away. "My thanks, Azrael. I couldn't have gotten this far without you." Elli cleared her throat behind them. "Or you, Elli. You were a true guardian angel."

"Seriously, if this gets any more cloying I'm going to puke," Asmoday groused.

Azrael clapped him on the shoulder, then launched himself onto the dragon. "Let's go, ghost girl!" Elli drifted up behind him, waving goodbye. A shower of grit, the buffeting wind of the dragon's wingbeats and they were gone winging away through the shuddering clouds.

"One more question, Asmoday."

"Only one?" He rolled his eyes, angel blue again. "Shoot."

"What was this about?"

"You heard the boss. He's only allowed three trials—physical, temptation and deception. You got through all of them. I think you cheated on the Labyrinth, the physical one, but I'm not the one who's keeping score. Now, get out of here." He looked pointedly at the spiral of gray flagstone leading from the center of the room. "I don't know how long the Lord will keep the halls straight and we don't want you lost down here, do we?" He snickered. "I'd get going if I were you." He winked at Serafina. "See you around, sister." With a *pop!* he disappeared in a puff of acrid smoke.

Taking her hand firmly in his, not quite believing that she was there beside him again, Rue gestured toward the spiral of brick. "Shall we go?"

She smiled up at him. "I thought you'd never ask."

CHAPTER TWENTY

They were waiting for them. He should have known they would be. The second they stepped from the place between the worlds into Serafina's apartment, there they were. Simeon – his red hair glowing in the light streaming from the windows at his back – frowned at them. "Did you think we wouldn't know?" His voice, choral and indignant, wrung a little squeak from Fina.

"Tone it down, brother," Michael instructed in a much more soothing tone. He stepped forward to take Serafina's hand. "Allow me, my dear. We've all heard so much about you from Ruvan. It's a pleasure to finally meet you face to face. I am Michael." He gestured to golden haired Gabriel behind him. "This is Gabriel and the disappointed one is my colleague Simeon." He smiled, his moonshine eyes gleaming, "He's always disappointed."

Rue had dropped to his knees. "My lords," he stammered.

"Get up, Ruvan," Gabriel pulled him to his feet.

"Yes," Simeon snapped, "you need to explain." His furrowed brows nearly met over his brilliant blue eyes. "What were you thinking?" He flung out a hand as if to encompass every decision Rue had ever made. "Abandoning your post? Delving into the depths? Enticing Azrael away from his duties! Do you know the trouble that caused? Four days here on the surface when no one died! No one!"

"The authorities were beginning to take notice," Gabriel mused.

Michael nodded. "It's been the highest volume of devotion we've seen in eons."

Simeon shook his head in scathing negation. "Be that as it may, it was irresponsible. All to save a mortal who was doomed at any rate?"

"To save Serafina," Rue corrected, sidling in front of her, blocking her from the princes' view. "I would do it a hundred times over if only to give her a few more days with those who love her here on earth."

"Unrepentant!" Simeon snarled.

Rue merely lifted his chin, defiance in every line of his body and every shudder of his wings. He knew what it looked like and he knew the punishment.

Michael, his moonshine eyes reminding Rue a little bit of Lucivar's silver and gold spirals, studied them without a word. He turned to have a silent exchange with Gabriel, who spoke for both of them. "Simeon would have us strip you of your wings forever, Ruvan, drop you with no memory in some mortal city and wash our hands of you."

Simeon sputtered off to the side, but said nothing.

"No!" Serafina shoved at Rue, shrugging his wings out of her way. "No, you're not going to do that to him." Hands fisted on her hips, she glared at the trio of heaven's princes. "He did it to save me. If you want to punish someone, punish me." She held her hands out to them. "Go ahead, I'm doomed already. I let Asmoday trick me. Go ahead, take me away." She looked over her shoulder at Rue. He could see the tears she refused to shed. "It'll be a bad enough punishment for him anyway."

Michael nodded and took her hands in his. Rue felt frozen. He couldn't move, couldn't yell, couldn't even think as the Archangel grasped Serafina's hands and the room erupted in golden light. A rush of warmth, a chorus of angel voices and the light dimmed. Fina still stood there, her hands in Michael's.

She blinked, as if just waking. "What?"

He bent to kiss her forehead. "You've been taken, Serafina. I have taken your humanity."

Rue started forward. "You mean...?"

Gabriel nodded. "She is mortal, yet not human. She has been marked for our purpose." He reached out, tugging up her sleeve. A small pair of angel wings, as meticulously inked as any of Joss' work, adorned her upper arm. His voice rang. "You are now an Ascended, Serafina, charged by Heaven's princes to guide and guard humanity. Find those pockets of evil and stamp them out, bring the light of Heaven's love into the darkness."

"What about Rue?" she demanded, fingers brushing over her new mark.

Simeon shrugged. "What about him? He'll return to Hell's Gate and his duties. You will stay here and help us in the upcoming battle."

"It's that late, is it?" Rue asked, understanding beginning to bloom.

Michael nodded. "You are but the first volley in a much longer war."

"Then take my wings." He twined his fingers with Fina's. "She's going to need help. She is a guide, someone who inspires others to goodness, but she'll need a guard. The demonkin and Asmoday himself will be focused on her now that she's been angel-touched."

"Can't fight your way out of a paper bag, can you?" Gabriel rolled his golden eyes. "Very well then, here is my gift to you." He extended a hand, pulling a celestial blade from the place between the worlds. "Here," he said, pressing the hilt of the long dagger into her free hand. "Rue can show you how to use this. It will bend to your will, but I want you to promise me that you will not leave it behind."

Mutely, she nodded.

"I think we're done here," Simeon announced. He turned to Rue. "You are certain about this?"

He nodded.

"As you wish it." Simeon gestured and that blinding light once more filled the small living room. When it faded, Rue's wings were once more nothing more than ink on his skin. "When you pass from this world to the next, you will both become true Ascended Angels, those charged with battling the denizens of Hell. We –," he gestured to the seraph princes, " –hold the Covenant. We cannot interfere, but you are of the earth and not bound to such promises."

"Nice loophole," Fina murmured.

Michael grinned, "Isn't it?"

Gabriel nodded. "It's not over. In fact, it's just beginning. You both saw the passways from Hell into the mortal realms. Rue, you know more than most what lives in the corners of the darker halls." A chill skated up the former angel's spine at those words. All the nightmares of mankind lurked in the depths. Which would Asmoday and Lucivar loose next on mankind? He was certain that the demonkin were nothing more than the advance guard. Cannon fodder, if you would. Gabriel continued, "Call on us, if you have a need. We'll send more to you as they are chosen."

Rue stood at attention, fully embracing the duty they laid on his shoulders—the general of Heaven's army here on earth. "I will not fail you."

"You never have, Ruvan," Michael assured him.

They turned to leave. "Wait a minute," Fina grabbed Gabriel's wrist. "When you said that I wasn't human anymore, did that also mean…." She trailed off.

He nodded. "Yes, Serafina, that means you're healed. The Ascended do not succumb to such illnesses."

"Cured?" Her fingers trembled on the angel's wrist.

"Cured," he repeated. Rue reached into his tunic for the vial, warm against his heart. Gabriel shook his head. "Keep it, Ruvan. You never know when you'll need a miracle."

His hand fell to his side.

Michael took one more look around the little apartment. "I would suggest getting a larger place soon, Ruvan." One corner of his mouth tipped up as he regarded Serafina. "I think you're going to need more room soon." Her cheeks flushed in embarrassment, making the prince laugh. "Shall we leave, my brothers?" He stepped into the beams of sunlight and disappeared.

Gabriel clapped Rue on the shoulder. "Call on me when you have a need."

"I will."

He too shimmered once in the light and vanished.

Simeon shuffled his feet on the worn carpet. "I took the liberty," he began, handing Serafina a note that had been sitting on the kitchen counter, "of making certain that your loved ones here worried less than they might have otherwise." He bowed stiffly and vanished.

Rue looked down at the note in her hand. In Simeon's beautiful script it explained how Rue had come back and whisked her off to Switzerland on the chance that the specialists there could do something for her. It asked them not to worry and assured them that she would be home for the holidays no matter the outcome. On the bottom, Dan had scrawled a demand that she call him as soon as she got in. He also promised to not hurt Rue. Much.

"I didn't think he had it in him," Rue murmured.

"I'd better call Dan right away."

He nodded, catching her when she would have stepped away from him. "One moment." He reeled her in, pulling her against him, reveling in truly feeling her. He tipped her face up to his, pausing with his mouth a breath away from hers. "Dan can wait. This can't," he murmured and closed the distance between them.

Laughter lit her eyes when she pulled back. "Just one question."

His arms tightened on her. "Just one?"

She nodded to her arm. The delicately etched wings almost seemed to glitter in the sunlight pouring in through the windows. "How are we ever going to explain this to Joss?"

He threw back his head and laughed.

* * * *

"Well, that went better than I thought it would." Lucivar settled onto his throne. One of the little dragonkin slipped out from under the seat to stretch under his hand.

Asmoday looked up, frowning. "Uh, didn't we lose this one, boss?"

The devil chuckled, the sound of rattling bones. "We lost nothing other than an opportunity to corrupt one of the first Ascended."

"Ah," Asmoday breathed, his pulse kicking up a little in excitement. "It's time again for another Cleansing?" He rubbed his hands together memories of the last Cleansing dancing in his head. It had been millennia. The last time he'd been allowed to run free it had been chalked up to a plague. He chuckled. It had been a plague, a plague of evil. "I loved the Dark Ages, my Lord."

"Didn't we all?" Lucivar tapped one finger against his chin, his silvery gold eyes narrowed in thought. "Vampires and zombies are rather popular nowadays, aren't they, Asmoday?"

"Yes. Humans seem to look at vampires as something to desire now. Sex symbols. Zombies, yeah, they're gaining in popularity, though the werewolves and bloodsuckers still have top billing."

"Something to be desired?" He shook his head in disbelief. "Well, then, perhaps we should remind them of what they truly are? Release the lamia and empusa from the Grecian halls. Let us also send out the incubi and succubi, keep them confused." He nodded. "That will do for now. The demonkin have made enough inroads?"

Asmoday shrugged. "They've gotten through in several places. A few of those places are stronger than others. I was going to send some imps through soon to stake out a few havens for them. I'll send the lamia and empusa through instead, let them settle. The incubi and succubi can't stay out in the human world, but they'll be able to give us some information.

"Yes, that will do for now. Let's raise the level of terror. They think they've shined the light of science into every crevice of darkness. There are no myths anymore. There are no demons and the only evil they believe in is in the hearts of mankind. It's time to show them that there are more than shadows in the darkness and more evil than they can ever hope to wash away in the light of science. Release the dogs of war, Asmoday. We are on the forefront of the first battle and it is a battle I intend to take. Send Mammon to me. I believe I can use him to corrupt a few more souls."

"Yes, my Lord." The demon of money could definitely be useful. He was a master at spreading greed and discord.

"I hear we've had some news from Ruvan and his erstwhile bride."

"Yes, my Lord. She's expecting. A girl, I believe."

"Let's make sure we send something to the little mother, Asmoday. A bouquet of lilies, perhaps? I love lilies. They remind me of funerals. A rattle for the little one when she arrives, perhaps?"

"I'll see to it, my Lord," Asmoday assured him, rising.

"One more thing, Asmoday, before you go." Lucivar stood, his face rippling, his form shimmering. Huge white to black wings folded away. His face twisted revealing a human countenance with simple gray eyes and aquiline nose. A goatee drew itself down his chin. Tattoos scrawled themselves from shoulder to wrist. After a few moments he stood in black boots, jeans, a sleeveless t-shirt with a screaming demon head on the front. He was no longer Lucivar, Lord of Hell and fallen angel. He now looked like Luke Coven, lead singer of the band Hell's Gate. The real Luke Coven had made a deal with him a decade ago – fame, fortune and talent in exchange for using his likeness whenever He wished. The real Luke snickered whenever the paparazzi puzzled over his around the world sightings. As long as it kept him in the news and in the public eye, he never thought of the consequences of making so close a deal with the Devil.

The demon gave him the once over. "Perfect, my Lord. Though, didn't Luke have an earring last time?"

"You're right, Asmoday." He adjusted that, a silver skull punching through his left ear. "Now, five year old boys still like Hot Wheels, right?"

"Small cars that go too fast are always a big draw."

He nodded and snapped His fingers pulling a brightly wrapped gift from thin air. "It's only right that a father should bring his son a gift for his birthday. After all, it isn't everyday he turns five." He winked at the demon and turned, stepping through a portal of shadow that appeared at a command. "Hold the fort, Asmoday, and put some of our plans into place. I'd like to taste the fears of humanity again as I walk among them."

Asmoday bowed low. "Of course, my Lord. Your command."

Luke nodded and disappeared through the portal, the door shutting behind him with a small *pop*.

With a spring in his step, Asmoday headed out of the throne room. It had been a long while since he'd been able to craft such wonderful wickedness and while he was perfectly willing to follow his master's plans, he did have a few schemes of his own to put into practice. *While the cat's away*, he thought, smiling to himself.

The End

More Titles from Solstice Shadows

Eden's Mark
By
D.M. Sears

Eden Arik was a typical teenager who lived the typical teenage life...until the pale eyes showed up in her dreams. The birthmark, Eden had always ignored, burned at the new nightmares, raising questions about her past. Eden finds out she is part witch and fairy that is destined to save a world she never knew existed that inhabits people far more than human. Her only solitude is the woods behind her house where she meets a mysterious stranger with steel eyes. With the help of her guardians, two unlikely shape shifters, and a vampire who can bring her to her knees with one glance, Eden goes on to search the secrets of her past, present, and future. Along her way to discovery, Eden comes across Circenn; her grandmother, consort to the Darkness and the evil magic he possess. Circenn will stop at nothing to bring Eden to the darkness so she can harness her granddaughter's limitless power. Seduction, power, and death pave the way towards Eden's destiny and the fate of Ellethny.

Daughter Of Hauk
By
KateMarie Collins

What would you do, if you found out your life was a lie?

After you were dead?

Arwenna Shalian spent her life in loyal service to a God she was never meant to serve. Tricked by her fellow priests, she betrayed a man she thought she loved by binding a demon to him. One that would send him to the brink of madness.

Can she find a way to forgive herself? And what of Hauk, the God she was Marked to serve? Will He find her and give her the chance to undo what she's done, or leave her at the mercy of the creatures that torture her soul?

Son Of Corse
By
KateMarie Collins

It's been almost two years since Arwenna banished the Demon Corse from her world. Life has been good. Idyllic, almost.

The illusion is shattered in a heartbeat during her sister's wedding. Not only are once-dead enemies back, but they've stolen Arwenna's only child, Sera.

The price Arwenna will have to pay to save her daughter is high. Can she muster the strength to make a pact that jeopardizes not just her own soul, but that of an entire world?

An Element Of Time
By
Bebe Knight

A vampire and a slayer walk into a bar... Sounds like the beginning of a bad joke, but for Veronica and Mackenzie, it's the beginning of the rest of their lives...

The world has seen its fair share of evil, but Veronica Chase had no idea such monsters truly existed. Werewolves, poltergeists, witches... even vampires. Ignorance was bliss. But her reality was crushed on that horrid day her family was taken away from her. Now, Veronica has devoted her entire life to hunting those very creatures, searching for the werewolf pack that murdered her parents in hopes of finding her abducted sister. Nothing will get in her way of settling the score for the hand she was unjustly dealt. That is until her newest assignment brings her to her knees.

After one hundred and eight years on earth, Mackenzie Jones thought he had seen it all. With the exception of daylight of course, but that's what comes with the territory being a vampire and all. Perpetually damned to live his life as a bartender in the shadows of the night, nothing has sparked his interest lately. Just once he wished something exciting would happen in his mundane life. Little did he know, his wish was about to come true. Walking through the door to his bar, and into his heart, Mackenzie allows love to take the wheel for the first time. There's just one slight problem. She's there to kill him.

Earth's Magick
By
Mel Massey

Life in Trinity Hills, Texas goes from normal to deadly for Mela Malone. Whenever Mela falls asleep, a mysterious creature, called The Hag, tries to kill her. What begins as dabbling in protective spells from an ancient Grimoire, leads to her initiation into an ancient order of warrior witches known as the Elementai.

Mela learns war is coming with The Darkness and the Hag is only one of the evil creatures in its service. As an Elementai, Mela learns it's her duty to find four part-human sisters who can help defeat the evil that threatens to return to the world. With every new discovery, Mela uncovers ancient secrets that complicate her quest further.

As war approaches, everyone must make a choice - fight with the Elementai for all life on Earth, or fight for The Darkness…